The
Middle Man

by Coburn Hawk

ISBN: 0-9857813-2-7
ISBN-13: 978-0-9857813-2-3

Amazon.com/author/coburnhawk

www.coburnhawk.com | www.randombridges.com

@coburnhawk | @randombridges

•

○

∞

This story is dedicated
to my two heroes:

My father, Donald O. Hawk,
who taught me that anything is possible

and my son, Spencer J. Hawk,
who proves it, every day.

∞

○

•

CONTENTS

Awakening

Exploring

Balancing

Reshaping

AWAKENING

: : RANDOM : :

His eyes had failed him; the world he awoke to was nothing but blackness. He blinked his eyes a bit, trying to jump-start his eyesight. Nothing. His head was heavy, as if from too much sleep, but he felt his heart begin to race as panic found him, alone in the dark.

"Take it slowly..." the kind, warm voice put him at ease. The voice came from a young man but sounded thick with years. "...You are safe. Try looking again."

As he opened his eyes he could see soft light reflected off the floor, which his cheek seemed to be pressed against. The light increased slightly, or maybe it was his eyes remembering their purpose.

The room was still mostly black, but brightening now to the glimmer of light in which he lay. The floor was smooth and cool, made from some inky stone. He became aware of the warm hand on his shoulder blade and the soft, rhythmic breath of his companion in the dark.

The unknown man crouched next to him was calm and relaxed. His dark hair almost reached his shoulders but was neatly groomed. His complexion was light brown and his eyes deep wells in the weak light. He had never seen this man before, but he was strangely comfortable with this comfortable stranger.

"Your name is Random..." the voice flowed.

"The full name is even more ridiculous." He cleared his throat slightly. "Random Bridges." The sleep left his voice as he pushed himself up on an elbow. "But thankfully it's the product of a father with a twisted sense of humor rather than anything as unseemly as an acting career. He didn't even bother with a middle name, the bastard."

The man smiled, with his eyes as much as with his face. The smile was nourishing. "That opening never fails to get a laugh, does it? It must be nice..." His focus went a little soft. "...to always have laughter in your first meetings. Smart man, that 'old bastard' of yours."

Random had received many responses to his well-rehearsed little skits starring his uncommon name during his lifetime, but never one so incisive and disarming. He reeled at the respect for his father that suddenly settled on him like an ill-fitting jacket. He found himself taking a shaky breath in.

The stranger's smile retreated. "I, however, do not have such luxury. My name is Joe, and you are dead."

There are many different types of silences, from awkward to tense to foreboding. This one was distinct: it was completely empty. Joe simply looked at Random and added nothing to the moment. Random sat propped on one elbow on the stone floor, holding his gaze. The look in Joe's eyes left no room for the stages leading up to acceptance. It was simply a statement of fact. It left very little for Random to say, other than...

"I see. Can you help me stand up?"

His body reacted slowly, as if it was filled with cold paste. Joe patiently offered his arm and a firm stance. At last Random stood. He was taller than Joe -- but he was taller than most people. If he had to guess, Joe was a few inches shy of six feet.

"Joe?"

"Yes, Random?"

"Not Satan or Lucifer or Nick?"

"Not Jesus or Mohammed or Buddha, either."

Random looked around the featureless space in which he stood. "Well, if that's the case, who exactly are you, then...in the scheme of things?" Joe didn't answer. They took a few more steps in the strange light. "If I'm dead, why do I feel like someone just beat me up? I'm walking like I'm ninety years old."

"You are adjusting to things here, and you are doing it more quickly than most." Joe said still guiding his steps. "This is not your body; it is your memory of your body. You are a person who is accustomed to visualization, so it is easier for you. Some people can barely move when they first arrive."

"Well, it looks like art school was good for something, then," Random chuckled.

Joe stopped and looked him dead in the eyes. Joe's eyes were deep. One minute Random felt reassured, the next he felt uncomfortable as one so heavy with years looked through him. "Your skills are more important than you would think. I've been watching you and wanted to be here to greet you personally." He paused and did not blink as his dark eyes pierced into Random's.

Joe suddenly stiffened and his attention darted off as if he'd heard a noise in the distance. His grip on Random's arm was harsh and wooden.

"I'm sorry I have to do this, but we have run out of time." Joe reached to the left, where nothing had been in the featureless space, and slid open a rice paper door. Light blazed from beyond it. He grabbed Random by both biceps and easily squeezed his somewhat limp body together.

"This will be disorienting...and you may pass out."

"What are you..."

Joe rolled through the door as if he were jumping from a train, heaving Random's greater weight with him. They went into free-fall, the light blinding, and the sound of acceleration blowing past their ears.

Random screamed and closed his eyes, expecting an impact that did not come, feeling only wind and speed. No, not like jumping from a train at all. Like exiting an aircraft.

He remembered the time he'd shot off his big mouth one drunken night and found himself at Aeroporto Municipal de Ijuí with some Brazilian asshole that was going to make him keep his word. Fucking tequila. Random knew his ass had to cash the check his drunken mouth had written. Crammed into a gutted Cessna 182 and trying not to vomit during an ascent that took thirty minutes. The jump ended up being a welcome relief from the claustrophobia of the plane.

He opened his eyes. Free-fall. His body snapped into the position they had taught him that bleary morning in Brazil. He snatched a hand to his chest to check for his rig, then extended it again to re-balance his falling body when he found nothing but his shirt.

Joe grabbed his right wrist and swung quickly around to grab his left, bringing them face-to-face and belly to earth. Random could see the gentle curve of the horizon behind Joe, then glimpsed the green canopy below them with a river running through it.

Joe smiled and laughed. He yelled over the rushing air. "I could not have done better myself! Perfect!"

Random failed to see the perfection that was pleasing Joe so much in that moment, but Joe then locked eyes with him and gained his attention. The air rushing by them seemed to quiet and Joe's voice amplified. "Now think of the hike through the rainforest, the long one where the air was damp in your lungs and your leg hurt from the branch that had scraped it, and you heard the noises that you realized were spider monkeys..."

Random felt weight on the soles of his feet. He broke from Joe's gaze to find himself standing under the green Costa Rican canopy, in the exact place that he remembered, with the strange whinny of the spider monkeys in the damp hot air. Joe stood in front of him and smiled. He sat down on a log and heaved a sigh as he glanced at the ground and then back at Random.

"Welcome to the afterlife, Mr. Bridges."

: : VISION : :

Random threw down the walking stick he found in his hand and heard it thunk against the rocks. "What the fuck is going on here and who the hell are you? This is some lucid fucking dream, isn't it?" He no longer found comfort in Joe's eyes, and he didn't think he liked him anymore.

Joe still sat on the log with his forearms on his knees, trying to catch his breath. He had an involuntary grin of exhilaration from the skydive, but he wiped as much of it off his face as he could when he answered. He realized Random was no longer placid and docile. "A lucid dream? Not a bad way to look at it, but no. You are dead and we are surfing your memories. This is all your doing, but I am afraid I had to accelerate the introduction a bit."

"If I'm dead, why'd you say we've run out of time? Shouldn't I have all the time in the world at this point?"

"An astute observation," Joe said, staring down at the ground and tracing a figure eight in the dirt with the tip of his shoe. "There were others coming and I need to be the only one to talk to you at this moment. They would start filling your head with nonsense and it would become a screaming match." He stood and surveyed their environment. "This is a nice memory. This was quite a trip for you, wasn't it?"

Random looked around and all the details crystallized--the heat, the sounds, the light through the canopy and the exhaustion in his muscles. He was overwhelmed with the pleasure of being back here. He could hear that little stream he knew he would find about twenty yards ahead.

5

"Don't change the subject. What others?"

"Let us walk a little ahead and find that spot by the river you love so much. I will answer your questions there while we eat that jerky from your pack."

"How do you know about that jerky? Or this place? Or that I ever took this trip?"

Joe turned his back on him and started walking toward the river Random longed to see again. "Like I said, I have been watching you."

The water was as clear as he remembered and the jerky just as delicious. He'd searched for months when he returned stateside to find anything that could compare to the twisted strips of meat he had bought from that twisted old woman in the village. For several years after he returned, he would catch himself checking airfare to Costa Rica, with the sole purpose of finding her and filling an empty suitcase with as much jerky as he could buy. He was convinced she probably made it in her home out of rats, but he would sell his mother to be able to get it in LA.

Joe had promised answers, but Random stopped caring when he saw the river. He let himself become immersed in the memory and gnawed on the rat jerky with glee.

"A dream," Joe said, gazing at the water, "is not a bad way to describe the afterlife we find ourselves in. You just have to add in the variable that...you are just one of the dreamers." The water babbled over the rocks and Random did not focus on Joe directly. "Here, dreamers can also be Builders, as proven by this place you have built for us to sit quietly and eat this-- what is this?"

"Rat...I think. But some of the tastiest shit to ever grace my mouth." Random gestured at the jungle around him. "So I built this with my memory?"

Joe looked at him. "Yes, but you only used your memory as a starting point. Look closely at the details. Is there anything different from the actual place? Anything that does not quite match?"

Random stopped and considered it. "There aren't any bugs. As much as I loved this spot, I couldn't stay too long because the bugs were eating me alive. I didn't care and just let 'em have their way with my legs so I could stay as long as possible." Random looked at his legs. They were bare and free of the bites he had spent the next two days treating with some smelly ointment.

"You are already editing the memories, making them unique and new. This is why I was watching you. This is why they want to get you away from me."

"Who are you talking about? The same ones you said would fill my head with crap?"

"Yes. They call themselves 'Truthers,' which is not just bad English but also the worst kind of ironic. They have an agenda and are trying very hard to change things here to match their own beliefs. They try to get to new arrivals before we can, to plant their ideas before the soul knows what is going on." Joe tore a new piece of jerky with his teeth.

If Random was dreaming, he wasn't sure how he had imagined anyone like Joe. He was peaceful and calm, despite the strange formal way he spoke. His heritage was hard to determine. He definitely had some Asian blood, but his heavy eyelids were mixed with a European nose. Random was fairly sure that English was not his mother tongue. "And who's this 'we' you're aligned with? Some angelic welcoming crew?"

"Not angels. Just the caretakers in this place. The Truthers don't seem to be willing to accept the way we have done things for thousands of years. They claim we have knowledge of some divine truth and that we are hiding it from everyone. Ultimately, they are not willing to accept what we told them and everyone else that arrived here. They decided to pass their time with this fabricated revolution, but they only struggle with the void they cannot confront."

Random made the face he used when he wanted to inform someone that they were talking out of their ass. "What is it you tell everyone that pisses them off? All you told me was that I'm dead."

Joe stopped chewing and swallowed hard. "I started to tell you when you asked whether I had other names, but we were interrupted and I was in no mood to have them appear and start raving at you."

Random thought back to what seemed like a long time ago, in that dark room. "I asked whether you were the devil. You said you weren't, but you also said you weren't Jesus or Mohammed..."

7

"Or Buddha." Joe said, pointing at his flat belly.

"But you didn't say who you are when I asked, and you still haven't, and this is all starting to sound like something you're making up. How do I know I'm even dead? Maybe I'm just really high on some drug I've forgotten taking because I'm so high."

Joe stood up and took in a deep breath. "Look, I am really sorry to do this, but I know they are still looking for you and I do not have the time to talk philosophy with you right now." Joe raised his arm, pointed a large silver pistol at Random's head and pulled the trigger.

Rocks, sky, grass, sky...the sound of water filling his ears. Random heard a piercing ring and then felt fingers weave into his hair and pull his head up and out of the cold liquid that muffled all sound.

:: OFFER ::

The soft world came slowly into focus. Random felt a dense pillow under his head. The ceiling fan he was looking up at stirred the thick air. The ceiling was cracked and dirty. The fan looked old, and he doubted it had ever been turned off. The dampness on his head and the moisture running down his face were sweat.

He touched his forehead where he was sure the bullet from that huge pistol had entered. He found no hole, just a wet cloth laid there by someone in a vain attempt to cool him in the oppressive heat. He removed the cloth and heard Joe's voice from the other side of the room.

"Yes, you are dead. And yes, I am still here. I am sorry I had to do that, and I am even more sorry that this was the only memory I could think of quickly. I wish you could have woken up in a nicer place."

Random wanted to jump up and punch Joe directly in the face, but his body had that same weak, thick feeling as when he first found himself in the dark room. Moving the washcloth from his head had taken all the energy he had. He couldn't even turn his head to locate Joe visually.

"Let me talk a bit and see if I can answer some of your questions. We have more time now; I do not think the Truthers will think to look for us here."

Random was angry and his head hurt, but he relaxed and took a breath. "I'm listening."

Joe stood at the window of the dingy little room, looking out at the bustle of the city below him. He tried to gauge the approximate year of this memory by the technology he could see--1970, if he had to guess. He knew this wasn't one of his memories, merely a reflection of one of the thousands he had experienced through others whom he had shepherded into this strange afterlife. He suddenly remembered the soldier whose memory this was, but pushed the image of his face aside. He had to honor his word and give Random the information he was so patiently waiting for. He needed to get Random's trust back.

"I have been helping ease the transition of those coming here for thousands of years. I was born in the same world you were, only a lot earlier. I lived my first life and died on a battlefield. When I first arrived here there was no one to welcome me. The afterlife was chaotic and confusing.

"I wandered through the worlds constructed by all these dreamers. Some thought they were still alive, some knew they were dead but constructed the mythological afterlives they had expected to find. The heavens and hells of countless souls blended into an ocean of chaos, gluttony and sadness. Many wept. There was so much sorrow…sorrow that was not necessary.

"I was lucky. I found the Conclave, a group who knew both that they were outside the mortal realm and that they were the ones building this world. They had set up a sanctuary where they had collectively pooled their creations. They were peaceful and wise. Some of them spoke of more than one life. They said they had lived many times and always found themselves back here."

Joe chuckled softly as he remembered the kind face of the woman who would become his teacher. "I demanded to know how they did it. I wanted to get out of this place and back to the battlefield I stupidly missed. I tried to force them to show me their secrets, but they laughed at me and ignored the threatening images I tried to construct. They knew I could not hurt them. They knew my threats were illusions."

Random had managed to turn himself on the damp bed and prop himself on one arm to watch Joe speaking to the open window. Joe felt his gaze and turned to face him.

"I was a warrior in life, a ruthless warrior. I died violently, which suited the way I had lived. Yet these men and women had much greater power in their stillness and silence than I had ever seen in an adversary. I finally stopped pursuing the secret of returning to Earth. I found myself more interested in how they could be so at peace. I became their student."

Joe smiled at the disbelief he saw on Random's face. "I know it is a lot to consider. I know you probably want to break my neck more than you want to believe anything I say. But give me just a small leap of faith for a moment longer. You should know what you are dealing with here."

Random struggled to shift his weight. He was not recovering his strength the way he had in the black room. "Well, it looks like I'm not going to be able to break your neck anytime soon, so you might as well continue. You were saying you had run into Mr. Miyagi running the purgatory Kung Fu studio. So what'd he have you do next? Paint a fence to build your strength? Wax his car?"

Joe's eyes flared with a deep rage and he hissed forcefully. "Te Nig Pizda!" He strode forward like a predator, and Random would have rolled off the bed and scrambled away like a frightened dog if he'd had the strength to.

Joe stopped on the second stride and breathed heavily through his nose. His eyes still burned but the fires were cooling. Random saw Joe fall into what was clearly a practiced state: his breath became deep and rhythmic as he closed his eyes and calmed his rage. When his breath slowed and he opened his eyes, the comfortable stranger had returned.

Random ventured, "Look, I'm sorry, it was a smartass thing to say. This has been a hell of a day for me, what with the dying and all." He dared a look at Joe, then looked away.

Joe stood very still and then Random saw his face move in his peripheral vision. Joe began to chuckle, then let it build into a small laugh. Random looked at him directly again and relaxed.

"That mouth always did get you into trouble, yet your sense of humor always seemed to get you out of it."

"It almost always worked that way," Random spoke with a sudden stiffness. "Almost always." He held Joe's gaze and they shared an unspoken memory. Random was assaulted by the vision of his own death. Wherever he was, he found himself believing that he was truly dead. The noise of the ceiling fan laboring against the stale air filled the room.

11

Joe spoke first and dodged the thought that was on both their minds. "Whether you choose to believe me or not is always up to you. But I will ask that you at least let me finish before you make up your mind."

"Of course. Please continue."

"We are in the middle here. We are without our mortality, but we do not have the answers we all thought we would have. Some do call it Purgatory. The true nature of the place is up for interpretation. Not every soul who passes from Earth finds itself here, but many do. I have met those who were pious and those who were wicked and everything in between. I am not sure what the selection process is, or whether there is one at all."

"So..." Random asked softly, "...there is no creator? No divine presence?"

Joe slipped into his most comforting tone, the one he'd perfected by answering this question more times than he could count. "We are here. We have each other. There are many things that are divine, and beautiful, and holy. I have met some of the prophets that they speak of in life, but most of them have come and gone on their own paths. But none of us have met any of the divine creators we were told of." He paused, as he always did, to let that thought settle. "There are things that we do know--more than we did in life--but that mystery remains."

Random felt a bit sad. Even though most of his friends had been either Buddhists or just straight-up atheists, part of him still held on to a more agnostic view. He supposed he was an atheist who held out hope. "So what do you know now that you didn't when you were alive?"

"That is a large question and more than I could answer briefly, but there are a few things I can tell you. My teachers did finally show me how to re-enter the mortal dance. I eventually did choose to return to an earthbound body. I have lived twelve lifetimes--thirteen if you include my first trip on the wheel. Now I no longer seek to return." Joe turned his head slowly to the window. "Now I seek to move on into the unknown."

"What's that supposed to mean?"

Joe turned to him slowly. He looked somehow younger, like he was talking about leaving for summer camp. "There are some who neither go back into a body, nor stay in this place. They simply let go and are never seen again. Where they go is a mystery, because none of them have ever come back. My teacher spoke of this and eventually made that transition, leaving me to carry on her work here and on Earth. This is what is next for me." He smiled a silly smile and his eyes twinkled.

Random was surprised when he realized he was sitting on the edge of the bed and able to move freely. He stood carefully. "So if I believe you, and I'm not saying that I do, what happens to me now?"

Joe did not smile in victory as Random had expected. He stepped forward until he was a little too close. "I want to take you to the Conclave, the place my teachers first built. There you can get all your questions answered without some zealot trying to sell you on the 'Truther revolution' or whatever they are calling it. Then you can make your own choice on what the next step in your path is. Your skills are needed. There are fewer and fewer of us. Many have made the transition into the mystery and more than a few are on Earth. We would like you to help us imagine a new existence here. You could be an architect of the next version of this world."

"So you came to meet me right after I died and whisked me away to offer me a job before the competition could?" Random couldn't help the smile on his face and the chuckle in his voice when he asked this question.

"Yes." Joe said simply.

"It is on Earth as it is in Heaven..." Random shook his head at the irony in which he was swimming. "Well, before I accept any job offer, I like to see where I'll be working. How long will it take us to get to this Conclave place?"

"You will have to adjust your thinking in many ways for us to reach our destination. If your thinking were pure, we would already be there. However, you are still gripped by many illusions that will slow us down, the greatest of which are the illusions of distance and time."

Joe paused, gauging Random's reaction to this piece of information. He was moving faster with him than with most, but he had to. Random was too important to his plans. The Truthers had been watching him also. Joe had gotten lucky with the timing. He had gambled and won, but his jackpot had only been a small head start. The Truthers would not give up, especially with her leading the charge.

Her name was Erminia, and she was a formidable opponent in this game in which he'd found himself. She had been small in stature in life, and she chose to remain that way even though she could easily re-imagine herself as thirteen feet tall if she wanted to. Her small size threw people off here even more than it had in life, and she used this to her advantage.

Random took a moment to process, but nodded as he considered the new information. "OK, so how do we break those illusions?"

Joe was impressed, but didn't show it. "We cannot do that yet. I have tried to tackle those two with other new arrivals in the past and it never ends well. The illusions of time and distance are too deeply ingrained. You need to have success destroying other, smaller illusions before you can take those two on."

"So what do we do? Can we at least start walking in that direction while I keep imagining it being closer and closer?"

Joe paused. That might just work. He had forgotten how quickly Random could apply even the most basic concepts into advanced strategy. "The first step is to allow other dreamers into your world. I am here because I forced my way in. But until you open the doors a bit, no other dreamers can enter. You are in a bubble of sorts. There are some who have locked themselves away in their own private heaven or hell so tightly that even I can't reach them anymore."

"So these 'Truthers' learned how to 'force their way in' to bubbles just like you do?"

Joe was cool and collected as he responded to the question; however, inside he was screaming at the top of his lungs. Random was quick and smart. He had to keep ahead of him. True, he had over a thousand years' more practice than this disoriented soul, but he had long ago learned the price of underestimating a new arrival. Random would start remembering all too soon, and then...well, Joe wasn't sure what would happen then. He had to get him to the Conclave by any means possible.

"Yes. There is one who was educated in the Conclave. She is the one who concocted this ridiculous 'movement' or 'rebellion' or whatever they're calling it these days. She has been here long enough and learned enough to cause me grief." He waited to see how this landed. Joe hoped he hadn't hesitated too long before answering the question.

"I take it you know her well."

"Yes."

14

Random was pacing the dingy room and feeling more refreshed by the moment. It wasn't as hot as it had been, and the room seemed cleaner as he walked the floorboards.

Joe grabbed his arm and looked at him intently. "Stop that! You are going to attract her attention." The sweat began to flow down Random's face again as the oppressive heat returned suddenly. A smell like rotten fruit assaulted his nose.

"Stop what? Pacing?"

"Changing things. You were changing the temperature and making this place less of a dump than it is. She cannot find us here because we are hiding in someone else's memory."

"Who is this chick you keep bringing up? You two use to date or something?"

Before Joe could answer, a huge explosion rocked the street below their window, the force of the sound so intense that they both hit the floor. Joe sprang up and ran to the window. From the carnage on the street, it was clear to see that the explosion had detonated in the middle of a crowd. Joe remembered the soldier he'd borrowed this memory from. He remembered the stories of the war being fought in the neighboring country and the time the soldier had spent in this city covertly. The soldier had told Joe about booby traps and suicide bombers in the theater of battle, but he had not mentioned any here.

Random had scrambled over to the other side of the bed, and was surprised to hear the old Bakelite phone on the bedside table ring weakly. It was as if the bell was muffled by the webs of the spiders that had most likely taken up residence inside it. The phone itself was otherworldly. It was a work of art with all its art deco curves and cloth-encased wire leading from the rotary base to the sculpted handset. It reminded him of a painting by Dalí he'd seen at a museum once.

The absurdity of the moment gripped him. Who could this be? Santa Claus? Mark Twain? His mother? What could he possibly have to lose if he really was already dead? He grinned mischievously and reached for the receiver, hefting its weight to his ear.

"Hello?"

Joe was sprinting across the room to reach him, but it was too late. Random's view of the scene faded to darkness and all sound ceased.

:: COUNTER-OFFER ::

Fuzzy edges coalesced into the image of a tiny, dark-haired woman sitting patiently in a chair looking at him. She had pale skin and high cheekbones. She looked Eastern European, perhaps Romanian. Her face was just at the border of stunning and severe, but it was hard to choose which was winning. She had tiny freckles across the bridge of her nose that looked like they'd been earned by a girl who played outdoors. Her hair was the color of bittersweet chocolate, and hung straight and shiny.

He found himself captivated by all these details as his mind raced to find a context for the piercing eyes that punctuated her face. They were darker than the darkest chocolate streaks of her hair. They drew him in, but did not offer much. She appeared to be in her mid-thirties, but she was one of those women who was probably older than she looked. She didn't blink, nor offer a smile.

His head cleared a bit more and then he was even more struck by how petite she was. She had full breasts that were a bit distracting, but she was tiny. She looked like a pixie from the woods, a nymph with a thousand-year-old stare.

"Hello. My name is Erminia." Her voice flowed across the table.

"Wow. And I thought my name was messed up." He smiled his best naughty-little-boy grin. She stared at him blankly with those dark wells. He began to feel heat up the back of his neck and wished he hadn't opened with an insult. He wondered how long she would keep staring at him, and whether she was intentionally trying to make him uncomfortable.

17

Thankfully, she finally moved. She leaned forward and looked at the table in front of her for a moment before standing up gracefully. She was lean, but curvy. As she walked across the wooden floor her high heels clicked and he realized that she must be even shorter without them. She wore expensive-looking black tailored pants and a black form-fitting cashmere sweater that was tucked in, emphasizing her tiny waist. Her heels were shiny and black and the soles were blood red; they flashed as she walked away from him. Her posture was perfect.

Without the distraction of her eyes, he finally noticed the room. It was simple and clean with hardwood floors with a stunning grain pattern. The table and chair at which she had been sitting were Mission Style, in a wood that complemented the floor well. He was surprised to see the Bakelite art deco telephone receiver still in his hand, its cloth cord snaking towards the rotary base that, strangely, still sat on the nightstand from that hot, dingy hotel room where he and Joe had been talking.

The walls were white and the room was awash with the sunlight spilling through a window behind him. There were no other windows, and he saw a single door, toward which she walked. Erminia stopped her clicking gait and pivoted silently to face him again.

"I figured that you were probably tired of hearing his lies, so I sent you a lifeline." She pointed at the phone in his hand. He gently placed the receiver back on the base. "Joe weaves a sweet little story to explain our existence here; however, it is nothing more than a lie meant to pacify the blind sheep. Would you like to know the truth?"

There was something disturbing about her referring to Joe's account as a 'sweet little story.' Given her size, it made it seem microscopic.

"Why should I believe you would tell me the truth? Why should I believe your story over his? Lemme guess: I'm not actually dead."

"Oh, your body is quite dead, I can assure you. I watched the whole thing myself; not much hope of a recovery from that." Now was the moment she chose to finally smile. It left him off balance and flooded with the images of his last moments. Joe had at least shown him the courtesy of not speaking about them directly. Had this woman also been witness to that scene? Random suddenly felt self-conscious. He pictured her standing in some hidden room behind a one-way mirror with a clipboard and a tiny pair of designer reading glasses. He felt as if she had intruded on a very private moment in his life--his final one.

She began to walk slowly back across the room. It was the poised walk of a public speaker, each click of her heels placed with precision so as not to break the rhythm of her voice. "Yes, it is true that you have released the mortal coil that held you and now find yourself...here...in the same riddle as the rest of us. That much is true, and the sooner you stop questioning that, the better. It is a fool's musing to question that. It leads to either a private hell or a Glory Bubble, but it does not reveal the truth."

"I'm sorry, a what bubble?" he asked.

She took on the air of a kind teacher. "It is what we call them. Souls who have invented their own personal Heaven, or Nirvana, or Asgard, or whatever. They are lost deeply in the illusion and refuse to believe that they are the creators. The world becomes locked and others can't get in. They have created their own 'Glory Bubble.'"

"But they believe they're dead. How would my questioning whether I'm dead have me end up in such a construct?" He saw her dangling information in front of him and leading him as an 'expert' on things he didn't know. He used to have a boss who did the same thing, and he wasn't having it.

"Yes, but they all started that way. They would not believe it until Buddha or Odin or Jesus told them. Before too long they construct the deity they want and it starts. The process speeds up, and they are lost before you know it." She leaned up against the table with her legs crossed at the ankles. "The other side of the coin are those who become Hellocked. It is the same concept, but with whatever hell their minds concoct to punish themselves for what they believe are their transgressions."

She walked back around to her chair and sat down crisply. "This is all our creation, Mr. Bridges, and it is important to remember that." She waved her hand across the desk and several screens appeared on its surface. She began to touch the different screens and images began to float in the air around the desk. They were images of him at different times in his life. There were captions noting his age and location when the 'picture' was taken.

"You had a very full life. Your accomplishments were not trivial. Both the Conclave and our humble family have been watching you and waiting for you to arrive. I had hoped to reach you first and--"

"And make me an offer before the Conclave did?" Random finished her sentence crudely. She paused, and Random knew she was not used to being interrupted. He knew how to play this now. She was used to respect and awe. He would give her none. This would keep her from using her standard parlor tricks, like this floating dossier or her charismatic stagecraft. At least, that was his hope.

She narrowed her eyes and flicked her wrist and the images vanished. "I see he has learned to talk faster. Yes, I want to have your talents on my team. You do not know the depth of the deceit the Conclave has spread. I was there in their 'sanctuary' for years. I was a true believer. When I realized the lie I knew I had to stop it. Those who listened to me named themselves the Truthers, and I agreed to lead them."

Random stood up and began his own crafted walk. He glanced at the light source behind his chair and saw a window looking out on a postcard vista of rolling green hills. He dismissed it and stayed on purpose. He turned back to the tiny woman. "So what's this 'grand truth' you're the champion of? Is the Conclave hiding God under the bed?"

He made the statement to elicit a response, trying to gather information. He had to find out whom he was dealing with. Erminia was subtle, and obviously practiced at being hard to read. But Random had played poker professionally for too many years not to catch the tell she gave him. The micro-expressions that shot across her placid face told him that he had hit the core of the recruiting message for her movement. More importantly, he was sure that the message was propaganda she did not believe. There was another game being played here. Given where they were, it couldn't be about money. Given her icy demeanor he doubted it had anything to do with love. That left only one possible motivation for this couture pixie. This had to be about power.

There was a knock at the lone door that saved her having to respond. She seemed both annoyed and relieved. She stood up smoothly. "Pardon me a moment, Mr. Bridges." She walked to the door and opened it enough to view whoever stood on the other side. The door swung in such a way that Random could not see beyond it. Another tell. If she had designed this room that way, she had things she was hiding.

As she stood there, she said nothing. At first he wondered whether there was anyone even there or she was just stalling. "Well? This had better be good; I was very specific that I was not to be disturbed. Spit it out."

The voice was nervous, apologetic and male. "I'm so sorry, Erminia, but the Recorder has detected...someone listening. They may already be aboard the Square."

"How is that possible? Aren't we at speed?" She stopped herself and looked back at Random. She addressed the unseen visitor again. "Keep on it. We will meet you in the control room shortly." She closed the door and pivoted in place to face Random. Even though they were both standing and it was now very clear how much bigger he was than she, she did not seem bothered.

"You are suspicious, manipulative and cunning, Mr. Bridges. That is precisely why I want you working for me. You obviously do not trust me, and there is no reason for you to." She once again reached for the door but opened it wide this time. A tall, thin man was standing outside it; he and jumped in surprise. He looked like a kid who would run an IT department: pale and twitchy, with a headset on one ear, its microphone curving in front of his mouth.

"This is Salvo. He came down here to inform me that someone is trying very hard to find you, Mr. Bridges. They have managed to home in on you even though we are aboard a moving target that is very difficult to track. Shall we go up to our main control room and see how dear old Joe managed to pull this off?"

She seemed to be laying her hand out on the table for him to see. He knew this wasn't true, but he wasn't going to pass up the chance. "Lead the way."

The hallway matched the stark cleanliness of the room. It had the same wood floors and trim with rich grain that continued to frame the perfect white walls with their ever-so-subtle texture. Salvo was hesitant to look him in the eyes and obviously not too happy with Erminia's sudden transparency. He gave a mumble and an awkward nod and began leading them down the long hallway.

Salvo was in front, but kept turning back to look at the tiny woman, her heels clicking with purpose behind him. Salvo shuffled sideways and sometimes walked backwards as he kept looking at her, waiting for instructions. Random brought up the rear and strolled easily with his long gait. The features of the long hall remained consistent, but somewhere ahead he could see that the hall turned right, and three framed paintings there got larger in his view as they approached. There seemed to be no other doors.

21

Erminia waited until Salvo had his back to her to finally speak. "So what did the Recorder say, exactly?" Salvo pivoted and resumed his half backwards, half sideways shuffle, struggling a bit to keep ahead of her brisk pace.

"It was just moments after the extraction... " He paused and glanced at Random.

"Go ahead; we have nothing to hide from Mr. Bridges."

"The Recorder began to talk about..." He opened the small notepad that dangled from a cord around his neck like a backstage pass. "...someone is listening hard in the Ether, they know who they're looking for, they have locked on, he is here, he won't be stopped, he has found him... Then there was a long string of nonsense before the Recorder stabilized and plainly told us that someone had just boarded the Square with the express intention of finding Random Bridges. He then told me that we had very little time, that the seeker would be here in minutes."

Erminia had quickened her pace just a bit. They were quickly approaching the end of this insanely long hallway. "What were some of the highlights of the nonsense?"

Salvo flipped pages quickly. "Ummm... gold buttons on red jacket, twisted metal burns in snow, blue butterfly does not remember the taste of yellow, and...this one was odd: the liquid chooses an old man..."

Erminia flicked her wrist in the same dismissive way she had made the images vanish at her desk. "It is all misdirection; he was masking his approach. I still have no idea how he managed to find us so quickly, especially when we are at speed." They arrived at the three paintings that marked the end of the hallway, and she stopped abruptly. She turned and looked up at Random. The paintings behind her were set in thin gold frames. He recognized the triptych immediately and flashed back to the moment when he was first assaulted by these images in his art history textbook. It was Bosch's *The Garden of Earthly Delights*, and it looked like the original triptych he had seen in Madrid.

She waited patiently for his focus to once again be drawn to her unblinking eyes. When she had his attention she spoke deliberately, but was cautious not to be condescending. "I will translate what Salvo and I were just saying without the jargon. We have a member of our group who is what they call a Recorder, who listens to the Ether. He can hear the voices of all those here as they create their realities. He is very old and mostly speaks in riddles." The schoolteacher persona was gone. She obviously just needed to convey a large amount of information quickly.

"OK..."

She continued. "The Recorders hear everything and everyone all at once. It drives them a bit mad and makes them hard to decipher. However, if they focus, they can hear specific things. We used our Recorder to find you. We also use him as a watchdog to let us know when someone is trying to find us. This time someone is looking for you, and I bet you can guess who."

"So what was all that about butterflies and liquid men?"

She rolled her eyes a tiny bit. "No one can sneak up on a Recorder, but you can confuse them by thinking of nonsense. That bit about 'tasting color' is very similar to a distracting thought Joe used to try to locate us not long ago. He might as well just tell me it is him, it's that obvious. He must be desperate to get so sloppy."

Random was fascinated by the whole concept but he was still playing a hand of poker with this woman and he had to stay on target. "You keep saying we're 'at speed.' What does that mean?"

She crossed her arms and tilted her head a bit. She was not going to want to talk much longer, he could tell. "We are aboard a very old construct that has been here in the Ether for many lifetimes. It is a mobile city that moves frequently to avoid the Conclave. It is a home for those who do not wish to be found, an alternative to the arrogance of their sanctuary, and a place where you can find just about anything for a price." She pointed to her left casually. He moved slowly in that direction and around the lone corner of the white hallway. It ended unceremoniously and opened into a huge space knotted with pipes, steel, wood, wires, sparks, steam and, above all, noise.

Above the industrial cacophony was a sky of sorts that streaked with colors, light and shapes. They were very much 'at speed'; he could think of no better way to describe it. Erminia and Salvo had followed and were standing close behind him. Her voice was calm and deep.

"Welcome to Transit Square."

23

:: TRANSIT SQUARE ::

His senses were overwhelmed. The noise of the city's movement was the sound of muted voices babbling endlessly rather than the rush of wind. It was a soft but consistent babble that had peaks and valleys of volume and intensity, as if waves of voices were breaking against the hull of a vessel sailing an ocean of thought.

He felt very much as if he were on a huge ocean liner as he took in the scene before him. The deck was wooden planks set into an iron framework. There were pipes big enough for a man to stand inside of snaking across the planking, sometimes in concert with other pipes that mimicked their path, other times shooting off from the rest. Many found their way to a giant stack in the distance that billowed plumes of white smoke, which seemed to indicate their direction of travel.

What made him doubt the idea of this being a ship was that he couldn't see the edges of the deck. Every bundle of pipes and sparking wires just led to the next. Whatever type of vessel Transit Square was, it was huge.

His roving eyes stopped and locked on Erminia standing on the deck in front of him looking like a Chief Financial Officer who had wandered into the boiler room by mistake.

"I know it is a lot to take in all at once, but I am afraid we need to keep moving, Mr. Bridges. Please follow me to our control room." She pivoted smoothly and strode off. Random followed and heard Salvo shuffling close behind him.

They walked through the wood-and-iron forest, and she began to lead them into tighter passages between the rust and sparks. They made several turns and Random became even more disoriented. There was no sun in the sky to use as a reference point, only a strange glow from the horizon on all sides.

They came to what seemed to be a dead end and she stopped. He could feel Salvo behind him. "We need to blindfold you before we go any farther. I'm sure you understand." Random shrugged, and let Salvo cover his eyes and take hold of his arm just above the elbow. They led him through a few more twists and turns, then stopped again. There were sounds of metal sliding on metal as some sort of portal was unlatched. The creak of rusted hinges told him the door was extremely heavy. He was led into a quieter space that was warmer. They kept on walking and he could hear their footsteps echo off the metal walls.

Slowly he began to hear voices that grew louder and spoke in panicked tones. They entered the room and several voices stopped at their arrival. The blindfold was removed and Random looked upon the control room of the Truther rebellion.

He was not very impressed. It was a large, circular room with tables and chairs strewn haphazardly about. There were about twenty-five people either sitting around the tables or rushing back and forth like confused messengers. Some who were seated scribbled on paper or poked at screens. The room was dark and rather dirty, and was organized around a large sphere that took up the center of the space. It was about fifteen feet in diameter and just barely managed to fit without touching the ceiling. It was the color of worn parchment and the surface was mottled. A spiral staircase in the back corner wound up to a second level.

"Relax, everyone," She spoke as a captain returning to the bridge. "We will handle this challenge." She gestured to Random. "Mr. Bridges is right here, so anyone targeting him would have to find their way in past all of us. We have nothing to hide from him."

A young girl with straight black hair and a slim build rushed up to her. She had an earpiece and microphone that matched Salvo's. "We need you to comfort the Recorder. He's been asking for you in between rather violent outbursts." Her eyes darted up toward Random. She had obviously not been comforted by Erminia's introduction.

26

"Thank you, Raven." With another runway-model pivot, Erminia turned to him. "Please excuse me for a moment, Mr. Bridges. Have a seat and I will be right back." She walked with purpose toward the large brownish globe and passed right into it. It dented slightly when she made contact and then engulfed her, ripples running across its surface. It was as though she had entered an opaque soap bubble. Raven gave him one last suspicious look and followed right behind Erminia, creating her own ripples on the surface of the globe.

Salvo had returned to his work, which seemed to be as a supervisor of this motley crew. They brought him screens and notes scribbled on paper for his review. Random felt the eyes upon him and moved slowly to the edge of the room. The crew members seemed more at ease with him as far from the sphere as possible. Most of them were young. He realized the irrelevance of that statement in this place. If he were to believe the common threads in what Joe and Erminia had told him, all these 'kids' were just souls like him who were no longer bound by age. The images he saw were how they remembered themselves. Didn't we all want to remember ourselves in our prime? He considered his own body for the first time. As he looked at his arms he knew he was remembering the strength he'd had in his early thirties. He looked around for a reflective surface and was shocked to watch as a mirror coalesced from the dirty wall.

There he was. Young. Strong. With that arrogant little smirk on his face that had always made him popular with the ladies, even when he was older. He nodded with approval at himself; then the mirror rippled and sank back into the wall as if it had never been there. Did he do that? He looked at the wall again and thought "mirror" very hard. Nothing happened this time. If Joe had been telling the truth, he had conjured up an entire rainforest from memory. If this place was simply the thoughts and memories of everyone made manifest, he just had to think anything and it would appear.

"Toast." He said it aloud as he thought it and watched his hand. It was the first thing that popped into his head. He watched as a warm piece of bread, perfectly browned with exactly the right amount of butter on it, became a reality. He sniffed it and juggled it a bit in his hand as it was hotter than he'd expected. He moved it toward his mouth but was interrupted by a loud, howling scream that made all heads turn to the sphere. He dropped his creation on the grimy floor and watched it land, butter side down.

The room was silent as the scream wound down and was replaced by a deep hum that made him feel comforted and safe. The hum faded and the activity of the room started again. More rushing and passing of notes and poking of screens. Three of the crew had formed a circle and were touching foreheads. He wondered whether they were praying.

He sat in a chair and leaned back against the wall. He was suddenly tired. Tired of this nonsense. Tired of these insane strangers and the shifting world he found himself tumbling through.

"Would you like a drink?" The husky voice came from beside him where no one had been a moment before. He turned his head slowly to find a barrel-chested man with a stubbly beard offering him a silver flask. The man looked worn from travel and seemed just as tired as Random felt.

He accepted the flask and held it below his nose. "Bourbon," the man said, leaning his arms heavily on his knees and looking at the toast on the ground. Random's nose confirmed the contents and he took a small swig from the flask. It was strong and warm. The noise of the room quieted and he felt refreshed even as the strength of the bourbon made him wince a bit.

"Take another, don't be shy. After the day you've had, you need it." Random didn't hesitate; he took a deeper pull. He shook his head a bit after that one. It was cheap bourbon, but not rotgut. It was exactly what he wanted right now. He offered the flask back and the older man looked up to meet his eyes.

He looked to be in his late fifties, with an unkempt coat of graying stubble that wasn't quite sure whether it was a beard or not. His skin was sunbaked and the lines in his face ran deep from squinting and, undoubtedly, smiling. He recovered his flask and gave a smile that warmed like the bourbon had. It was then Random realized that his eyes were not the same color. One was a grey-blue, while the other was a light hazel that leaned toward the yellow side of the spectrum.

The man took a swig from the flask himself, capped it and put it in the inside pocket of his brown duster. "So how'd you like to get out of this shithole and go someplace you have room to think?"

Random wanted nothing more desperately. "How would I do that?" he asked, indicating the room of frantic people. Before the man could respond, another series of wails came from the sphere and several people dropped their papers and dashed into it, sending ripples across the surface, now more the color of burlap than parchment.

Random winced at the sound and put his hand on the stranger's arm insistently. "Can you get me out of here?"

The man smiled slowly and winked his blue eye quickly. "You bet your ass I can, son." He reached over and took Random's hands in his. The bubble rippled wildly and Erminia came soaring out like she had jumped from a trampoline located inside. She landed perfectly, despite still wearing heels.

The man broke eye contact with Random but kept a firm hold on his hands. He smiled at the tiny woman and gave a small nod. "Payback really is a bitch, isn't it?"

With a sharp pop, Random and the man with the flask winked out of existence. The toast lay where it had fallen, still warm.

:: FABRIC ::

Random heard the pop and watched the scene behind the man shift from a noise-filled metal room to a dark and quiet night sky. The man released his hands and smiled. "Want some grub?" The man turned and leaned down to tend an iron pot hung over an open fire. "It's not much, just some simple stew. Potatoes and rabbit. I started it earlier; didn't think I'd be having company."

Random didn't answer. He looked around to assess his surroundings. He was sitting on a log in front of a campfire. His host sat on a large rock, tending the iron pot, which hung from a metal frame straddling the crackling flames. It was dark, and the night sky only offered up a few lonely stars.

Random felt fine. The air was cold and crisp. The fire warmed him. The stew smelled good. The man gave him a look as he tasted the stew with a wooden spoon. He gave a small grunt and reached into a satchel near his feet. He pulled out a half-full fifth of bourbon and handed it to Random.

They sat quietly for a while. The sound of the fire, the smell of the stew, the occasional slosh of the bourbon as they passed the bottle. Another trip into the satchel produced two rough bowls and a crude wooden ladle. The man filled the bowls and handed one to Random along with the ladle. He took the remaining bowl and used the spoon he had stirred it with as his utensil.

Their sounds became a concert of blowing on hot soup and slurping broth punctuated with hums of appreciation for the meal as they ate. They cleared their minds as only men can do, forgetting the past and disregarding the

31

future. There was only stew. There was only now. They savored the quiet as they did the stew. Random served himself a second bowl and used his ladle to serve his host another helping. They did it all without words, and went right back to the ritual of blowing on steaming spoons, slurping broth, and humming even more appreciation for the second bowl, which was thicker with meat and potatoes.

They finished at almost the same time. They locked eyes briefly with sleepy nods of satisfaction. The man collected the bowls and utensils and tossed them unceremoniously on the ground. He once again grabbed the bourbon and drank deeply. He held it for a moment with his eyes closed in a state of gratitude. He passed the bottle and Random followed suit.

They sank to the ground and used the log as a backrest. The man pulled a long pipe from his jacket. It was bone white with a thin, curved stem. He packed the bowl slowly from a leather pouch. Using a small stick he lit from the coals, he stoked the bowl and puffed on the pipe before handing it over. Random was pleased with whatever they were smoking. It had a sweetness like apple.

The man leaned back and smiled as he tapped out the pipe and loaded it again. He let the silence be, clamping the unlit pipe in his mouth, staring at the fire.

Random finally broke the silence. "Thank you."

"'Welcome," the man grunted.

The fire continued its dance and crackle. A soft breeze fanned it a bit. The man searched for a new twig to light his pipe.

"My name's Random." The man lit his pipe and puffed slowly. "Something tells me you knew that already."

The pipe was stoked well and he leaned back in a halo of smoke. "I'd heard your name. Pleasure to meet you." His yellow eye caught the firelight and made him look wolf like.

Random found himself considering his next words carefully. The man studied him, slightly bemused, and offered no help.

"May I ask what your name is?"

"Sure." The silence was still thick, but he only left Random hanging for a moment longer. "Fabric is what they call me."

"Fabric? Is Joe the only one here with a normal name?"

"You're one to talk about the kettle, Mr. Pot." He chuckled softly and puffed his pipe. "But you're right, Fabric is an odd name, even here. Souls rename themselves and do tend to make some odd choices. I believe that young Joe chose that name because it was common. It was a strategic choice, given all the newcomers he meets. His original name was something pretty damn hard to pronounce, as I remember. As for my name, I didn't pick it. Others started calling me Fabric and it seemed to stick." He shrugged. "I don't mind it."

"Why?" Random looked down at the brown duster and simple jerkin Fabric wore. He was dressed like a mountain man who had misplaced his coonskin cap. "No offense, but you don't seemed too concerned with fashion."

Fabric smiled and gave a small grunt. "None taken. Fancy dress is not the origin of my nickname. I'm a wanderer here. I explore and map the Ether, keeping track of how it all fits together. It's a hobby that still fascinates me. They say I know the fabric of the place better than most."

"Why'd you help me?"

Fabric laughed and took his last drag off the pipe before tapping it out on a rock. "I was repaying a debt. That little bitch crossed me on a deal a while back. She probably thought I'd forgotten by now. I hadn't. I could see how hard she'd worked to snatch you. I don't particularly know why, nor do I care. But I knew it'd piss her off and screw up whatever she's planning." He smiled broadly. "Now we're even, according to me. She probably don't see it the same way."

He stowed his pipe and leaned back again. "Plus, you seemed like a nice kid. I was watching those two bouncing you all around without givin' you a moment to mourn your own death. I figured I could do a good deed by giving you a safe haven for a spell." He looked up at the few stars that twinkled here and there. "But mostly I did it to piss in her oatmeal."

Random believed Fabric. He sat at ease, and seemed satisfied with a plan well executed.

"She thought it was Joe who was coming after me."

"I know, that was the brilliant part!" Fabric sat up and the fire reflected in his mismatched eyes. "The two of them really went at it a while back. I was just watching from the shadows. My Recorder picked up that bit about 'the taste of yellow' that Joe used to sneak up on them. Them idiot cultists thought it was some communication from the divine! He damn near caught them with that bit of nonsense. That Joe is a smart kid, and I took note of it. I knew I could use it to pin my approach on him when I was ready to move. Thanks for dying when you did. The timing was perfect!"

Random looked a bit confused. "You said 'your Recorder'..." He looked into the shadows, wondering whether there was a large bubble hiding just out of sight.

Fabric reached into his satchel once again. It was the same buckskin color as most of his clothing. He pulled out an ornate silver cube about five inches across. He held it gently. It was covered in interlocking spirals engraved into the metal surface. It looked like an artifact that might have sat on Cleopatra's dressing table.

"An old friend who likes to travel with me. We travel light; she has all the space she needs." He smiled at the cube fondly and placed it back in the satchel. "I'd introduce you, but...well, you've already had a full day."

Random was glad to let that go for the moment. "What do you want from me?" His voice was a bit sleepy.

Fabric smiled. "Not a damn thing, son. You helped me settle a score. My payment to you for this service is a hot meal, a stiff drink, and a place where neither Joe nor that little bitch'll find you for a while. Relax. Close your eyes and sleep if you like. I'll keep watch."

Random was asleep in minutes. Fabric tended the fire and waited until he knew Random was down for the count. He took out the silver cube again and placed it on his belly. He sang softly to the Recorder like a parent singing a lullaby.

: : CIRCLING THE SQUARE : :

"How do you know this is the place? It does not seem big enough for them to set down." Joe's voice was betraying him. He was out of his element and it showed. The woman he'd hired crouched like a panther behind a small gathering of boulders she had conjured up to provide them cover. She was used to stupid questions from clients. They came to her when they were desperate and needed something no one else could deliver. As a result, her services were expensive. Answering stupid questions and babysitting those not familiar with the wilds of the Ether was just an occupational hazard.

"This be the place. Be patient, and be quiet...please." She normally did not give such courtesy to clients, but she never thought someone like Joe would engage her services. She was treating him more kindly because this one was really going to cost him.

She had shown her normal unshakeable confidence at the request, but inside she struggled with doubt. She wasn't clear whether what he had requested could even be done, but she loved a challenge and this payday would top anything she had done to date. It would either solve her problems, or create a whole new set of them.

"I am sorry. I do not mean to question your work." He sat down on the ground, leaned back against one of the rocks, and adjusted the thick cloak she had given him.

She relaxed her ready stance and folded herself silently back down into a simple squat beside him. She moved like a shadow during a swift sunset.

Joe peered out of his cloak. Tazir was a sight to behold. Her limbs were long and lean. She seemed like the spawn of African royalty and extraterrestrial intelligence. Her skin was black as night and tinged with a blue iridescence where the light could find the edges of her form. She was close to seven feet, but nimble and silent in every motion. Her head was bald, with a slight hint of the high hairline that honored her tribal roots. Her features had both the chiseled beauty of a queen and the dangerous lines of a warrior. A long, serpentine scar raised above her smooth flesh ran from the base of her neck down the length of her right arm, ending near her elbow. It was a distinctive wound: old, deep, and very intentional.

Tazir spoke in a deep hush. "The Square be running a bit late, but this be the place. They'll make the room they need when they arrive. Ever seen it land?" Her eyes searched his light brown face slowly as he peeked from the hooded cloak.

"I saw it take off once...but that was a long time ago." He thought back to the day so many lifetimes in the past.

"It's a sight." She reached into the small bag slung across her chest and resting at her hip. She withdrew a gold cylinder about the size of a large mason jar. She spoke to it in a whisper that became a muted song. The metal cylinder reacted by sliding open in a way only a watchmaker could have foreseen. Its top bloomed like a gilded lotus, in a symphony of clicks and whirs. Warm light poured from it, and a tiny humanoid form floated free of the mechanical wonder, moving to curl its arms around Tazir's neck in a loving embrace. It moved alternately as liquid, then as smoke. It formed and reformed itself, always returning to the form of a small human-shaped being no more than fourteen inches high.

It came to rest on her shoulder, nestled near her left ear. It began to speak, a trickle of words building to the more audible range. Its voice was that of a child chanting a stream of consciousness.

"...long rivers flow, green fields and wildflowers, dark prism beyond his reach...it is moving close, long circle, engine room was afraid...great mountain hall, family of laughter, warm garden filled with squash and strawberries...they cannot delay any longer, the clients are waiting, they must stick to the original destination...lonely man on an endless plain, so much sorrow, monsters pursue him...they are here!" The chanting stopped and the tiny form flowed like mercury back into the container, the metal parts already clicking and whirring as it re-formed into the sealed golden cylinder just as the last drops of the Recorder dove back inside.

Tazir held the cylinder gently and whispered a final incantation before putting it back in her bag. She coiled back up to the rock and hugged it again like a great cat ready to pounce. Joe poked his head over the edge of a stone, taking care to keep the cloak wrapped tightly, just as she had instructed. They waited.

The clearing they looked out upon was a flat plain, featureless other than a few tufts of reeds and the small grouping of rocks behind which he and Tazir crouched. The light was a nondescript version of twilight. Surrounding the small clearing, rising up on all sides, were three huge bubbles that sat like dark, shimmering marbles on a slab of concrete. Nearly two hundred feet high, they almost touched before sloping away from each other to their own apexes. The strange twilight filtered through the cracks between them and lit the clearing feebly.

Joe hated being here. This was the intersection of three very nasty realities. The three souls who had constructed them were the ones the term 'Hellocked' had been coined to describe. They had created a living hellscape together in the time of confusion before the Conclave had become widely accepted. It was said they had been three brothers in whatever life they had lived on Earth, and had all died in one tragic moment. They had arrived here together and decided as a group that this was whatever hell they had been warned of. The reality they had constructed with their shared torment was so horrific that it was still spoken of in hushed tones. One day, it was said, the nightmare closed off into a sealed realm that no one entered and no one left. It had been such a powerful vision that others who had been near the nightmare found themselves trapped inside with the brothers.

Joe remembered when the one great blemish had begun to split, first into two, and then finally into three. There were many theories as to the reason for the division after hundreds of years as a whole, but it was all rumor and speculation. These hells were all still locked; no souls entered and none left. Joe remembered the sad look on the face of the ancient woman who had been his teacher when he'd asked about it. She would not confirm or deny the stories. She simply told him it was a place to be avoided and to be remembered as a warning. She did say once that this was one of the reasons why she had helped to form the Conclave in the first place. He always felt a darkness from her, like that of a widow, when he dared mention it.

The small clearing was silent. He trusted his guide, but failed to see how Transit Square would fit in it if it was as large as he remembered. He understood the choice of location. There was a sadness that overcame anyone who looked at the dark, opaque swirls that filled the huge mucous structures like a thunderstorm in a snow globe. No one wanted to come here. It was the perfect place to hide a city.

Then he saw it. The first few glimmers. Small winks of light that flicked on and off at the three corners of the roughly triangular clearing. With a sharp pop, three small, identical craft appeared. They each held three people sitting astride them with heavy overcoats and goggles. One crew member sat higher and toward the back of each craft, and appeared to be the pilot. The other two sat lower, and held flared tubes over their shoulders that they panned across the area furiously.

He closed as much of the cloak as he could while still allowing himself to see. He was not going to miss this. Each craft hovered and turned in a practiced dance while the teams pointed the tubes around. They were scout ships looking for any last-minute signs of trouble. One by one the teams completed their scans and stowed their strange tubes, giving an all-clear sign to the others.

Tazir's cloak seemed to be doing its job; it masked him well. The scanners moved as far back as they could from the noses of the strange little ships. The front of each craft was fitted with a disc of iron about twenty feet in diameter. The discs ruined the lines of the otherwise sporty little rockets and looked like they had been bolted on as an afterthought.

The pilots aimed the ridiculous noses of their crafts so that each faced one of the gloomy spheres. They hovered higher until they were about seventy-five feet above the ground. At a silent signal, their engines roared and they each went hurtling towards the surface of their chosen target. Joe gasped as he realized their intent.

The spheres dented as the ships reached the surface. The sound of the engines grew louder as they pushed against the huge objects, leaving deep dimples that grew slowly. The Hellocked realms would not allow them entry, but their surface was elastic. The clearing was getting bigger. They were making room.

Flashes of light began to fill the clearing, just a few at first, then like ten thousand cameras flashing silently. The sound would come soon. He had heard it once, but knew he would still be unprepared for its intensity. He was right.

The sound that accompanied the arrival of the city had been likened to the tearing of a planet that was filled with high-pressure gas. It was so uncomfortable to hear that even those awaiting the arrival of the Square stayed miles away. Joe and Tazir were alone in the clearing because they were the only ones stupid enough to be this close.

The sound came and made both Joe and Tazir cringe. It was physically painful at this proximity, and lived up to its reputation as being one of the most thoroughly unpleasant sounds you could ever be unlucky enough to hear.

With the sound came the city.

It ripped and popped into the space from the center outward. The scout ships had made room but it wasn't enough. The massive tangle of bronze, copper, wire, concrete, sparks and smoke assaulted the boundaries of the three hells and sent ripples rushing over their surfaces with the sounds of screams. The scout ships had chosen their altitude with precision. The decks of the city rolled out just below them.

And in an instant, it was before them. The behemoth still hovered just a few feet above the ground, jets of steam pouring from its belly. The central smokestack marked the highest point, rising high above the deck. Below the deck, a woven nest of pipes, wires, superstructure and walkways formed an inverted pyramid. It was like a large industrial city had grown bored of its location, built itself a mechanical lifting system and gone off on a holiday.

Out of the mechanical roots of the city came an array of enormous landing gear that creaked and moaned as it unfolded from the mess. Each leg locked in its own time, and the city descended like a clockwork flying saucer that might have been built by naval engineers at the turn of the 20th century.

When its weight finally came to rest on the landing gear and huge plumes of white smoke filled the clearing, Joe found himself repeating the words that Tazir had spoken to him.

"It is a sight..."

:: NEGOTIATION ::

Joe sat very still. His head was still throbbing and his ears still ringing from the intense sound of the arrival. Tazir was also frozen in her catlike pose on the rock. He was watching the mountain of twisted metal as it settled into its new location, jets of steam firing off at odd intervals, as if the city were breathing a sigh of relief after a long run. The inverted pyramid of mechanical chaos that was its undercarriage began to crawl with activity as hatches opened and crew members began to fill the knotted network of walkways. Sometimes an alert siren blew, spewing its own tiny puff of white smoke, signaling something to the men and women who crawled over the superstructure like ants. All sounds were muted for Joe now, after the appalling noise he had just survived.

Tazir grabbed his arm and shook him gently. He looked at her and saw her mouth moving but did not hear her words. She realized that they were both temporarily deafened. She pointed to her eyes to gain his undivided attention.

Her face began to shift. Her high forehead dropped and her cheekbones softened. Her skin faded to a warm brown and her eyes became emerald green with flecks of brown. Her long, thin limbs shortened and became plump and full in his peripheral vision. In a few moments, he watched Tazir transform into a stunning Latin woman in her early thirties who looked as if she had just stepped off a beach in Brazil, still warm from the sun.

This was why he had agreed to pay her fee. She was one of the best; she could transform herself faster and with more precision than almost anyone he had ever met. It was a gift that only a rare few seemed to have. They could recall the nature of others with such depth that they could assume their forms. It was said that it took a true love of the subject to accomplish effectively. Tazir had a diverse palette of forms to choose from, and was forever collecting new subjects. Joe had often wondered what it would take to love so many, so deeply.

His eyes dropped to the base of her neck. The thick scar remained on Tazir's new skin, tracking over her shoulder and down her right arm, winding its tortuous path toward her elbow. This was her touchstone, the marker she took with her as she assumed each new form. Without such a marker, she might lose herself as she wore the skins of those she loved. He had seen one who had fallen prey to this fate. It was a great risk that was carried by all her kind.

The full Brazilian lips began to speak, and Joe found his hearing had returned enough to make out her words. The voice matched the new body; it was thick and seductive. Her green eyes flared and her thin, dark eyebrows danced as she spoke.

"That is the first step. Now we need to get aboard. What payment can you offer the boatswain?"

"What will interest them the most?" Joe still held the heavy cloak tightly at the neck.

Tazir's new hands moved to his with grace and her very touch had his grip loosen before she even spoke. "You won't need that; they're not looking anymore, meu querido." She slowly dropped his hood to his neck and adjusted how it lay. She touched him like a woman who was a mother of many, a matriarch who had not lost the fire of sexuality that had given her so many children in the first place. Joe now knew why she had been so highly recommended. She didn't just look like this new woman; she moved, spoke and behaved like her. The transformation was complete and seamless. He now realized why she had chosen such a large, brutal scar as her touchstone.

"Food is always best. The more complex the flavor and texture, the better." Her head tipped slightly as she absentmindedly adjusted the way the cloak hung on his chest. "Do you have any fresh memories of unique food? They seem to have a preference for very rich flavors."

Joe had not walked the earth for hundreds of years, but he had a wealth of memories to draw from. Almost none of the memories he searched belonged to him. He greeted those who had just arrived and bathed in the fresh treasure trove of memories they brought with them. At times the visions they trailed were nightmarish, if they had passed violently or with deep regret. Other times he would be wrapped in love and hospitality, often sharing a meal.

He knew the value the memories of food carried here. A soul inhabiting the Ether did not require food, but there was comfort in a meal. The longer they were here, the more their memories would fade. Soon a soul might do anything to remember the taste of a bowl of grits, or a shank of lamb, or the burn of a hot pepper that made their lips go numb. He had learned to mine these memories in his first meetings, and it had made him a very wealthy man who could afford almost anything, even Tazir's exorbitant fee.

Joe's eyes darted back and forth as if he were scanning an invisible book. He stopped and looked back into the sensual eyes of Tazir's new countenance. A wicked smile drew the corners of his mouth up slowly.

Tazir smiled wickedly in return. "Whatever that is, it's perfect. We have little time before the masses arrive." She removed her bag and withdrew a flowing, long-sleeved blouse, which she donned to cover her scar. She also extracted a skirt the color of the Mediterranean to complete her outfit. She held out her hand to Joe. "The cloak, please."

He returned the large, heavy cloak and she packed it in the small bag easily, even though logically it was far too big to fit. She turned back to him and raised her eyebrow at him expectantly.

Joe closed his eyes and concentrated. He had chosen his disguise before he contacted Tazir, and had practiced it well. She made it look easy; it was more difficult for him. Slowly his entire body rippled as he took on the likeness of the wild-eyed boy he had met just a few months ago. He had the thin, wiry build of a basketball player. He had begged and pleaded to get back into a body as soon as possible. Joe had helped him bypass much of the waiting and delays that occurred at the sanctuary of the Conclave and sent him back without delay. If Joe hadn't helped him, the boy would have found another way. He would have found the black markets of Transit Square.

Joe opened his eyes and the disguise was complete. Tazir inspected his work. "You make it so hard, creating both the person and the costume together but this will do. Now all you need to do is act a bit desperate, pay the toll, and we're in."

It wasn't long until the others began to arrive. Most came on foot, while some went streaming by the crowds in shining cars, hovering craft, flying carpets, and even one couple on the back of a camel. They traveled mostly in twos, but occasionally there were parties of three or four. They all gathered near one of the mammoth mechanical feet, where a lone gangplank was pivoting down to meet the ground. Tazir and Joe mixed in with the other travelers on foot and took their time.

By the time they reached the entry point to Transit Square, the crew had set up a small tent near the base of the gangplank. All the vehicles were parked haphazardly and there was a queue of about forty people waiting to speak to those in the tent. Joe saw a young man in jeans and a white t-shirt being led away from the tent by a woman dressed like a gypsy. They checked in with two large, surly crew members that guarded the base of the gangplank and handed them a yellow card. The gypsy and the man then ascended the first steps of what would be a long climb before they reached the main deck of the city.

Tazir led him, holding his hand to comfort him. He was having a hard time with the sudden change in her behavior, having met her as the almost alien warrior queen. Her actions were not just an act; they were part of the package when she was in this form. She was, quite literally, a different person.

The line moved slowly. As they stood, about ten more couples lined up behind them. These appeared to be the last of the applicants for the day. The final applicant arrived with flair, astride a pegasus. Some in line made noises of approval and wonder as the beast touched down. The rider was a flamboyant man in a red turban and flowing robes. He vaulted off the steed before it even touched down, and struck a pose. He then helped the rather frail-looking old woman who was his passenger down to the ground. Tazir pointedly ignored his grand entrance; her disdain was noticeable.

By the time they neared the front of the line, seven applicants had been turned away. They each came out of the tent visibly upset, their handlers comforting them.

There were many hushed conversations in the line between the guides and their clients. No one chatted idly, and there was the distinct feeling of competition in the air. Those who had been sent to the back of the line spoke nervously in huddles with their handlers. The guides would take their clients aside and have a private consultation before going to the back of the line to wait for a second chance. The clients did not hide their growing desperation.

Tazir and Joe stood at the flap of the tent and stepped back quickly when the applicant before them came storming out. He was a large man with a beard and a chest you could project a film on. He wore a loincloth and fur boots that looked like they had come from the same animal hide. He was shouting and being chased by a tiny elfin creature with dragonfly wings that buzzed loudly as it flitted around its client, trying to calm him.

"Next!" came a bellow from within the tent.

The simple exterior of the tent belied the lavish interior. A grand mahogany desk trimmed with gilt fittings sat in the center. It had to weigh several thousand pounds. The floors were covered in plush Persian rugs. The canvas walls were adorned with painted murals that moved gently as the breeze buffeted them from outside. A massive crystal chandelier hung suspended in the air, secured to nothing. Behind the desk were several polished wood tables loaded with platters of food, two sculptures in marble that looked like they were straight out of the Louvre, a multi-layer fountain that gurgled softly, three large red-lacquered chests with traditional Chinese latches, three or four framed oil paintings, and one perfect Les Paul hollow-body electric guitar propped in a shining chrome stand. All of the items were tagged, as if ready to be auctioned.

Sitting behind the massive desk was a slight man in a crisp white shirt, a green bow tie, a royal blue vest and round glasses with gold frames. The light from the chandelier glittered off the rims of his glasses and the gold watch chain that disappeared into his vest pocket. He didn't look up from the paper on which he was writing with a long white feather quill. Joe noticed the ornately carved wooden stand that held an immaculate waistcoat and bowler. They waited for the man to finish his task and grant them his attention.

The dapper man finished his scratching and replaced the quill in a crystal holder on the desktop. He read over whatever he had been scrawling and mouthed words silently. Satisfied, he placed the parchment in a large file folder that sat on the desktop. It was then that he sighed and looked up at the pair in front of him.

His eyes skipped off Joe and landed squarely on Tazir's very pleasing visage. "Sarah! What a pleasure to see you again! It's been lifetimes since you have graced our doorstep with your enchanting beauty." He stood briskly and formally and walked around the desk to greet her. She extended her hand and actually curtsied as he kissed it gently.

"Oh, Doctor Morris, your flattery feeds my wicked soul!" Her eyebrows danced over her glittering green eyes.

"Sarah, please, call me Cyril. We have known each other too long to use titles." He released her hand after another soft kiss and then glanced at the thin, slightly desperate-looking young man that was Joe's cover. "But I see you are here on business." He strode back to his leather chair behind the polished desk and sat down with authority. A new sheet of parchment rolled out of thin air and rested on his blotter. The long feather quill floated deftly from its crystal rest and hovered so that he could pluck it out of the air at any moment. "I take it this is your first visit to Transit Square, young man?"

Joe nodded his unfamiliar head nervously. Tazir had made it clear in their rehearsals that he should try not to speak, and follow her lead.

"Well, as I'm sure your lovely guide Sarah has explained," his eyes darted to the Brazilian beauty posing for his pleasure, "coming aboard the Square requires a toll. As you can see behind me, the types of memories we accept are varied. What they have in common is that they are all vivid and complete. Today is the first time I've accepted a guitar as a fare, but this is a memory from a musician who had a love for a very rare instrument. He lived with it for much of his life and knew every curve, every imperfection, and every intricacy of tone. I was astounded by the texture of the memory and granted him passage."

Dr. Cyril Morris plucked his feather stylus from the air and adjusted himself in his seat. "So, what memory do you have for me, young man?" He looked expectant, and it was clear, though he wrapped himself tightly in formality and protocol, that he loved his job.

Sarah-Tazir chimed in with her melodic voice. "Oh, come now, Cyril, can't I simply pay his toll with a visit to your chambers once we're back at speed?" Her brown body twisted slightly. The good Doctor's eyes grew larger behind the gold rims of his glasses as his eyes considered the suggestive movement of her hips.

"That grants you passage, my dear, but you know the rules. He must provide his own payment, just like everyone else." He turned his attention back to Joe. "It is what keeps this a vibrant city. We are an ever-changing metropolis fueled by the fresh influx of new recollections from the world that you are obviously very keen to get back to. Don't be shy; show me what you've brought. Anything would be better than the last applicant. I can't believe he had the gall to try to sell the memory of his favorite weapons."

Doctor Morris shook his head slightly. "As if anyone here would have a strong desire to remember the tools of destruction."

Joe moved as if he were a much younger man at a recital with his whole family watching. Tazir had coached him well, and this entire interaction was playing out much as she had expected. He held his palms up and a red and black nylon, reinforced backpack appeared and fell into his grasp. It was a modern-style rucksack of the kind often sold in expensive outdoor stores in sprawling cities to urban professionals who would probably never use it for much more than a short hike in a national park. However, this pack was heavily used, with scuffs and marks that made it clear it had been on an excursion worthy of its design. There was a hydration hose clipped to the shoulder strap, and a large tear in the side that had been stitched back up roughly using a dirty leather bootlace. Complementing its well-used exterior was a damp, earthy smell of underbrush with a musty hint of mildew. Wherever this backpack had been, it had been a hell of a ride.

Joe took the weight of the bag as it came to be, then caught it by its shoulder strap before lowering it to the ground. Dr. Morris sat higher in his chair to watch the nervous young man unzip the large main zipper and begin to rummage through the pack. Joe jumped back as a five-inch centipede crawled out of the compartment and across the Persian rug. He then began extracting the contents and arranging them on the thick carpet: a micro-propane cooking set nested like Russian dolls, a shank of soiled rope with a sharp hook tied to the end, a rain poncho that trickled drops of water and several high-impact plastic boxes that were locked securely to keep out moisture.

Sarah outwardly feigned building excitement as each item was extracted, but inside, Tazir was unclear what the hell Joe was thinking with this offering. She had assumed he would have something truly wondrous to offer, given all he had seen. She began to feel their chances of even boarding Transit Square, let alone achieving the more difficult stages of the plan, slipping away.

The Doctor stayed transfixed and somewhat amused as he waited patiently. At last, Joe withdrew a bright red plastic box with heavy latches and a white cross on it. It appeared to be a first aid kit. He pulled hard on the latches and they snapped loudly. He stood up and placed the box on the desk blotter, with the unlatched side facing Dr. Morris. He stepped back and folded his hands, looking down at the floor meekly.

Cyril Morris released his quill and it floated away. He touched the box gently at first but found he needed both hands to force the tight plastic clamshell open. There were no first aid supplies inside. The watertight container was filled to capacity with thick, stiff, dried meat in rough strips.

The Doctor stayed frozen and his eyes moved back to Joe. The thin, nervous young face that Joe hid behind gave a clear signal that communicated "try some" with a tiny flick of the head.

Cyril took a large strip of the dried meat and sat back in his leather chair. He considered the ugly brown strip for a moment and then tore into it with his side teeth.

The stream of expressions that ran over his face was like watching a passenger on a roller coaster. Soon they were followed by grunts of approval as he chewed loudly and tore in for another bite.

After chewing the dried meat vigorously for a long time he finally spoke. "What is this?"

"Rat...I think." Joe mumbled.

Dr. Morris quickly opened the desk drawer and extracted a bright yellow card, which he handed to Joe. Still chewing the jerky vigorously, he said, "Welcome, young man! Enjoy your time aboard Transit Square!"

:: SUBVERSION ::

They climbed through the maze of catwalks for almost an hour. Often their progress was slowed by what seemed like complete disregard for human beings: at times, the walkway narrowed and devolved into a ledge without railings. Other times, the metal path simply stopped at a bulkhead and they had to double back to find some way to climb the knots of tubing to reach the next level, as some pipes were too hot to touch. Every problem in the design must have been solved with the addition of more switch boxes, additional tubing, or loops of dirty electrical wire. An otherwise clear path would have to be abandoned due to the sparking of fouled wires, or a blown valve spouting steam.

Tazir had made this ascent before and thus saved them some time with her memory. She did notice that every obstacle seemed to bother Joe quite a bit. She would catch him shaking his head or just standing tracing the paths of rusted spaghetti in an attempt to decipher the logic. She speculated that he must have spent too much time in the crisp, ordered halls of the Conclave. The shifting chaos around him must be upsetting by comparison.

Finally they reached a landing with a passage that led them away from the open air and deep under the city. The walls and floor became stone, and the smell of damp soil surrounded them. Now and again a pipe with a large valve wheel broke through the stone like a mechanical root structure, but it was clear that the stone was much older. They were in the catacombs of the original city. The mechanical mess had been added later.

They reached a ladder. A rusted sign showed an arrow pointing up. They looked up the shaft that ran straight up to a small point of light at the top. It would be a very long climb in a tight space.

"I wish we could just fly up." Sarah ran her delicate finger over the slimy rungs of the metal ladder with distaste. Joe had walked over to a wall and was running his hands over the stone. He found a small square block about six inches from the floor and began dusting it off.

Joe spoke without taking his focus off the wall. "She has made sure that can't happen. There is no flying anywhere in the city. It is easier to control the masses when they are grounded." He touched the stone he had finished cleaning softly. He stood up and turned to face her. "Can I lose the disguise now? I need all my concentration for this."

She gave him a puzzled look. "You don't really need it now; my companion is masking us both." She touched the satchel at her hip that contained the gold cylinder. "Need your concentration...for what?"

Joe morphed back into his preferred appearance. The nervous young man was gone and he felt relief at being himself again. Tazir was so at ease in her new form that he had been calling her Sarah as they climbed. It wasn't as easy for him; he had had to constantly remember the nervous boy to maintain his appearance.

"We may not be able to fly, but there is more than one way to enter the Square." Joe unfastened the clasp of the necklace he wore against his chest. Two items were strung on it. He removed one of the items and held it in his teeth while he refastened the necklace, tucking the remaining pendant back into his shirt. The item he had removed was a pewter color with a tinge of copper. He plucked it out of his teeth and held it by a gold handle on its backside. It was an exquisite piece of workmanship, a filigree of metals so delicate it looked like lace. The way he held it made it look like a stamp that would be pressed in ink and then used to print the design on paper.

He turned back to the wall and pressed the metal on the small stone he had cleaned. It sank into the stone when he applied some pressure. He then released the handle and rubbed his fingertips like a safecracker.

She crouched beside him and watched intently. He blew on his fingertips and ignored her, focusing on the metal embedded in the stone. "You shepherd the impatient, to serve us all...my love."

He touched the handle and turned it ninety degrees. The sound of stone sliding on stone announced the appearance of the doorway that opened in the wall. He removed the metal key and stood up. He walked through the door and she followed. As soon as they were through, torches mounted to the walls ignited to light their way. He turned back to the opening and swallowed hard. "Thank you." The stone slid again and the doorway once again became a solid wall.

He turned his head and gently took the hand of the beautiful Brazilian woman in front of him. He placed the delicate key in her open palm. "I will still honor our original terms. Consider this a bonus." He took a lit torch from the wall and began leading the way down the passage. "I won't need it anymore."

She followed behind him but was transfixed by the item she held in her hand. More subtle details revealed themselves the longer she looked at it. The key's pewter base had a tiny rim of copper and the handle was a warm, soft gold that looked as if it had been hammered by hand. She realized that she could get lost in studying the details of the workmanship and walk into a wall. She wrapped it carefully in one of her scarves and placed it in her satchel. She then quickened her steps to catch up with Joe, who walked swiftly through the catacombs, choosing passageways and turning corners with the confidence that comes from familiarity.

The small stone passageway opened into a chamber. For the first time, Joe stopped and looked at the two arched doorways in front of them. He looked at one, and then the other. He touched his forehead and traced an invisible map in his head.

Sarah walked to the wall and ran her fingers over the graffiti that had been carved in the stone. She whispered the words as she traced the letters with her touch. "Vandal Square welcomes all."

Joe's attention turned to her voice. The light from his torch cast a flickering shadow of her on the wall. "This place has not been called that in a long time. I suggest you not speak that name again; it will make it harder for your companion to mask our presence." He turned back to the archways and moved toward the one on the left. "This way."

They walked the catacombs for another half hour or so. At times he paused to assess their position and then continue on. He obviously knew the place well, but it had been lifetimes since he had walked this path. They were climbing as they walked, sometimes ascending stairs, other times gradual inclines, but always up.

At last they reached a wooden door with heavy iron hinges. He placed the torch in a holder on the wall near the door. She met his eyes for the first time since he had placed the key in her hand. She touched his forearm and brought his hands up, holding them tenderly in hers. "You are very kind to have given me such a gift. I've been guiding souls here for hundreds of years. Guides are known to be gossips but I've never even heard whispers of these tunnels. How do you know of this place?"

He was overcome by her tenderness and the firelight in her green eyes. He touched her face gently and her lips parted instinctively. The creases at the corners of his eyes accompanied a smile. "Because I was one of the Builders of what is now known as Transit Square, before it became a moving target. These catacombs were part of the original design and allowed us to move in and out of the city undetected, back when the gatekeepers were far more fierce than your friend Doctor Morris."

Her eyes widened at the thought. He pulled away and held her hands in his. "Now we need to ready ourselves. Beyond this door is a shop that is in the very heart of the Square. I am not sure how much it has changed, as it has been a long time since I have been here. I will need your skills to get to our destination. Have you thought about what is next?"

She gathered herself and remembered she was on an assignment. A renewed professionalism came over her, as she now had a new sense of the difficulty of the job and the nature of her uncommon client. "Yes, of course. You will resume your disguise and I will continue to be Sarah. It's been several years since I've been here, but I was a respected guide. No one will think twice at seeing me lead you through the Square." She stopped a moment. "What shop does this door lead into? The more I know about what we're stepping into, the better."

His focus went soft as he looked back, deep in his memory. "It was a tavern on the corner, a place to eat rich food and drink thick ale. It was three stories high and had paned windows with red awnings. The walls were lined with cherrywood and gold. There was a obsidian fireplace in the center that was always lit..."

"Genseric's? This door leads to Genseric's?" She did not hide her surprise.

"I see she kept the name. Never underestimate the power of nostalgia." He read the dismay on her face. "It leads to a storage room in the basement. I designed it to provide entry without attracting attention. There is a stairway that leads to the kitchen."

Tazir was not comforted. "Genseric's is a place to see and be seen. The other guides know Sarah and would be suspicious if I walked out of the kitchen."

Joe smiled as he turned the knob and opened the door. "Well, we will have to create a diversion."

· · · · ·

Erminia sipped the warm beer from a pint glass so large, it made her look like a child. Genseric's was bustling with commerce. There were a few new arrivals and many who had become regulars. Today was busy, as they had just landed the city in a location that would provide safe haven for a while. She remembered how much Joe hated this dismal nook between the Hellocked souls, and doubted the Conclave would come looking for the Square here. They would be able to stay here for at least a month until they had to move again.

The first day after touchdown was always filled with excitement. Only those guides who were in the know would arrive today, but soon there would be a flood of new souls bartering their memories. When they started to arrive alone without the aid of guides, Erminia would know it was time to relocate. It meant that their location had become common knowledge.

The Tavern that bore the name of one of her heroes was populated mostly by those having a final drink or purchasing a sumptuous meal before disembarking. No one left when they were at speed and, normally, no one got on board either--that is, not until that old bastard had somehow managed to stow away and steal Random from her grasp, right in her own control room.

She should have known better than to cross him. She sipped her beer and cursed herself for her arrogance. She was the queen here, running things and shaping the world to her desire while fueling her manufactured 'movement' of young fools seeking the 'truth' and forwarding her larger plan. She had gotten overconfident, and had welched on a deal she'd struck with Fabric. That was at least fifty years ago. She hadn't realized he would wait so patiently to return the favor. He had waited for her to want something very badly and be fully committed with her guard down. He had waited for Random the same way both she and Joe had, but for a different reason.

She doubted he had any idea why either she or Joe wanted Random so badly. He probably didn't care. He was known for pulling off elaborate plots and fantastic pranks just because it amused him. He was very old, and had been here longer than most of the Recorders. It wasn't even worth it to try to guess his motives. She was rather impressed with his deviousness; she just wished she hadn't been the target of it.

Delays. She hated delays. So much planning had gone into this. She now had to wait for Fabric to grow tired of his new toy and turn his attention to the next shiny thing that grabbed his attention. He had a notoriously short attention span, but she would still have to find Random and gain his trust. Even when she did, and she knew she would, who knows what crap Fabric would have filled his head with by then?

For now she just sipped her beer and sat in her private booth surveying the pandemonium that was Genseric's Tavern. The large obsidian fireplace roared and crackled in the middle of the chaos. It was an open bonfire bordered by a smooth obsidian bench in the shape of an octagon. Many sat on the bench, their backs to the fire, chatting with their parties at tables and chairs all along the perimeter. The once-lustrous cherry walls were blackened with soot. No matter how many times she tried to re-imagine them, the patrons always pictured them stained with soot from the fire. They imagined the tavern as dark and a bit seedy. She finally stopped fighting their shared illusion and just let them have it. She had managed to keep sconces filled with orchids on the walls, especially near her private booth. The delicate flowers looked ridiculously out of place in the otherwise stale and dingy tavern, but everyone knew they were her creation and let them be to avoid her wrath. The flowers always perked up when the patrons noticed her enter, like little floral soldiers.

One wall of the great room was occupied by a long bar, carved out of the same rich cherry wood as the stained wall paneling. It was crowded with patrons shouting orders and providing payment. Behind the bar was a team of workers. They gathered the items offered for trade and placed them on tables. It was an odd array of memories. Just as in the small tent of Doctor Cyril Morris, they were all tagged methodically. The bartenders would return to the patrons and conjure up whatever had been bargained for--mostly food and drink today.

On the opposite wall was a line of small booths with sheer curtains drawn across them. As was the case most days, they were fully occupied and the sounds of all types of sexual activities rang from them. Silhouetted by flickering flames, the orgy continued perpetually. Sometimes patrons moved from the bar to a curtained booth to collect whatever carnal pleasure they had been able to afford.

Some couples had no need of the privacy of a booth and pleasured each other openly for all to see. For the most part, the flesh worshippers tended to stay on the one side of the bar, to avoid distracting those who were just here for a good meal.

Erminia's booth was near the back, and raised to oversee whatever scene was unfolding below. The swinging doors of the kitchen were just below her little balcony. The 'cooks' really just needed a quiet place to recreate the complex memories of food, but it worked much like a standard kitchen, with trays of delicacies being carried out by servers or just floating out on their own to the appropriate table.

She enjoyed the debauchery and felt it paid homage to the man after whom she'd named this place. But today she was not amused, having just recently lost her prize and wondering how long it would take to get her plans back on track.

The saloon-style doors flew open and a voice called out loudly enough that it was easily heard even over the noise of the patrons. "Huzzah!" The man in the red turban who had arrived on the winged horse stood triumphantly in the doorway. Some looked up from their meals and one exhibitionist couple even paused mid-stroke to consider him before continuing to screw each other loudly.

The man did not seem pleased with his reception. He turned to help a frail old woman, who was his current client, through the doorway. He led her slowly to a table and clapped his hands loudly for service. Within a few moments, a buxom young woman in an outfit that left little to the imagination came hovering down to the table. Although flying and even hovering were not allowed anywhere in the city, Erminia had made it possible for the staff here to bend that rule; it just made it easier when things got too busy.

Erminia watched as the man in the red turban placed his order and pointed at the old woman. He had sat her away from all the sex and faced her in the opposite direction. He made a flourish with his hands and produced a ripe watermelon that caught the attention of the rutting couple, who had switched positions so that they could both watch while continuing their activities.

The waitress evaluated the melon and then tagged it. With a wave of her hand it zoomed back to the kitchen.

She held her hands over the table and a complete tea service appeared. The old woman was delighted and began to shovel sugar into her cup. Erminia was transfixed by the old woman, as were others in the tavern. Not many people remembered themselves as anything but young. However, every once in a while, a soul would arrive who was locked in its last memory, unable to recall being anything but old. They were usually very ready to get back to Earth, no matter what the cost.

The man in the red turban looked at the walls and noticed the fresh orchids, in full bloom. He looked up at Erminia and met her eyes. He was tall and tan with a sharp black goatee and an almost cartoonish swagger. He rolled his eyebrows and bowed his head in acknowledgement of her presence. When he spoke, his voice was close, as if he were right next to her. "Do you mind if I come and join you for a moment?"

She stopped sipping her beer and answered him curtly. "You have a lot of nerve. Why would I want to talk to you?"

He bowed respectfully and spoke again. "A thousand apologies, dear lady. I had a piece of information I thought might interest you. However, I see I have offended you. Perhaps another time."

"What kind of information?" She despised him but knew that he traveled extensively through the Ether ever since he had left her employ.

"Oh, just a little random rumor I heard. Probably nothing." He smiled wickedly.

He might just be playing her, but she was willing to take a chance. "I will hear you out. Get up here immediately."

He bowed again. He glanced at the kitchen door for a moment and then stretched his arms wide. Slowly he floated upwards and his colorful robes twisted in the air. The reaction from the patrons was more along the lines of what he had hoped for with his entrance. He soared above their heads to the sounds of yells and shouts. He flew effortlessly across the tavern and came into a seated position across from Erminia in her booth. The crowd was not pleased that he had somehow managed this flight when none of them could. Several shouting matches erupted and a few tables were overturned. The chaos seemed to spread and patrons were shouting insults up at the balcony. The staff rushed around in an attempt to quiet the disorder. The man sat with a cocky look on his face, proud of the bedlam he had caused.

"You know you are not supposed to do that. Are you trying to cause a riot?" She ignored the shouts from below and held his eyes in her unblinking stare.

He finally shifted his weight. "Well, you did say 'immediately,' and I figured, as a former employee of this fine establishment, I still might have the exemption. Turns out I do...or at least I did." He chuckled.

"Speak your piece, Jared; I am not in the mood for your games. What information are you looking to sell?"

He nodded slowly. "To the point, as always, I see. It seems that there is a nook, out past the eastern sea, wedged neatly between some Glory bubbles. In many ways it's the polar opposite of the little corner of hell you've chosen to land in. I mapped it several years ago and put a tracer on it, figured it would be a good place to hide if I ever needed to."

"Why should I care about this?"

"The tracer just went off a week or so ago. It seems someone is squatting in my hideout. I dropped by to have a peek and if it wasn't that old coot Fabric with a newcomer...what was his name again...?"

Erminia was angry. She hated having to deal with Jared. She wished he had just gone back to Earth after he paid his debt to her. Instead he became a guide and a royal pain in the ass. He was a little too thrilled to have his former employer over a barrel.

"What do you want for the location?"

His eyebrows hopped a bit, but he didn't hesitate to name his price. "I want that little spot down at the other end of the Square we've discussed before. I want to own it outright with no rent or tributes to you, and free rein to build whatever I want."

She breathed a sigh. It was a high price. Not just the prospect of the loss of the space, which was at a premium here, but also the thought of seeing him strutting the Square constantly as a full-time resident, made her stomach turn. "Done. But only if the information is accurate."

He spit in his hand and held it out. She spit in hers with the gusto of a sailor and shook it.

He looked over the railing at the chaos that was only now subsiding. "A pleasure doing business with you. I'll take the stairs back down to avoid any further disruption to your day."

• • • • •

The saloon doors swung open as Sarah led the nervous young man out of the Tavern and into the Square.

:: CONFRONTATION ::

"Choose your parents! Live a life of luxury with a rich couple! We have Americans, Saudi princes and wealthy Chinese families! You, sir! Are you ready to choose your destiny?" The barker pointed at Joe as he walked past.

"I have a Swiss family! Live in Europe and travel the continent! Less than a month to wait and you'll awaken in the Alps to start your ski lessons!" the second barker howled to all who passed.

"Fame awaits you! I have an actress in Columbia waiting for you to be her first son! Just a few weeks left! The rainforest will be your playground! Act now! This birth into a connected family will not last!" the third barker yelled when the others paused for a breath.

The shouts of the barkers in the Square rang with a well-rehearsed rhythm as they competed for the attention of the crowds milling through the market. Joe spotted the young man in jeans who had offered his cherished guitar to Cyril, his gypsy guide haggling with a huge man in a cowboy hat. "...they're a good family in the Midwest, a fine choice if he doesn't mind hard work..."

Between the shouts in English came other languages. French, German, Spanish and Mandarin all found his ears. Joe knew most of them well. Sometimes he translated the calls in his mind, other times he just let them be filler for the cacophony of sound in which they were immersed. The Square was busy with commerce, but not yet the madhouse it would become when the masses began to arrive in droves. The market became subdued when the Square was at speed and awakened when it found a landing. It would soon be overrun with new arrivals.

59

Tazir led Joe easily through the bustle, even though barkers called her by name to try to divert her their way. "Sarah! Bring him here! I have a special placement I've been saving! He can be a man of power and influence!" She acknowledged them with nods, but led Joe through the Square with purpose.

The Square was paved in huge blocks of limestone, fitted with the touch of a master mason. It was a large, open expanse rimmed by an array of buildings. Genseric's was at one of the corners of the Square and the largest and tallest structure in its quarter. As they moved swiftly away from it and toward the center of the Square, Joe saw many other structures that dwarfed it in newer quarters he did not recognize. Erminia had allowed her tenants a broad freedom to design their structures, but had kept the section near Genseric's as close to the original look of the city as she could. Joe turned his back on the nostalgic little corner and followed Tazir toward the center of the Square.

Most of the activity was near the perimeter. Barkers would take their customers into one of the buildings and complete their transactions. The customers paid handsomely and would receive a time to return that was close to the birth of the body for which they had negotiated. When the time was close, they would lodge in the establishment and be on alert. Then they would go into a chamber and be assisted back into the earthly realm. If they were lucky, and the proprietor had been honest, they would enter the body they had been sold. They might have more time to incubate in their new mother's womb, or they may be moments from birth; it varied.

As Joe and Tazir moved to the center of the Square, they had the luxury of space around them once again. Tazir slowed and let him catch up. They walked side by side for a few minutes, but then Joe stopped suddenly, his eyes slowly moving up as he considered the large structure that rose from the center of the Square and cast its shadow over them all.

The central smokestack rose almost one hundred feet before it fulfilled its function and billowed cloud-like puffs of steam into the strange sky. He followed the clouds up with his eyes and saw the enormous curves of the three ominous bubbles between which the city was wedged. The globes loomed with a darkness and despair that made him a little nauseated. He remembered where they were and dropped his gaze back to the base of the stack.

The well-fitted stones of the Square tilted, then broke, then crumbled into debris as they met the stack. It was a scene of frozen violence. The stack had obviously sprouted from beneath the stones in a single moment of creation. It was an alien that had become the central focus of this place, puffing away softly. Many other pipes snaked their way to meet it, most elevated to allow people to walk under them, others right down on the deck, dividing the Square like iron walls.

"She destroyed the fountain." He spoke to no one, but Tazir moved closer to hear him. "I never thought she would destroy the fountain..." He trailed off and his appearance began to change subtly as he lost concentration on his disguise.

Tazir grabbed his shoulders and shook him gently. "Stay focused. You need to keep yourself hidden." Joe met her eyes and once again became the likeness of the nervous young man eager to get back into a body.

"I am sorry. So much has changed. I forgot myself."

"Well, don't let it happen again. One slip like that at the wrong moment and all this'll be for nothing." She softened and touched his face. "There are many things here that may upset you if you truly were one of the original Builders. The landscape can change in a moment and we can find ourselves in a dark corner. Remember why you asked me to guide you here."

"Of course." He tried to ignore the looming smokestack and turned all his attention to her kind green eyes. "Do you know how to find the place of which I told you?"

She smiled. "No. But I know who to ask. Come on." She held his hand and led him away from the stack, toward a quieter quarter and off of the open Square.

· · · · ·

The alley was dark. The ground was not the same. It did not reflect the meager light the way the limestone of the Square did. The streets here were wooden planks set into an iron framework. The feel of a city center was replaced with the reminder that they were on a vessel that moved often. Streetlamps flickered with open flames encased in lumpy glass cubes. They did not do much to combat the strange twilight that filtered between the three private hells that loomed above them.

Sarah stepped up to a beaten door, heavy with age. She located an almost invisible tab of metal near the center hinge and lifted it to reveal a tiny letter slot. She dropped her note in quickly and continued down the planked alley at a pace she hoped would not draw any attention.

When she reached the second intersection, she turned right and headed toward the grimy cafe in which she had left Joe. She could see it a block and a half away, its bright yellow door mocking the gloom around it, when a hand grabbed her arm and she was drawn into a hidden alley. The man who held her was wide and stout. His skin was an inviting chocolate brown, but his eyes were blood red and inhuman. He had a thick, prehensile tail that moved behind him like a serpent while he stared her down. He did not speak, and she knew better than to engage him. She waited for whoever was holding his invisible leash.

"Who are you, pretty lady, and how'd you know about that drop point?" The voice came from deeper within the darkness of the alcove. There was no form with which to associate it.

"I am an old friend. It's been a long time since I've called on your family." The thick man's tail stopped dancing. Her tone was out of character for the green-eyed beauty he was viewing.

A shadow shifted in a dark alcove and formed into a wiry man with a bald head. He was built like a wrestler, lean and wound like a spring. His skin was black as the shadow from which he formed; his eyes were a pale green. He had a tiny tuft of snow-white hair that grew just below his lower lip and came to a point at his chin. "You don't look like any friend of mine. You look like a snotty little guide who shakes her ass and screws the staff to get what she wants. You look like a whore with delusions of grandeur to me..."

The supple young Brazilian beauty suddenly locked her arms down in front of her, palms facing the ground, her stance wide, and her feet flat. In a liquid moment, Sarah's clothes ripped apart as she grew to a height of nearly seven feet. Her skin became as black as the bald man's, but with a blue iridescence where the light could find her edges. The long, brutal scar that ran from the base of her neck down her right arm was revealed as the tiny blouse Sarah had been wearing was reduced to shreds.

Tazir towered in all her naked glory over both the bald man and his red-eyed thug. Her arm shot out and grabbed the little man by the neck, lifting him easily off the ground. The thug's tail swished as he awaited instructions from his master, but the thick presence stayed calm and quiet, watching with its unblinking red eyes. The bald man grabbed at the hand that was locked almost completely around his throat, and kicked his dangling feet a bit. He then grinned and began to laugh as best he could, given how he dangled in her grasp.

"You always were a son of a bitch, Otto. If we weren't already dead, I would kill you just for sport." She released her grip and the man dropped easily to his feet. His laugh grew fuller but remained quiet enough to not attract attention.

As he laughed, his skin changed to a warm olive color, but his tiny beard remained a white tuft of cotton. When he stopped being amused with himself, he held his arms wide, palms up, and leaned back as he looked up at her. "Oh, come on, Tazir! It was a joke! You have to be the most oversensitive giant African warrior goddess I know!"

Otto glanced at the red-eyed thug and the thick creature relaxed a bit. He turned his attention back to the towering nude woman in front of him, wearing only the satchel strung across her chest. His wheezing laughter stopped and his face became serious. He could see she was not amused. "Tazir, you know I loved Sarah almost as much as you did. I just had to make sure it was you."

Tazir softened her stance and managed a smile. "I know you did."

"Forget it! How the hell are you? It's been years since I've seen you on the Square. What brings you sneaking around my dark alley?"

She squatted down so that her knees rose high on either side of her. "I need your help, Otto. I have a very important client and we need to find something that's been hidden here since before this was Transit Square. It was here when this city had a different name..."

His eyebrows rose and his head tilted. "It must be a very special client if they know of anything hidden here that long. Who is this mysterious benefactor who has you risk so much? I know how dangerous it is for you coming back here, even disguised as Sarah."

"You really think I would tell you?"

He grinned. "No, but I'd bet you didn't come looking for my help unless you had something very shiny to offer in return for my family's services."

"Very shiny." She reached into her satchel and brought out the scarf. She carefully unwrapped the key to the catacombs.

• • • • •

The sliding of the stone door released a cloud of ancient dust as a shaft of light entered the forgotten chamber. Otto thrust the heavy flashlight in first, then followed it with a few darts of his head, first to the left, then to the right. He stepped just inside the door and squatted low. He ran the beam of his light across the floor and panned it slowly up the walls to assess the entire space. He stroked the tiny white tuft of hair just below his lower lip thoughtfully. "Huh. Learn something new every day, I guess."

A fluttering light buzzed in and circled him like a firefly drawn to a flame. He paused his beard-stroking and smiled as it hovered before him. "Yes, darlin', fetch our guests and tell them we've found what they were looking for." The light hopped and buzzed out the way it had come.

He clicked off his flashlight and sat silhouetted in the doorway for a moment. A ball of flame ignited and hovered in front of him. He cradled it between his palms for a moment and then sent it out into the center of the chamber, where it illuminated the room before him. He stood up slowly just as Tazir and the nervous young man who was her client came up behind him. The fluttering light flew to his shoulder, where it dimmed to a tiny woman with dragonfly wings who held his ear for stability.

The ceiling was high and the walls of the room were draped with tapestries and dozens of framed oil paintings. The cold, dusty fireplace that dominated one wall was flanked by two Ming Dynasty vases so big a man could stand inside them. Opulent overstuffed couches, ornately carved wooden chairs and filigree tables from every era of mankind decorated the chamber, while a massive ebony desk lurked in a corner. It seemed that the only design mantra that had been employed in assembling the furnishings was to take one museum-quality piece from every culture and time and use it as an everyday item, despite the fact that each was priceless.

Otto turned and looked hard at the nervous man, but Tazir moved her body to block his stare. He looked up at her proud jaw and held up the exquisite key. "So this works in lots of different places, I see. And it's mine to keep? Does the full access to the ancient catacombs you promised me include this little rumpus room also?"

She shot a quick look to confirm with Joe, then nodded at Otto. "As soon as we're done, it's yours to use as you wish. Consider it a bonus."

"Some would make the mistake of being curious at this point," Otto paused and pocketed his prize with a smile, "but I know when to mind my own. But I will not consider this marvelously hidden nook a bonus. You have a credit on your account with me, old friend. Feel free to call in the favor when you need it. You'll most likely find me here. I'll be moving the family's base of operations to this little gem when you and your client are done with it."

Otto held his hand in front of his forehead and a red bowler appeared in it. He promptly tipped it and placed it on his shiny head, strolling out briskly as the sound of sliding stone sealed the portal behind him.

The fireplace roared and the room came to life as if it had been waiting for this moment for generations. Pools of light formed on their own and Otto's little ball of flame winked out. A formal dining table supported by Egyptian gods offered up platters of steaming food and a sitar in the corner began to strum itself softly. A stone carving of the Buddha with his head in his hands began to weep water, a gurgling fountain to provide accompaniment.

Joe's disguise melted as he strode to the ebony desk. The lamp on it lit on cue as he reached the chair behind it. Joe sat with purpose and began shuffling papers as if he had just returned from a long trip. "Help yourself to whatever you find. I need to gather my thoughts for a moment before we begin." He paused and looked at the dark, sinewy woman. "I have never done this before. I admit I am a bit nervous."

"It'll be fine as long as we're not disturbed." Tazir took in the surroundings. "How did you keep this from her for so long?"

Joe smiled slowly and looked up at the high ceiling. "I put it right under her feet."

• • • • •

Erminia's feet were bare. She sat on a bench in her private chambers staring at the small patch of floor between them.

The room around her was elegant and lush. The floor was a patchwork of materials fit together with mastery: travertine, hardwoods, and variegated marble woven between patches of lush green grass. A Balinese daybed with teak latticework, enhanced by the living vines that crawled through it, seemed to sigh as its white curtains moved with the breeze. The room was both a bedchamber and a delicate garden, with a stream running gently through it, past the stone bench on which Erminia sat. The stream continued on past the eighteenth-century dressing table with beveled mirrors, through the stand of curling bamboo, and into the sitting room with its carpet of grass and flowers framing the deep cushions that begged visitors to sit low to the ground surrounded by ferns. The breeze through the open window was fresh and smelled of the Mediterranean. A hummingbird paused near her to kiss a white orchid, then moved on with a whisper of its wings.

The beauty around her did not shake the dark mood in which she found herself; in many ways it made it deeper. Every curve of wood, every gurgle of the water, every butterfly that landed unexpectedly had been designed by him. It had been an act of pure love that now tasted bitter in her mouth. Some days were worse than others. Today wasn't looking good.

She had come back to gather her thoughts and decide how to approach Random once Jared gave her the location of the nook where he was hiding. She could arrive in a blaze of glory, landing Transit Square and presenting herself as a powerful Queen, but the more she thought about it, the more she knew that would not appeal to him. Despite the fact that Random was a new arrival in her world, she had watched him for years on Earth. She needed a different approach to gain his trust.

She got to her feet and walked to the dressing table. She held out her arms and looked at her form in the beveled mirror. A sheer nightgown revealed her curves and her hair hung soft. Her freckles were more noticeable on the bridge of her nose. She looked young and vibrant. She flipped her head down and gathered her hair into a ponytail. When she looked again into the mirror, she wore a fitted skirt and a tailored top, all in black. She touched her lips and they turned blood red. She turned and her high heels clicked on the stone path. The door opened before her and Salvo jumped; clearly he had been trying to working up the courage to knock, but never found it. She rolled her eyes at him and clicked her way down the hall. He scurried behind, reading his notes.

"The Recorder again?" She knew the answer.

"Yes, but it's very strange: very quiet and subdued. If I didn't know better, I would say it sounds intoxicated. Nothing concrete, but a single word came up a third time..."

"What was it?" she snipped as she turned a corner with precision.

"Vandal."

She stopped so abruptly he almost ran her over. "Are you sure that was it? It was not garbled or unclear?" She looked intently at the floor.

Salvo consulted his tiny notebook almost by habit. "Quite sure. It was one of the few things we've been able to make out since we landed."

She turned to him and grabbed his arm so hard it made him flinch. "We are going there now. Mind your ears." In a ripping snap they winked out of existence.

A moment later those gathered in the Truther control room recoiled as the sound of Erminia's and Salvo's arrival hit them like a bat upside the head. Some grabbed their ears by reflex and pitched forward. Salvo's knees gave and his body went limp. He collapsed in a heap, hitting the floor loudly as his eyes rolled back. He had not minded his ears. Erminia left him where he lay and walked into the bubble in the center of the room, which was now a dull milky white.

She emerged in a child's nursery. It was disturbingly immaculate, with a painted mural of the ocean on one wall. The other walls were a pale sage green and every piece of furniture was snow white, from the rocker to the dresser to the crib she approached with caution.

In the crib was a being that was mostly light. Its form tried to assume that of an infant, but it flowed and pulsed like liquid. It was on its back and its soft-focus mouth was moving silently. Raven sat on a stool with a notepad, trying to decipher the being's words. Muffled voices crackled in her earpiece. She stood up and moved away as Erminia approached the crib.

Erminia leaned in closer. "What have you heard of the Vandals, old one?"

Two dark spots on the smooth face appeared to mimic eyes. The Recorder recognized Erminia and the whispers stopped. Suddenly it spoke in a clear register, rejuvenated by her presence. "...vandal...sss...underway, red hat, dragonfly...old ways, disguise, daring, masquerade, mimic, marriage...van...vandal...sssss." The dark spots turned to her.

Her heart sank. Probably just an errant thought the Recorder had picked up. The name of her people had long ago become a part of the language, reflecting only the devastation they had caused when they sacked Rome. Everyone here knew to listen hard for the term, but only when it referred to the name she and Joe had chosen for the city when they decided to build it.

For a moment, she could hear their drunken laughter the night they chose the name. She pushed the memory of his joyous face from her mind.

The Recorder's stream of consciousness was not what she had hoped it would be. She was glad that Salvo had passed out from the violence of their transit. Served him right for wasting her time.

She touched the being softly on its chest. "Sleep, kind one. We will have much to do in the days ahead." But her touch made the strange infant twitch and its lumpy arm of light hardened and grabbed her hand hard.

"Vandal....Square! He is here. He is close. He is here..." It released her and the dark spots turned to sleepy slits. "...he has it with him..."

Her heart almost stopped. Raven was at her side, a finger on her headset, ready to mobilize the troops. Erminia was frozen. She turned slowly and looked at the girl. Her eyes questioned whether she had heard what she thought she heard. The girl nodded slowly, reverently, in supreme awe of this moment, of what it meant.

Erminia remembered to breathe. She wanted to scream, cry, dance, and bark orders like a drill sergeant. She composed herself and took stock of the fragile form in the crib beside her. In a soft voice that did not veil her excitement, she spoke to the girl. "Get someone else in here to listen. We need to get everyone together and let them know so we can coordinate our next steps. If he has truly been stupid enough to come back here and bring the key with him, the Truth we have all been seeking may be just a few steps away."

Raven nodded and whispered into her earpiece. Erminia walked out of the bubble, back into the control room. The room was already quiet, and fell into complete silence when she emerged. All eyes watched her as she strode to one of the large tables and took a seat at the head of it. The silence was barely stirred by the shuffles as they all drew closer around her.

"It seems we have a visitor from the Conclave aboard the Square." No one breathed. "This soul has had the audacity to come into our home uninvited, and the stupidity to bring with him the key to his own demise..."

"Sounds like my kind of guy." All heads spun to look at the tall, tanned man in the red turban standing near the doorway. Jared smiled with teeth so white they seemed a bit oversized in his mouth.

Erminia stood and leaned on the table with her palms flat. "I told you never to come back here. I am busy right now, Jared."

"As I can see. I won't interrupt your moment of glory much longer. I just wanted to drop off the map of the location we discussed." He held a carved ivory tube and showed the rolled parchment inside it before capping the scroll case and placing it on the table. "I'm staying in the house right next to the future site of Jared's Incarnation Station and await a visit from you once you've confirmed that this information is accurate." He smiled and gave a bow that was both formal and a bit mocking. He turned and walked back down the hallway.

Raven scurried after him and they all waited to hear the heavy latch of the metal door. She came running back down the hall and nodded to let them all know he was gone.

"Jared is an arrogant pest, but he has given us Mr. Bridges' location." Those assembled exchanged looks and sharply-hissed whispers with wild eyes. Erminia took the ivory tube and sat back down. She held her hand up to quiet the chatter. "This is the day we've been waiting for, my friends. We must calm our enthusiasm and act with precision."

The room was hushed. They waited breathlessly. Erminia held the scroll case like a scepter. "Our first task is to locate our visitor from the Conclave and take possession of the item he..."

"Erminia! Come quickly!" The voice came from the bubble in the center of the room. The head of a handsome young man with a headset was poking out, the rest of his body still inside the cold nursery with the Recorder.

Erminia stood slowly and looked at the huge bubble. It was no longer milky white but the color of tanned leather, and pulsed with light from within. The Recorder was awake. The head of the young man disappeared back inside. Erminia walked with purpose and breached the rippling surface, still holding the ivory scroll case.

The scene inside had changed drastically. The nursery was gone and she emerged in a huge park, its rolling green hills bathed in the golden light of a waning day. The young man with the headset was chasing a child across the grass. The child was a beacon of light that turned quickly and ran to Erminia. She held her arms open and it leapt into her embrace with a wave of giggles.

"Time is now! Found him! No hiding anymore! Blades of grass, bed of teak, marble floors, gentle stream, dressing table, he waits with hummingbirds, butterflies, soft breeze from sea..." The child of light appeared as a toddler, more detailed than the liquid infant form the Recorder had just shifted from. Its eyes remained nondescript, but Erminia could sense its pride at its discovery nonetheless. She touched its glowing cheek tenderly.

"Thank you, kind one. Run and play now. I will be back soon." She put the being down and it raced across the rolling grass, screaming in glee. Erminia touched the young man with the earpiece on the shoulder. "Stay with him. Play games if he wants to, but stay close." The man nodded without looking at her, his eyes fixed on the child. Erminia turned and went back to the control room.

The ripples flowed over the surface of the sphere and the nervous chatter stopped. All eyes turned to her. Salvo was now on his feet again and putting his earpiece back in as he approached her. She handed him the ivory cylinder.

"He is in my chamber. He must want a confrontation." She took a deep breath and lowered her eyes. "He will get his wish. Mind your ears, everyone!" Hands slapped to ears, and Salvo jumped away from her like a soldier fleeing a grenade. She paused to give them time to shield their minds and, with a ripping pop, left only a twinkle of lights where she had stood.

• • • • •

Joe sat on the edge of the delicate teak bed listening to the gentle sound of the stream that flowed through the room. He wore pressed pants and a white, collarless shirt buttoned to the top, the sleeves rolled to reveal his forearms. He was barefoot. Hanging on a leather cord around his neck was an exquisite golden amulet that lay against the linen shirt.

The door opened slowly and Erminia stepped over the threshold. He smiled with the corners of his eyes but kept a tight rein on his mouth. He sat quietly with his hands folded in his lap.

Her body was rigid and taut. The lower lid of her right eye twitched involuntarily from the rage that coursed through her. Her arms shot out before her and her mouth released a hellish scream. The delicate teak bed frame exploded in a shower of splinters and Joe was thrown against the wall. She dropped her arms and walked forward. The ferns in the cushioned seating area wilted into ash and several birds burst into flames. Joe managed to get to his feet just in time to see the beveled mirror of the eighteenth-century dressing table tear free and hurtle toward him. He crossed his arms in defense, but the mirror shattered before it ever reached him. Joe seemed surprised that the mirror had not found its mark, but was not prepared when the entire dressing table followed closely behind; it flattened him against the wall in an explosion of claw feet and inlaid wood.

She released another primal howl as his body rose from the rubble and was tossed against another wall like a rag doll. The babbling creek hissed and whistled as it boiled to steam. The stone bench tore from its foundations and raced to meet Joe's crumpled body. The bench burned to ash before it reached him and she yelled in frustration. Tapestries shredded themselves where they hung. Oil paintings in heavy gilt frames melted into liquid and oozed down the walls.

Erminia raised her hands, her fingers curled like claws. Heavy chains erupted from the floor and coiled around Joe's body before he could rise again. They grappled his limbs and pinned him to the ground. She approached him with demonic glee and extended her perfectly manicured nails toward the pendant that hung at his chest.

She paused, then snatched it violently, ripping the leather cord. She held the amulet triumphantly as the once-peaceful chamber burned around her. She turned her attention to her prisoner and spoke with chilling calm.

"Now you will know what it is to watch everything you have loved crumble before your eyes. I will destroy the precious sanctuary you cast me out of in your moment of arrogance. You will watch the Conclave fall. Then perhaps you will know a fraction of the pain I have known."

· · · · ·

Doctor Cyril Morris made the lines of people wait as he took a break from his duties. The crowds had grown; many had come to board Transit Square. He stood outside his tent away from the commotion and took his watch from the pocket of his blue vest. Time made little difference here, but he enjoyed the weight and feel of the watch and the whir of its tiny gears.

He watched as the applicant he had just granted passage presented his yellow pass at the gangplank. As the applicant and his guide walked past the guards and up the ramp, Cyril saw them pass the nervous young man whom Sarah had presented to him. He carried a satchel hung at his hip and was doing something odd: he was coming down the ramp, disembarking from the Square.

Cyril looked for Sarah, but the nervous man was alone. It was rare to see a soul give up their quest to return to Earth so soon. Perhaps he had realized that there was no hurry. Perhaps he saw that he had time to explore.

Cyril smiled when he thought of the night of pleasure that Sarah would give him. He knew she would keep her word. He watched the nervous young man walk away from the crowds. His only destination seemed to be the gap between the towering dark bubbles. Cyril experienced a slight wave of jealousy as he watched this lone soul, off to explore the wilds of the Ether. He realized the feeling was just a result of the dismal space in which they had landed. He had no desire to give up his role as gatekeeper.

He went back into his tent to see what treasured memory the next desperate soul would offer. He smiled when he remembered that he still had a few pieces of the delicious jerky the nervous young man had given him in his desk drawer.

EXPLORING

: : RANDOM MORNING : :

Random awoke to a brilliant dawn. The light was golden and the air was warm. The bare ground where he had fallen asleep was covered with soft green shoots of new grass he had not noticed in the dark. He rolled to his back and looked up at an improbable sky.

The clearing he lay in was wedged in between what appeared to be several towering soap bubbles. They shimmered iridescent in the glorious light of morning, soaring upwards and revealing patches of stunning blue skies, devoid of clouds.

He sat up slowly, almost fearing that the delicate vision would pop if he moved too quickly. The neat circle of stones held the remnants of the fire, long extinguished. The log where he had feasted was smooth and inviting.

His companion sat on the rock, whittling on a small stick with a large knife. "Glad you could join us again. How do you feel?" Fabric spoke without looking up from his task.

"I feel...good. Rested..." Random shook his head gently. "How long was I out?"

Fabric fixed his mismatched eyes on Random and replied with a snicker. "Do you really think I could give you a measurement of time that would have any meaning here?" He carelessly threw down the stick he had been focused on and returned the knife to a sheath on his belt. "You were out long enough to calm your soul. No one here needs sleep, but we remember it from life as a way to recover. No reason for night and day either, but we're all trained by our lives on Earth, so they remain a shared illusion, too."

Fabric stood up and Random was able to assess him in the full light of day. He was a thick man with a huge chest and a bit of a gut on him. His skin was weathered, heavily lined, and a deep russet brown from the sun. His one hazel eye was yellow when the light caught it.

Random looked past the barrel-chested man and changed his focus to the object behind him. Fabric saw his focus change and looked over his own shoulder at the rainbow of colors flowing over the surface of the bubble closest to them. "Pretty, aren't they? Deceptively so, I'm afraid. The Glory Bubbles may contain some soul's version of Heaven, but they're based on a fantasy so powerful that there's no room for others. If you broke the rules of their reality while inside, you'd be attacked like a virus." He gestured to the other bubbles. "Prisons, every one."

Random stood and turned slowly, considering the bubbles. "Why are so many clustered together?"

"A fine question! You'd be surprised how seldom it's asked. There've been groups of like-minded idiots who've attempted to create shared visions of Nirvana. It's when a creation becomes a bubble and shuts out other views that the trouble starts. They inevitably disagree on some detail, then a tiny difference of opinion becomes a civil war. Eventually the bubble divides into two, and this keeps up 'til there's one cell for every soul." Fabric paused and looked at a bubble as if trying to see inside. "No amount of beauty can change the fact that they're alone. They're so lost, they no longer remember they created them."

Fabric shook off his circumspect tone and turned back to Random with a mischievous grin. "Upside is, the spaces between them create lovely little nooks like this one. Fine places to hide when you don't want to be found."

Random paused and thought a moment. "Anyone can create what they visualize here, right?"

Fabric stretched his arms wide and was suddenly holding two ice cream cones. "Check!" He handed one to Random and began to eat his ice cream happily.

Random held his cone but continued his thought. "And these 'Glory Bubbles' were created by shared illusions that shut out all other perceptions?"

Fabric licked his wrist where the ice cream was dripping. "A little crude, but yeah. Where you headed with this, son?"

"Joe told me he was a member of something called the Conclave. He said they had a sanctuary he wanted to take me to." Random replayed the conversation he and Joe had had in that oppressive little hotel room. "So what's the difference between the Conclave's sanctuary and one of these Glory Bubbles? Aren't they both shared illusions?"

Fabric slowly sat down on the stone again. "My, you're an interesting one. I can see why they're fighting over you. You could take the inquiry farther and ask whether the memory of this place called Earth is not just its own little fantasy..."

Random remembered the Rinpoche he'd met in Philadelphia and the words that rang through his teaching that day, translated from the Tibetan he spoke as though singing. "All is maya..."

"...or you could eat your ice cream before it melts." The mismatched eyes smiled with mischief and peace. Random started at the thin trail of chocolate running down his wrist and traced it up to the frozen source. It was one of the most delicious ice cream cones he had ever tasted. He abandoned his logic thread and began to attack the cone.

"This is so good! Normally I prefer vanilla, but I've never tasted chocolate like this!"

Fabric smiled. "When you have chocolate, it's best to choose the chocolate." They fell back into silent feasting, chasing the cold streams of flavor down their wrists.

When eating became finger-licking, Random once again considered his host. "So, where do we go from here?"

Fabric leaned forward and slapped his knees. "We... don't go anywhere. I've done my good deed and settled a score at the same time. I've given you an ample head start on those who pursue you, and now I must bid you farewell." He stood and held out his arm. His worn satchel flew to his shoulder like a trusted pet. He held his other arm out and a walking staff appeared in it.

"You can't just leave me here! I have no idea where I am! Where should I go? One of them'll find me eventually. Which one do I trust?"

Fabric smiled. "You're a smart kid. I'm sure you'll figure something out." And after a sound like a champagne cork firing through a piece of dry canvas, Random found himself alone.

The sudden solitude collapsed on him. He hadn't had one moment to himself since he...died. Was he really dead? Was this all there was? There was no grand plan, no Creator to comfort, no reunion with those who had passed before him? He had often thought of seeing his father again and sharing a cocktail as they reflected on their lives. He wanted to hear that he had been there looking down when Random had married Karen, and had been in the delivery room when his grandson was born.

Karen. Random fell to his knees. What did she think when she heard how he had died? Had she been shocked by the details of the only secret he had ever kept from her, or had some kind soul just kept it simple? Your husband is dead. No, that would not have been enough for her. She would be unstoppable as always. She would know everything now. Random hoped she would remember how much he loved her and never question how authentic that love was...had been.

He wept. He wanted to hold her again. His sobbing intensified when the image of his son's face flashed across his mind. He fell forward on all fours and wept like he had never been able to in life. His life was over. He was alone.

He stood quickly and screamed at the shining bubbles all around him. He waved his arms and found he was suddenly holding a baseball bat. A dining room table filled with fine porcelain shimmered into existence on the soft grass about fifty feet from him. He let out a primal howl and raced towards it with his bat raised high. When he reached the delicate table setting, his throat was burning and sweat poured from his face into his eyes.

The table was set formally for a party of eight. It was an exact replica of the awkward Thanksgiving meal his family had attended at his Aunt Patty's house when he was nine years old. Her house was as compulsively impeccable as the table. The carpets were white and there were clear plastic runners that led to white furniture also covered in plastic. It was the first and last time his casual family had donned scratchy suits and endured a bland dinner at Aunt Patty's house.

The violence he inflicted upon this ghostly remnant of his past was severe. The hickory bat laid waste to the delicate crystal and fancy silverware. The dry, tasteless turkey flew in an arc as he finished destroying the china and went to work on the table itself. It put up enough resistance that he turned on the spindly chairs, then came back to finish off the table when he had perfected his swing. The sound it made when it finally gave way and was cleaved in two echoed off the Glory Bubbles.

Then, as quickly as it had gripped him, the rage subsided as he sat heavily on the ground surrounded by the broken shards that were his handiwork. He breathed like a child after a tantrum, with a mixture of huffs and whimpers. He hefted the bat and saw that he had split it in the final strokes of his attack. He threw it aside and looked at the shards around him.

He had made these. He had conjured up a weapon and a target for his anger out of nothing. These things had simply come to be, much like the mirror and the piece of toast he had imagined right before Fabric had brought him here.

He stood slowly and looked at the plain ground with its tufts of tender grass. Between bubbles, he saw the flat plain extending to the horizon, where it rose sharply into distant mountains. They looked inviting, and he imagined there was a cold mountain stream there, just waiting for him to find it.

"Well, I'm not walking." He spoke aloud to himself. "Anything I can imagine, huh?" He closed his eyes and a slow, devious smile crept across his face like a crack across ice. Random opened his eyes slowly. He took in a sharp breath as he viewed his creation.

The motorcycle was exactly as he remembered it. It was the 1941 Indian (model 841) he had first seen six months ago at Sturgis. He had ignored all the other shiny bikes as soon as he saw the restored WWII monster in all its original olive-drab beauty.

The owner tolerated him at first as another tourist there to gawk, but became friendly when Random had returned the next day with charcoal and paper, begging to draw the bike. He spent three and a half hours drawing every last detail as the beaming owner drank cheap beer from cans and answered questions from the crowds watching Random's drawing come to life.

Now it was here, and it was all his. Random swung his leg over and sat down on the worn brown leather seat. The huge bike matched his large frame well. He ran through the start-up sequence he had watched with envy and, with a single kickstart, the engine growled to life. He reached up and pulled down the vintage goggles that he found on his head because he had expected them to be there.

He put the bike in gear and twisted the throttle. He pointed the front wheel toward the gap and shifted up to gain more speed. After a second shift, he was accelerating to freedom from the bubbles, the pain, the guilt, the despair that he wanted to escape. The bike roared as the engine wound up and he leaned forward, anticipating the exit. In a last burst of speed, he emerged from the forest of bubbles onto a vast open plain. He made his final shift and opened the bike up, the horizon his only destination. His screams were drowned out by the sound of the engine and the rush of the wind.

The space between the bubbles was once again silent as the light danced across the shards of crystal surrounding the thoroughly decimated Thanksgiving table. A breeze tossed a fabric napkin that had escaped its silver holder.

The silence was broken by a ripping sound ending in a sharp bang that echoed off the bubbles. The tall, lanky man examined the abandoned fire while the two women with him walked the remains of the dinner party. The thin young girl with straight black hair had located the turkey and was poking it with the leg of a chair. The tiny woman in the tailored dress and high heels squatted down to look at the bat. She touched the split that ran through the thickest part of the wood.

The lanky man raced up to her holding a large shard of blue-and-white porcelain with a blue windmill baked into the glazing. "This is very fresh; look at the crispness of detail! He couldn't have gotten far!"

Erminia stood slowly and took the shard from him. "Actually, Salvo, the rules of degradation do not apply to Mr. Bridges. He could have left months ago and his creations would be just as vivid." She threw the shard down and it shattered against other debris.

Raven joined them, pocketing a tiny crystal elephant that had escaped the violence. "So what now?"

Erminia gathered her thoughts as she crossed her arms and fingered the large, ornamented key she had taken from Joe, which she now wore as a pendant. She looked at the ground and noticed the tire tracks leading away from the site. "We figure out where he wants to go and meet him there. In the worst-case scenario, we do it without him." She laid her palm flat over her pendant, reveling in her prize. "I need to get back to our guest. He may have an idea where to look, and I would hate to be a bad host."

With a sickening, ripping sound, they left the napkins to slowly dance among the splinters and shards.

:: DREAMING TOGETHER ::

The bike clicked and popped as it cooled in the shade near the creek. Its matte green paint was a vain attempt at camouflage and only made it more alien in the quiet glade Random had found at the foot of the steep mountains.

The light coming through the old-growth trees was mottled and the grass was a cool carpet on the back of his neck. He looked straight up at the canopy and let the forest sounds quiet his mind. The ride had been all that he had wished for and it had taken him hours at full throttle to get here. He had felt the last of the rage burn off just as he reached the cool sanctuary he had invaded astride eight hundred pounds of hot, muddy metal.

He lay as he had fallen, his gloves and goggles cast away from him, listening to water dance over the rocks in the creek bed. His eyes were locked skyward, but unfocused; when birds shot past his field of vision, he didn't follow them.

After long minutes the bike finally cooled enough to be silent and he stopped breathing in heavy draws of air. He slowly sat up and took in the beauty he had stumbled upon. The glade was elegant in its simplicity. There were both shade and light, both gentle sound and blissful quiet. It seemed to lie as a manicured haven at the edge of the featureless plain on which the Glory Bubbles sat. They were far enough away that they appeared to be nothing more than the abandoned toys of an enormous child who had wandered off.

He looked at the creek and managed a smile. He loved rivers more than any other body of water. This one was pretty, but a bit too sleepy for his taste.

He preferred more current to make the water cascade over obstacles. More water wouldn't do much here, as the rocks were modestly sized and the terrain rather flat.

Could he change that? Wasn't this just some memory of a shady place, some illusion with no more validity than the Indian on which he had roared up? Logically, he should be able to sculpt the landscape itself, if it was made of the same stuff. He stood up with the energy of raw curiosity and shook his hands a bit to prepare.

Would it require more effort to move land than it did to dream a motorcycle out of thin air? It shouldn't, but he reckoned it might seem that way in his mind, given that he had lived so long in a world bound by physics. Joe had told him that time and distance were illusions that were habitual, and thus harder illusions to break. This was physicality. It didn't have to be hard if he could get his mind out of the way.

"This is easy... none of this is real…this is easy, this is easy…this…" He hesitated and realized he hadn't thought of what he wanted to make. The bike had been easy…but he had known every detail the moment he thought of it. The hours he had spent drawing it had burned an image into his memory that was, in many ways, more permanent than the drawing he had given to the drunken biker when he was done.

He closed his eyes and thought of a waterfall he had seen in Yellowstone Park during his youth. He pictured it with as much detail as he could. He opened his eyes. No change. He closed his eyes and tried again, adding the sounds and the smells he remembered. He opened his eyes to a scene unaltered by his efforts.

Maybe what he was trying to build was too different. Maybe he needed to work with what was here already. He got closer to the creek and looked at the simple stones. He kept his eyes open this time and concentrated on one section, imagining how the water would fall if there were a greater difference in elevation.

When the ground began to move it was accompanied by the sound of stone on stone. He was both startled and thrown off balance, as he was moving the very ground on which he stood. The moment he lost his concentration and focused on trying not to fall, the movement and sound stopped. He looked again and saw that he had indeed reformed the creek bed and created a small waterfall.

He laughed and forgot the thoughts from which he had been running. The instant gratification of seeing the world change at his whim was intoxicating. He focused on the same spot and imagined the waterfall doubling its height.

This second attempt was easier to accomplish, but he found himself thrown to the ground by the movement of the terrain. He jumped up and bellowed at his accomplishment: the sleepy creek now dropped water about three feet. He had created a rift that ran like a scar across the soft grass. It extended thirty feet from each bank. As he examined his handiwork, he saw that he had pushed the hunk of land down. The creek was now filling the depression and a pond was forming.

He wondered how he could increase the flow of water. Would he have to focus on the source of the creek farther up in the mountains?

"Excuse me, young man." The words came from behind him and made him jump. He spun around to face two old women standing shoulder-to-shoulder facing him.

On his left was a small Chinese woman in a blue silk caftan and a black knit cap that sat high on her head. She squinted up at him with a face that was stern, yet soft with many traces of laughter carved into it. She held a pink-flowered parasol perched on her frail shoulder. His eyes fell immediately to the large black amulet, a tortoise with a snake coiling around it, which hung around her neck. Her face was round but her forehead high, with wisps of steel-gray hair escaping from the cap.

The old woman on his right was Indian in heritage but had skin that was burnt to nearly black in the deep lines of age that covered her face. She had smudges of both white and red pigment on the bridge of her nose and over the center of her forehead. She clutched a green shawl around her neck with her roasted brown hand. One simple silver band encircled a dark finger in brilliant contrast to her skin. The amber eyes that seared through him amplified her ancient, intense beauty.

The woman with the parasol spoke again. "We didn't mean to startle you, but we must ask you to stop what you are doing. This is a sacred place. My name is Sister Del." She gestured to her companion. "This is Sister Darśana. We are the caretakers here."

Random looked at Darśana. Her eyes made him nervous, but it was she who recoiled as his eyes met hers. She did not look away, but her eyes widened and her hand clutched her shawl a bit tighter.

He looked back to the round face of Sister Del. Her face was easier to be with, at first, but then he found himself squirming under the air of authority radiating from her. She was not to be trifled with, and she somehow let him know that as they considered each other. He opened his mouth to speak but found that no words came. The back of his neck was hot and he felt blood rush to his face.

Sister Del didn't wait for him to find his voice. "How did he find us?" Sister Darśana answered in a deep reverberation that made him jump again. "He has been here before. We have guarded his sleep."

Sister Del continued to look at him but answered. "Yes, that makes sense. He has the lost look of a new arrival, but this is not his first spin of the wheel."

Darśana's voice reverberated again. "He is an old one. He altered the Glade and reformed the river. Yet he does not remember who he is. He is a monkey swinging a sword, with no thought to the world he is in."

Random was a paralyzed child being spoken of as if he were not there. His mouth tried again to speak but only wisps of air passed his lips as he stood under their unrelenting eyes.

Sister Del reached out and touched his arm. He managed not to jump this time. "Relax, sweet one. We are surprised both by your visit and that you've managed to alter a landscape that has remained unchanged for thousands of years." She gifted him the smile of a kind elder and he managed to start breathing normally again. Her hand was warm and he felt his pulse slow. "What do you think your name is, child?"

The question gnawed at him even as he managed to answer it in a whisper. "Random..."

Sister Del retracted her hand quickly, as if she had laid it on a hot stove. Darśana drew her shawl over her face and her eyes widened. They both took a step back and moved closer to each other.

He managed to find his voice. "I'm sorry, ladies; I meant no harm. I didn't mean to..." He stopped. He knew the body language. He had passed six foot by the time he was fifteen and he had learned this one well. They viewed him as a threat.

Sister Del straightened her bent spine as best she could as Darśana clutched her arm. "Why did you come back here? What do you want from us?"

Random tipped his head and raised an eyebrow curiously. "I don't remember ever being here before. I mean you no harm; I was just looking for a place to stop and collect my thoughts." He paused as the gnawing question returned to him. "What do you think my name is?"

Sister Darśana released her grasp on her shawl, her face revealing panic. "We watched over you here. We kept you sleeping longer than any before or any since. When you began to stir, I told them not to let you awaken again. You do not remember yourself, but I remember well! Leave the sleepers at peace! Leave this sacred place!"

Sister Del touched Darśana's shoulder but the dark woman deflected the gesture and walked away from them both. She turned her back on them and went to stand under one of the thick trees. She laid her palms on it gently.

"Sister Del, I don't understand. How do you know me? What does she think I've done? What's this about 'sleepers,' and why does she ask me to leave them at peace?"

The tiny woman's parasol rotated gently as she touched the black pendant of the tortoise and the snake with her translucent hand. She looked up at him cautiously. "Come, I will show you the sleepers."

He followed her as she led him away from both Darśana's refuge and the rapidly forming pond. They stopped when they reached the tree Random had first lain under, his goggles and gloves still littering the ground. Sister Del folded her parasol and hung it in the crook of her arm. She walked over to the trunk of the old tree and placed her palm on it gently. She then waved him closer and pointed at the bark.

As he looked closer she gave him the stern shush of a librarian, then hummed low. He looked at the surface of the tree and saw it shimmer and become less and less opaque. As he watched, the image of a young man with his arms folded became visible, locked deep in the heartwood of the massive tree. He appeared to be in his early twenties and clutched a rifle to him as he dreamed the dream of a corpse.

Sister Del whispered reverently. "There are those souls who arrive with deep wounds. They have fought wars, witnessed destruction, or seen horrors

87

they cannot release. The Conclave brings them to us and we help them sleep. They need time to heal, to forget, to forgive themselves." She hummed again and the image of the soldier faded, leaving only the bark of the tree that was his sarcophagus.

She gestured with her crooked arm as widely as she could to the trees that stretched out around them for miles. "They all sleep. We guard them and keep them safe. We listen for when they start to stir, and help them awaken when they are ready." As tiny as she was, she somehow managed to look down her nose at him. "You were here longer than any of them--more than a thousand years. Some wished you would sleep forever, and Darśana was among them. We warned the Conclave when you stirred, but they chose to allow you to awaken, against our advice."

He furrowed his brow and looked at the ground. He sat down as one would in a graveyard rather than a park. He crossed his legs and looked within. The top of his head was just a few inches lower than hers, now that he was sitting. Sister Del waited.

He kept his eyes locked on the ground. "What had I done to be so reviled?" The breeze made some leaves dance as the question hung in the air. He looked at the wrinkled woman directly. "Why did you put me to sleep?"

Sister Del crossed her delicate arms and down at him. "There are many Builders here but, as with all things, some are more gifted than others. You were a powerful creator in this plane of existence for many, many years. You helped build some of the bigger and more permanent features of this world. You designed this very Glade yourself, when you saw the suffering souls around you. You designed it to be a haven that was hard to find and resistant to change. It was the ultimate irony when you became its most long-term resident..." She held her palms together and nodded at him. "I know your question remains, but the answer is not simple and much is lost to the thousands of years that have passed. Sister Darśana and I had been sequestered here for many lifetimes, insulated from most things. The Conclave came to us when they had no other option. I only know what they told us."

"What did they tell you?" His breath was shallow.

"They told us that you had allowed dark thoughts to take hold of you. You had allowed your inner demons to take shape. The deeper you went into the dark spiral, the more darkness became real in this world. Your nightmares were not yours alone; rather, they used your gifts of creation to take real and lasting form. Your dark thoughts became manifest and found others to torment."

She paused. "They told us that you had gone insane. Given who you were and the powers of creation you wielded, we had no choice but to put you in a deep sleep."

She lowered herself to the ground and sat with him on the grass. "When you began to stir, they were in need of you. The Conclave had become fractured and a new movement had arisen to attempt to seize the minds of the masses."

"The Truthers..." he whispered.

She nodded. "I see you have been here long enough to learn of the struggle. I do not know their overriding purpose, but in any case the Truthers seek to change the very structure of the place. Your awakening was kept secret from them, and the Conclave convinced you to enter a new body and walk the earth. You seemed renewed and the darkness no longer gripped you, but the Conclave was taking a big risk. Unfortunately, the fractures in the Conclave were much deeper than they expected. The rebellion learned that you were back on Earth, and began to watch for your return." A bird flew by with a song streaming from it. "Given that you know the name of their rebellion, I assume that you have met her?"

"Erminia? Yes. I was greeted by someone named Joe, but she chased us and managed to snatch me away from him."

The old woman nodded. "Yet you walk free of both of them. Now you find yourself in the place most familiar to you, confronted by a past you did not know you had." She smiled. "When you began to stir, I secretly did not agree with Sister Darśana. I knew you before. I knew the man you were and the kindness in your soul. I felt you had slept long enough."

Once again she touched his arm with her warm hand. "You have a fresh start, a new chance. The choices you make now are for you, and you alone. But I must ask you, kindly, to leave this place. There is a war going on and both sides are seeking you. I must protect those who sleep."

He managed a thin smile. "I understand." He stood and gathered his gloves and goggles. "Before I go, may I ask you something?"

"You may ask; I will answer if I can."

"I've been to the control room of Erminia's rebellion. I heard what she had to say and got a sense of her character. I'm not sure I gave Joe a fair chance. To make an honest choice, I want to see the Conclave for myself. I don't want the grand tour reserved for a guest he wants to impress. I want to arrive as others do and see it, warts and all. Can you tell me where to look?"

Sister Del gave a small chuckle. "Take the road on which you came in back toward the bubbles. When you reach the plain, turn left and follow the line of the mountains until you find the main pass. It is well-traveled and easy to spot. Through the pass, on the other side of the range, you will find what you seek."

Random started toward the motorcycle, then turned back. "You said you knew the kind of man I was. What kind of man is Joe? Is he someone I can trust?"

She stood and opened her parasol again. "He is a soul with both great gifts and great faults. He was once a dear friend to you, but you grew apart. I am not sure why. To judge the measure of a man is a very personal thing. I would only counsel that you listen to your heart." She approached him and touched his chest. "From what I remember, it was a good heart."

He bent down and kissed her cheek, then sat astride the motorcycle and went through the start-up sequence. The engine roared and he guided it out of the Glade as quietly as he could. Sister Del watched him until the sound became distant.

· · · · ·

Sister Del found Darśana kneeling on the bank of the new pond. She sat near her and shared the shade of her parasol.

"Do you think it was wise to tell him so much, Del?" Darśana played with the grass without looking up.

"Destiny is no longer ours to write, dear sister. The world wants a change and nothing can stop that. I choose to have faith in his heart. Will you have faith with me?"

Darśana removed her shawl and took in a deep breath. "I have long had the gift of sight. I have spent lifetimes gazing into tortured souls to help them find what they need to heal. But I see nothing when I look into him. I see only the void."

"Perhaps you see a blank canvas, waiting for paint."

:: MIND THE BOX ::

Random was glad to emerge from the trees, and took a long, wide turn on the flat plain. He brought the bike to a stop and looked back. He wasn't sure what to think about what he had just heard. He did, however, have both a destination and a direction. Those were two things he hadn't had since he arrived here. He flipped the bike into gear and opened it up, the forest of souls on his left and the bubbles on his right.

The vibration of the bike numbed his palms but calmed his mind. What Sister Del had told him could just be the manipulation of an old recluse eager to be rid of him, but he could not ignore it. The glade had felt familiar. He had found himself drawn to it. He somehow believed he had slept there. Even the relentless Indian could not shake the truth he felt from his bones. Movement and sound were his only solace. He watched the jagged hills to his left in search of the pass of which Sister Del had told him.

What did it mean to go insane here? If he believed her, what demons had been released from his subconscious that would have this 'Conclave' contract the Sisters to put him to sleep for a thousand years? Most of what he had witnessed here seemed insane. How dark had these demons been? He needed to get to the Conclave and see it for himself. He needed to know who they were before he decided whether he trusted their judgment.

His mind was ripped from its meditative trance by the alarm of danger ahead. He got off the gas and grabbed the brake too hard. He considered a downshift but the bike had already started to wobble. As he raced to meet the obstacle in his path he decided to release the brake and use the speed to turn.

He could still miss the bright red phone booth that grew larger by the second, but clearly he was going to lay the huge bike down.

Time slowed. All sound muted. He found himself in that slow-motion world of long thoughts and thick moments. He used the stretched time to choose carefully the moment to release the handlebars. He moved his foot to the seat and launched his body up and clear of the mass of metal that was beginning its death roll.

He secretly loved moments like this. He thought back to the tree he had fallen out of as a child and the way it had taken him what seemed like hours to reach the ground. He had run through at least four different scenarios for landing in the stretched moments, but had still thrown out his arm reflexively in the last second and broken his wrist in three places.

The bike tumbled to the right of the phone booth in a horrific, slow silence. He judged the trajectory of his body and determined he was still bound to intersect with this artifact of London. Time continued to seep like cold syrup and he considered the details of the object he was destined to impact at high speed.

The red paint was thick; its numerous layers crowded the dirty panes of glass. This was clearly not a pawnshop reproduction but an actual booth that had sat on the streets on London for decades, shielding the chatter of tourists, the schemes of criminals and the moans of lovers. As his body approached it, Random could see a red-faced man inside holding the European pay phone with its alien geometry.

He turned his body sideways in midair. He could just miss it, or perhaps make it more of a glancing blow rather than a broadside impact. His calculation was correct. He found his face just inches from the glass, looking into the eyes of a man with unruly eyebrows and a very disturbing grin on his face.

A fraction of a moment later, time resumed its normal speed and he found himself tumbling across the hard-baked ground with the screams of ripping metal assaulting his ears. He tucked his limbs and rolled hard, his body skipping like a stone on a still pond.

He suddenly realized he was already dead. The motorcycle, the ground, and even his body were projections. He had no bones left to break. He was tumbling through a lie.

He imagined himself landing on his feet. A moment later, his rolls stopped, his feet planting solid on the ground in a landing any gymnast would have been proud of. The Indian finished its racket a moment later with a long slide to a final stop.

"Hey!"

Random turned from the sight of the shattered bike to face the man who was leaning out of the phone booth and holding the receiver out. "It's for you! God wants to know why you wrecked such a pretty bike!" There was a pause as Random clenched his hands into fists and ground his teeth with rage. The man's face softened and he began a wheeze that built to a chorus of laughter. He dropped the receiver and his laughter rose to a howl as he bent over and made no attempt to conceal how thoroughly amused he was with himself.

Random began closing the gap between them with a walk only used when preparing to kick the living shit out of someone. The man's laughter intensified and he began to point and squeeze words out between laughs. "...Your face! Ooowaa, you are so pissed! Priceless!"

"You think it's funny, you son of a bitch?! What the fuck are you trying to do? You could have--"

The man stood up straight and finished his sentence. "Killed you?" Random stopped just out of arm's reach of the man. He was exactly the kind of opponent Random avoided fighting. He stood with his feet planted firmly and a puckish grin on his face that just dared Random to take a swing at him. The flood of rage was halted first by the man's confidence, and then by the words.

"Well, I mean...what are you-- That was a shitty thing to do!" Random's patented quick wit was suddenly the stupid flailing of a twelve-year-old boy in a schoolyard, trying to act tough. The man stood shirtless in the bright sun. His skin was almost as red as a tomato. He wore a bright blue patterned sarong and khaki work boots. His eyebrows were unruly and curled in all directions. He was containing his amusement but it shimmered just below the surface.

The man could not hold it in any longer. He released a blast of laughter right into Random's face as he continued to look him dead in the eye. Random squirmed and tried hard not to let his anger subside. But the more he thought about it and watched this buffoon cackle, the more he found his own face holding back a smile. The man spotted it and pointed. "Ha! Could have killed you! Hahahaha...wooo hooo hoo!"

Random was still attempting to be upset with his hands on his hips. "Well, it was still a shitty...I mean--" He lost his composure and found himself chuckling. The man's laughter was raucous and contagious and the absurdity of the situation finally hit him. He was pissed that a man in a dress had put an imaginary phone booth in front of him and made him wreck his imaginary motorcycle.

Their laughter finally wound down and the man wiped tears from his eyes. "Well, it's good of you to be such a sport about it." He offered his hand to shake. "The name's Will."

Random shook his hand firmly. "Random. Nice to meet you...I guess." They chuckled a bit more. Will's face had the lines of a man who laughed as a lifestyle choice. He looked like a guy you would see on a construction site, if you didn't count the blue sarong that made him look like a surfer in work boots. His eyes were dark and his hair was a sandy brown that hung in wild curls to his shoulders.

"Let's take a look at that bike." Will began a series of long strides toward the lump of metal. Random hesitated, but then caught up quickly. The more delicate pieces like the mirrors, pegs, speedometer and headlamp had ripped off in the violent tumble. The front wheel was still spinning when they reached it. Will leaned over and touched the deep dent in the tank.

"Nice! Damn, look at the detail! This is as good as they come. Tell me, Mr. Random, where'd you come by this?"

Random was a bit confused. "I made it. You know, from memory. Where else would I get it?" Will's expressions were hard to read. Random wasn't sure whether he was about to be the butt of another joke.

Will straightened up slowly. "You're a Builder?" He squinted a bit, suspicious. "Then you can you put it back together...right?"

Random's eyebrows shot up in surprise. "I suppose I could, couldn't I? ...Sure!" He looked at the bike and forgot everything else. He focused on the dented tank. With a sharp pop, the dent was gone and the paint no longer scuffed. He held his hands out and the bike lifted onto its wheels and balanced perfectly. Random concentrated hard on the way it should be, the way he remembered it, and in a rush of movement, all the wayward fragments of the bike rushed to their source. The Indian was flawless again. The kickstand swung down with a creak of the spring and the bike leaned its weight over onto it.

Random laughed at the sky, then turned to Will. "I just love that! Being dead does have its advantages, doesn't it?"

But the joy seemed to leave Will's face. His eyes darted back and forth until he found his voice. "How long have you been here, Random?"

Random walked to the bike and swung his leg over. "I guess you could say I'm new here. Why?"

"I've been here a lot longer, and I've never seen anything manifest that fast before." Will stepped closer and touched the headlight that only moments ago had been shattered glass. "Can you build...anything?"

Random wrinkled his brow. "I suppose...if I could picture it in my mind first. You can't?"

Will shook his head. "Not like you just did. It takes me a lot longer. I was never much for memorizing details of stuff. I guess you could say I'm a bit short on patience, at least in that department." Will turned and pointed at the phone booth. "That stupid thing took me three days. I just moved it in front of you when I saw you blasting this way. I've been out here practicing, trying to get better, but my skill is not for objects."

"What's your skill for, then, Will?"

Will took a short step back and closed his eyes. A calm emanated from him as the breeze stopped and a silence descended. Random was scanning the space around Will, looking for something to shimmer to life, when the long, low note of an oboe filled his ears. The sound was soon joined by other wind instruments and then a symphony of strings behind it. The complexity and richness of the sound was overwhelming. Random was sure he was standing surrounded by an invisible orchestra, hearing not just the music, but also the breathing of the performers as they coaxed magic from their instruments. The music rose to its crescendo and dropped to a quiet pause. Will opened his eyes and the breeze returned. Random sat in the worn leather seat and could feel his body swaying gently. The music had been like nothing he had ever heard.

Will smiled. "Everyone's always going on about Mozart, but you have to hand it to Bach on that one. His artistry is masterful. Did you like it?"

Random felt his eyes welling up a bit. He had never been moved by a piece of music in quite that way. "It was beautiful. If you can do that so quickly, why does a phone booth take you three days?"

Will shook his head again. "Like I said, never thought much about the details of 'stuff,' but music..." A warm smile of joy washed over him. "Music was everything to me. The style didn't matter, it was the forms and patterns that held my love. I love all music, not just classical concertos. I could just as easily give you the blues, or speed metal, or country. I love all of them, in a way."

"Why would you practice imagining a phone booth at all?"

Will laughed. "The size was the important thing. I've never tried anything that big before. It was an assignment. I have an instructor at the Conclave who's a big fan of assignments. She says it'll help me become more well-rounded, whatever the hell that means."

Random sat up straight. "Are you a member of the Conclave?"

Will laughed again. "Wow, you are fresh off the Rock, aren't you? I'm a student at the Conclave. I've played around here in dead land long enough. I want to get back in a body, but not just any body. My last life was a bit rough for my taste. I want to choose a good birth this time, with a better set of circumstances. I'm willing to do the work to earn it. If that means throwing phone booths in front of lunatics riding motorcycles in the desert, so be it."

The way Will had said it was playful, but being referred to as a lunatic brought him back to the thoughts he had been wrestling with before the crash. He set his jaw and looked at the ground. Then, with a sudden shift, Random sat up with a bright look on his face.

"I have a proposition for you, Will. I'm headed to the Conclave, but I don't know exactly how to get there. If you showed me the way...I could help you with your homework."

The same wicked smile seemed to bloom on both their faces. Will nodded as he spoke. "Oh, this sounds like an all-around bad idea. Deal!" They shook on it. Will rocked back and forth like an impatient child. He looked at the rear fender of the bike, just behind the single seat Random sat in.

"No, you can't ride bitch on this thing. Have you ridden a bike before?"

Will bristled a bit. "Hell, yes. I had one for a couple years."

Random stroked his chin in thought. "Well, I'm not going to start you creating something that complicated if a friggin' phone booth took you three days." He stopped and closed his eyes. He thought back to his memory of Sturgis and flipped through the images in his mind. The smile he felt on his face let him know when he found the right one. He dropped his hands and focused hard on another bike that had caught his attention. The air around his head grew warm and he found himself racing around the image in his mind.

Random opened his eyes. Will was giving him a puzzled look. Random pointed over his shoulder. "That should do." Will turned around and let out a hoot. A vintage Ariel Square Four with a red and chrome tank sat patiently waiting. The fenders were black and the raised fin on the front fender bore the designation "FZ1944" in large white letters.

"Normally old British bikes are more trouble than they're worth, but I don't think we'll have to worry about it breaking down here." Before Will could reply, Random had fired the Indian to life. Will raced to the Ariel like it was Christmas morning. He went over the gauges and switches to get his bearings. He then flipped the kick-starter out and it fired up on the first jump. His laughter was drowned out by the roar of the motors.

Random rolled up alongside him. He held out the set of vintage goggles. Will went to grab them, but Random kept them out of reach. He shook his head and held them up for Will to see, but not touch.

Will understood and looked at the goggles hard. He held out his own hand the same way. He wanted to ride so badly he could hardly stand it. Random kept motioning him to look at the goggles, not his own empty hand. Then Random snapped the goggles over his eyes and pointed at Will's hand.

This time Will's laughter could be heard over the rumbling bikes as he pulled the goggles he had just created over his eyes. They dropped the bikes into gear and Random motioned for Will to lead the way.

: : THE SCAR : :

They rode until nightfall, keeping the throttles wide open. They played games of chase, alternating who was in the lead. Their speed was not regulated by the machines' limitations but by their intent. They rode until exhaustion exceeded exhilaration. Random slowed and motioned toward the tree line.

Before Will had even gotten off his bike, Random was already assessing the campsite. He was tired and in no mood for another lesson. He focused his mind, but kept his eyes open. Two tents, a fire ring, and matching camp chairs appeared. Random sat in one chair and reached to his right, where the cooler he expected came into being. He dug in the ice and pulled out a bottle of beer. "Start a fire for us and come have a cold one."

Random was surprised when the fire burst to life in mere seconds. Will sat down with what seemed like a permanent grin. "Fire is easy; I just think of how it sounds." Will looked at his empty palm. "Hey. What's wrong with my hand?" Random handed him the beer he was holding and fished out a new one for himself. He popped the top of his with an opener tied to the cooler. Will forced his off using the edge of a rock. They held the bottles up to toast.

"To a damn fine ride!" Will raised his bottle. The beers were the brand Random had always brought on camping trips. The men were silent except for grunted approvals they exchanged in appreciation for their beers.

Random waited until they had cracked open their second round before finally allowing himself to ask the many questions that had been rolling around in his head during their ride. "So, what does it mean to be a 'student' at the Conclave?"

Will swallowed a mouthful of beer. "Well, it means different things to different people. For me it's mostly about patience, which is a pretty annoying lesson." He grabbed a stick and started poking the fire. "I used to be like the majority of souls here, racing to get into another body and not too picky about which one I got. Like I said, my last go on the wheel was a little rough. Turns out I made a deal with a rather shady character who was peddling incarnations on Transit Square."

The name brought Random back to the memory of the mobile city and walking the decks with Erminia and her lanky minion. "And is Transit Square the Conclave's competition to put people back on Earth?"

Will didn't smile as he continued to poke the fire. "More and more it seems that way. The Square has always been a black market for those who don't want to go through the hassle of the Conclave. The births offered through the Conclave are more reliable and in very high demand. As you can imagine, there's a lot of competition, and usually a long wait."

"People compete for parents?" Random had a hard time imagining it.

Will finally looked him in the eyes. "At the Conclave, people petition for parents. They try to find a good match between a soul who's looking to evolve in a certain way and a family that can support that evolution. It's pretty subjective, and most of the time there's more than one match, so there are usually competing candidates."

Random forced a laugh that ended up sounding awkward. "So then what? Do they flip a coin? Arm wrestle for it? Answer a riddle?"

Will leaned back and held the smoldering stick like a spear. "I'm not really sure. I've never gotten that far in the process. This is my first time trying the Conclave's way. I've always just rolled the dice in the past."

"Do you remember all your...lives? Do you remember being here before?" Random had stopped trying to look cool. He sat forward in his chair soaking up the words.

Will had brought the red smoldering tip of his stick close to his face and was rotating it slowly as he considered his answer. "Recently I've started to remember a little of the last time I was here. It comes in bits and pieces. The first memory came when I was on Transit Square, about seven years ago, shopping for a body. I ended up at the same damn place I'd gotten my last body. I recognized the guy who was running it, the same cheat I'd hired before. It was a deep memory; it shook me to the core. I got off the Square as soon as I could and started making my way to the Conclave." He tossed the stick into the fire and took another swig of his beer. "As far as the other lives I've lived, yeah, I remember them more and more the longer I'm here. Sometimes that's good and other times it fucks with me. It seems I wasn't always as 'evolved' as I am now--if you can believe it. I'm glad I have a teacher who was willing to accept me as a student. There were some memories that were...dark. She was there to help me sort them out and forgive myself. According to her, that's why I always chose the easy route before. There were things I'd done and people I'd been that I wasn't willing to face."

Random hung on every word. He was tired of being the stupid new guy who didn't know the rules of the game. "So when you get back in a body you forget everything, start over fresh?"

Will leaned forward with his arms on his knees and his face softened. When he wasn't smiling or laughing, he looked older and a bit ominous, especially with the firelight on his face. "Well, that's what the shysters on the Square will tell you. But the folks at the Conclave have a different story. They believe that you drag all that shit along with you no matter how many times you spin the wheel. I used to think they were full of shit, but now I agree with them." He polished off the last of his beer and stood up. "I plan on going back without a bunch of baggage this time. Now, if you don't mind, I'm going to take advantage of this nice tent you made for me and close my eyes for a while."

Random was visibly disappointed. He had so many more questions. "Why do you need to sleep? We're dead. Couldn't we just stay awake forever?"

"It's an old habit we all seem to keep. It's not really necessary, but it helps rest the mind. Sleep here is deep and, as far as I know, no one dreams. I guess every day here is enough of a dream world." Will, thankfully, smiled again. "But if I had to guess, you won't be sleeping for a while. Don't worry there, sport, I'll answer more of your questions tomorrow. I'm sure you have a sack of them." He ducked under the tent flap and disappeared inside.

The popping and cracking of the fire was more noticeable in Will's absence. His last words still resonated in Random's head. Where would you start if you wanted to settle up all the transgressions of not just the life you remember, but even those you had lived and forgotten? And where did that leave him? He was proud that the life he had lived had been one without much regret. Sure, there had been stupid choices he had made along the way, but he always felt that they were part of a path.

If he hadn't gotten thrown off the soccer team for getting all the freshmen drunk, he never would have refocused his energy on drawing and painting. If he hadn't gone to art school, he never would have met that batshit-crazy chick in his life drawing class. If she had been just a little less crazy, he wouldn't have left her and hooked up with her friend Karen out of spite. If he hadn't met Karen...he had no idea what his life would have been like without her. He ached at the thought of giving up one day with her or their son. His last bad idea was the only one he couldn't reconcile. That chain of events had ultimately cost him his life.

The sadness began to well up again, but was quickly replaced by the larger question that now pestered him. What of the inner demons he had supposedly released here? Did a thousand-year sleep settle that account? He thought of the look in Sister Darśana's eyes as she recoiled from him. She had not forgotten whatever he had unleashed in his insanity. It lay fresh on her face when she realized who he was. If he wanted to reconcile things the way Will did, how could that be accomplished? How could he atone for sins he didn't remember committing?

The fire dimmed to embers. He could hear Will's heavy breathing, and assumed he had succumbed to whatever version of dreamless sleep was available here. The buzzing of questions and theories in his head confirmed Will's prediction. Random would not be sleeping for a while.

He stood up and focused on the blackness of the night beyond the soft glow of the fire. He could hear what sounded like faint drums on the wind. He grabbed a fallen branch off the ground. He snapped off a few twigs and leaned his weight on it. It would do as a walking stick. He turned his back on the flatlands they had assaulted with the bikes all day. He followed the faint whisper of what sounded like drums into the forest.

The trees were different here. They weren't the thick old-growth ones he had seen in the Glade. These trunks were thin, and he doubted they held sleeping souls. The slope was gradual, but the darkness was making it increasingly challenging. He stopped and concentrated on the top of his stick. In a moment a glowing orb appeared as a cap, cascading light a few feet around him. He continued climbing toward what was now clearly the sound of drums.

The light was essential as the grade became more challenging. He could see that there was going to be a final steep hike ahead to what looked like a plateau. Beyond the rise were cliffs that shot up hundreds of feet--a wall of rock. He could see a flickering glow from the top of the plateau. Shadows and firelight danced to the drumbeats on the walls of the sheer cliffs.

His progress was slowed by waist-deep brush and grass. Even with his light he could not see the ground, and stumbled a few times as he stepped in hidden depressions masked by the weave of vegetation. He was near the base of the last rise and ready to start his final ascent to the plateau. A line of brush just taller than he was stood as his last hurdle before the climb. He focused on it and imagined it parting before him, but he found this landscape ignoring his efforts. There was something different about this place. The only choice was to go through it.

He didn't care. He was enjoying the physicality of the hike as a distraction from his noisy mind. He checked the density of the brush and knew that he could break through if he could get his body moving forward up the slope. Random planted his staff in the ground and leaned on it to make sure he was on a firm spot below the spongy underbrush. He stepped back, then rushed forward, using the stick to pole-vault his mass at the wall of bushes.

It worked. The plant life gave way with a chorus of snapping twigs and rushing grass. He crashed with his feet reaching forward for a landing. He found himself falling past the point where the ground should be and releasing his staff as he fell into the darkness of the hole he didn't realize was there until too late.

He was in free-fall just long enough to feel his stomach jump. He made contact with the hard bottom of the hole and rolled, slamming his head into stone. The impact dazed him and hurt like hell. He lay still for a moment, then sat up in the darkness. At first he thought it was his head that was pounding, but then realized it was the drums. Somehow the drumbeats were louder in the hole than they had been topside.

He managed to find his stick by groping around the stone floor of the pit. He felt the globe still on top, but the light had gone out. As he sat in the dark, his eyes started to adjust. He stopped messing with the globe and looked around. The pit was about seven feet across. The walls and floor were all stone. The vegetation he had fallen through was about ten feet above him.

He followed the sound of the drumbeats to a wide crack with light filtering through it weakly. Random crawled over to the crack and could feel air blowing out of it, carrying the sound to him.

He stuck his fingers into the crack and gave it a few tugs, using the weight of his body. The stone moved by inches at first, but then gave way all at once to reveal a dimly lit passage beyond. A few more minutes of removing stones and he had created a hole just big enough to squirm through.

He was able to stand up once he got through. The sound of drums echoed in the passage. Light and sound guided him forward. The stone of the walls and floor was rough but sturdy masonry. It was a single squarish hallway that continued to take him toward the mountains and slightly uphill. At the end of the hallway, some fifty feet away, a door stood open. The light source and the drumming increased as he approached. The door was iron. It would have made sense on an ancient ocean liner but was out of place here. The heavy hinges were bent; it hung slightly askew.

He peered cautiously into the chamber beyond the door. The room was a lumpy oval, fifteen feet at its widest, and appeared to be the casualty of an earthquake or a bomb blast. The tall bookcases had vomited books and papers onto the stone floor. A delicate wooden table had been crushed by what appeared to be a marble bust of a pharaoh. Oil paintings in heavy frames lay atop the debris. One painting was speared on the sharp leg of a chair, its canvas torn beyond repair. All the splintered furniture was once ornate and of very high quality. It was like a cave that had been furnished by a nobleman.

At the other end of the chamber, opposite where Random stood, the stone hallway continued for about three feet before the walls, ceiling and floor all ended abruptly. He could see a rock wall and a small slice of the night sky. The firelight and shadows flickered from beyond. He made his way past the debris in the room, taking care not to disturb the broken piles and cause any noise that would alert the drummers to his presence.

When he reached a point where he could see over the edge of the broken passage, he found he was looking out into a crater. The light was from a bonfire at the very bottom, some hundred feet or so below him. Around the fire were two drummers and three dancers. He couldn't make out much more beyond that at this distance. The broken hallway he stood in was high on the wall of the crater. The rim was some fifty feet above him, judging by the opposite wall. What he had thought was a plateau was actually an immense, ragged hole.

On the opposite wall, he could see other passages that had once been underground tunnels like this one, now just black doorways leading to nowhere but a long fall. In the walls of the crater he also spotted the remains of pipes, twisted and bent, their metal torn violently. Some of the pipes were big enough for a man to stand in, but ripped and torn even so. The network of rusted plumbing all pointed skyward, like hundreds of accusing fingers. It didn't look like an impact had caused this wound in the terrain. Rather, something very large had been yanked out by its roots.

He stepped back into the chamber. Random had no desire to call out to whoever was drumming and dancing below. His mind was uneasy and he did not like this place. It felt like a tomb. He would need to backtrack and climb out of the pit he had fallen into. With a final look into the crater, he turned back to the passage through which he had entered, but stopped when he saw the crooked picture that had managed to remain hanging from the wall above the arched doorway. It was a small, framed drawing and he took it down to see the detail better.

It was a hand-rendered map of two cities separated by a thick ridge of mountains with a single pass between them. The city to the west was smaller, high in the mountains. It was at the far end of a flat plain that ended in a box canyon. The words written in a curling script told him that the smaller city through the pass in the mountains was his destination, the Conclave. The pass through the mountains was narrow and made many turns before it reached the vast plain that led to the city. Nestled at the back of the canyon, the Conclave was represented by a series of circles.

The city on the east was large, and sprawling at the foot of the range. A statue rose from a fountain in the central courtyard. The larger city was just south of the entrance to the pass. Lettering in the same ancient hand curled above it: "Vandal Square." He remembered being aboard the moving city and how Erminia had told him that it was a home for "those who do not want to be found." Had "The Square" been right here on the other side of the mountains from their rivals in the incarnation business? The idea that an entire city had somehow picked up and gone on the run was hard to imagine, but the longer he was here, the more elastic his imagination became.

What did it say about the Conclave if an entire city had been moved to escape their scrutiny? He could hardly grasp the intensity of thought that would be required to accomplish such a feat. He wasn't sure what version of the Conclave he believed. Were they the benevolent teachers both Joe and

Will claimed? Or were they the arrogant elite, lying to the masses, as Erminia professed? He wasn't too sure now.

Random pored over the rest of the hand-drawn map. Some details were hard to make out in the flickering light. The forest of Glory Bubbles was not here, but he saw a group of trees that were larger and drawn with more care. If those trees represented the Glade where he had met the Sisters, he and Will could easily reach the mouth of the pass in the morning. Random took the frame and dropped it flat on the stone. The glass shattered and he carefully removed the map and rolled it into a tube.

It was time to find out what this Conclave was all about firsthand. He would pass into the crowds that must surround this merchant of high births. Perhaps Will could help get him deeper into the city with his status as a student. Once Random had made his assessment, he would find Joe again and talk with him on his own terms. He needed to know whether what the Sisters had told him was true. If it was, and if he and Joe had known each other, he needed to know what he had done to be ruled insane. It was time to get some answers. It was time to get out of this hole.

: : OFF THE MAP : :

The morning sun shone warm, and the droning sound of the motors was comforting to Random. He was still trying to shake the disquiet his strange night hike had left him with. The map was tucked safely away in his pack.

The landscape was mostly the same, but the wide, flat plain was becoming more narrow as clumps of twisted trees began to appear on their right, sandwiching the featureless plain against the forested mountains, ever-present on their left. The Glory Bubbles were far behind them now, their domed tops only visible if he were to glance over his shoulder. He did not take the time to look back. He had a destination now and forward was the only direction that interested him.

The twisted trees were joined by glimmers of what appeared to be pools of water. The bright morning sun danced off them, making them shine like gemstones. Random and Will rode with purpose, not as playful as they had been the previous day. Random took notice when Will suddenly changed his trajectory and began heading toward a large tree sprawled over a more substantial pool of water.

Random pictured the map in his head and questioned the new direction. He reminded himself that maps don't always tell the whole story. Will was still his guide in this unfamiliar world. He accelerated a bit and followed Will's new course.

They began to pass much closer to the shimmering ponds that dotted the plain. The light on the water was more than the reflection of the bright morning sun. The water itself had a strange glow that became apparent close-up. The trees gripping the water's edge were old and knotted, like full-scale versions of Japanese bonsai.

From a distance, the tree toward which they were headed had seemed a bit larger than the others. As they got closer to it, Random realized that its scale was truly massive. The water below it formed a small lake and the tree grew from an island in the center of it.

Will slowed the Ariel as they neared the shore, then brought the bike to a full stop and cut the engine. Random pulled up alongside him and silenced the Indian. Will dropped the kickstand and got off the bike without a word of explanation. Random was not sure why his guide had stopped here, but dismounted.

Will walked in silence and did not seem to care whether Random followed him. Random noticed a change in his demeanor as he approached the water line. His pace was slow, his steps carefully chosen. He looked like a man either entering a church or about to cross a minefield.

As they stood looking at the gnarled tree, Random realized that they were not the only visitors. Small groups of men and women were gathered at the opposite shore. Although his mind was buzzing with questions, Random could not convince his voice to ask any. There was something about the place that inspired the reverence that a temple might.

A wind stirred the branches of the colossal tree with sudden, violent gusts. Random looked into the great boughs and saw what appeared to be its fruit: lumpy masses streaked with yellow and green. They reminded him of summer squashes. The smallest were the size of basketballs, while the largest approached the size of a man.

The groups of people on the opposite shore began to stir. There was a noticeable excitement, but no clear organization. Random managed to find his voice as the gusts of wind grew more intense. "What's going on here? Why are those people..."

His questions were silenced when the snapping of branches echoed from high above and two ripe fruit began falling toward the surface of the water. Several travelers rushed to the edge of the shore and dove into the lake, just moments before the strange fruits followed them in.

As the first swimmer broke the surface, the water glowed intensely at the spot the fruit entered. The glowing spots appeared around every item that breached the surface of the strange liquid. The lights in the water were like silent fireworks. The wind increased again and four more of the hanging squashes broke free of their bonds. Those on the shore were now in a frenzy, some jumping in recklessly while others seemed to be waiting for some invisible signal. Eventually, even the most cautious swimmer had launched himself into the water, cannonball style.

As quickly as the wind had picked up, the air again became still and the great tree came to rest once again. The underwater fireworks faded back to a consistent glow. The silence closed in again. The surface of the lake became still. There was no one left standing on the opposite shore.

After long moments, Random realized that not one of the swimmers had resurfaced. As the time span most people could hold their breath passed, he began to pace nervously. He started pulling off his shirt and moving forward, but he was blocked when Will placed his thick body between Random and the lake.

"I wouldn't do that if I were you--unless you've grown so tired of my company already that you want to jump back into a body."

Random shook his head in confusion. "I don't understand. What just happened here?"

Will looked deep into his eyes without blinking. "These pools are all doorways. If you jump into one, you'll find yourself in the body of a baby on Earth. Without a guide of any sort, those who leap leave their next life to fate, to the next roll of the dice."

At that moment another snap sounded from overhead as one of the squash-like fruit fell from very high up in the tree. It bounced off a lower branch, then continued its fall toward the lake, ending in a huge splash and an explosion of light.

"And what the hell are those things?"

Will smiled and put his hand on Random's shoulder. "They say that those are new souls, born from the Ether itself. There's no reason to wait for them to fall if you intend to jump back into the world, but there are many superstitions around the timing. Either way, a jump into a wild pool is a leap of faith."

Will turned and began walking back to his motorcycle. He pulled on his gloves and raised the bike off its kickstand. Random walked back to the Indian, but he just stood next to it, puzzled.

Will paused in his start-up sequence to watch him. "Don't worry, they're always here if that's the path you want to choose. I only stopped because I suddenly remembered this tree. I jumped into this very pool, a long time ago. Some souls may get lucky, but I wouldn't call that particular roll a lucky one for me. The little I remember of that short life is enough for me to stay away from wild pools."

Will flashed Random a smile and motioned to the Indian. "Come on, fire up that beast. We have a ways to go yet."

· · · · ·

By early afternoon they had come to an overlook within sight of the pass. Random had expected to see a mist-filled gap in the sheer wall of mountains. He had imagined having a quiet moment of contemplation before taking the final turn toward the vaunted Conclave and all its mysteries. Perhaps he and Will would encounter travelers who clearly sought wisdom on the path, with robes and twisted staves.

The last thing he had expected was the bizarre parade of chaos shuffling toward the shantytown at the mouth of the pass. They stopped the bikes and Random shut off the Indian to take it all in from a distance. Will rolled up next to him and killed his engine.

Random had returned to the campsite the night before and studied the map he had taken from the room on the brink of the crater. What he was looking at was not on the map. "What the hell is that?" Random spoke to the wind more than to Will. He hadn't mentioned his late-night adventure to Will, and had opted to keep the map to himself for now.

Will was watching him intently, and let the silence hang. Random had been awake when he emerged from the tent to greet the morning. He had been silently making coffee in a tin pot over a fresh fire. Will shared a cup, but was surprised that no new line of questions erupted from his companion. They sat listening to the wind in the trees and sipping the brew. After a while, Random had simply stated that he wanted to get moving.

Will watched Random's confusion at the sight of the shabby encampment that lay less than a half a mile from them, where the narrow mountain pass spilled onto the featureless plain. "That is a checkpoint for the souls who wish to get back on the Rock, a final stop for those headed to the Conclave and a place of trade in all manner of things. It's not as shady as the black markets on the Square, but it has some darker shades of gray in the folds. That, my friend, is Lüdertown."

Random scanned the flat landscape that stretched to the horizon to the east of the mountains. It had just been the two of them with the world to themselves. Now he could see souls streaming like ants toward Lüdertown from all directions. Some were on foot in groups. Some drove vehicles with clouds of dust in their wake. The skies were abuzz with flying craft. Small planes, gliding wings, gyrocopters, even a small dirigible. All of them seemed bound for the squalid collection of camps. Lüdertown was laid out in a semicircle, its arms spread wide to the wasteland. The last rows of hovels stopped a few hundred feet from the beginning of the mountain pass. He could see a few specks of travelers, all on foot, beginning their trek to the Conclave. He noticed there was no air traffic crossing the mountains.

Pointing to the sky, Random turned to Will. "Why don't they just fly over?"

Will answered without a smile. "They can't, but someone tries, every once in a while. The Conclave doesn't want Mrs. Napoleon flying her city to their doorstep. Anything that tries to fly through the pass slowly loses altitude and stops working. This is the only access to the Conclave, and you have to go it on foot or not at all." Will patted the gas tank of his bike like he would a loyal hound. "It'll be a shame to let these babies go, but they should fetch a high price."

Random shook his head a bit as he incorporated all this new information into his perception of this place and the conflict that everyone he met seemed very aware of. He considered coming clean with Will and sharing everything that had happened to him, but he wasn't sure just yet how much he could trust him. Random decided to play dumb and fish for some information. "Mrs. Napoleon?"

"She's the 'midget queen' of Transit Square. She flies her little kingdom around and causes the Conclave headaches." Will paused. "Her name is Erminia. She isn't really a midget, but she is pretty small. I saw her once, the last time I was on the Square. She looked me dead in the eye. Gorgeous, polished, elegant...and crazy as the day is long. When she walks in a room, it just gets awkward. I bet she's a hell of a ride in the sack, but the level of crazy I saw in her eyes...well, it isn't worth it, in my opinion."

Random had also looked into those eyes. He had seen cunning and bitterness mixed with a kind of sadness. He wasn't sure whether he would classify it as crazy, but he hadn't ruled that out. He looked down at his bike. "What would a high price be? What form of currency do they use here?"

Will laughed. "I keep forgetting how new you are. There is no currency; it's more of a barter system. People here trade memories--" Will could see the thoughts racing through Random's head. "Look, think of it this way. So, one of the ways that physical stuff is created here is by things we remember. It's how you created these beautiful machines. Certain things rely almost completely on the memories we gathered from life." Will paused as he tried to think of a good example. "Food is a perfect example. We don't need it here, but we remember the joy of eating it. Do you remember what barbecued ribs taste like?"

"Yes, of course. I love good barbecue."

Will continued. "Perfect. Now imagine that you hadn't actually eaten real ribs for forty years. You remember that you like them, but after so many years, when you make them, they taste a little blander every time. Now you come across someone who is freshly dead. They just had ribs last month. If they can remember them for you, now you have a fresh memory to go off of. It's not as good as theirs, because it's a copy, but it's a lot better than your forty-year-old version."

Will was very animated explaining this concept. He paused reluctantly to make sure it had sunk in before he continued. Random was happy to put his pride aside and be a pupil. He noticed Will was waiting. "OK, I can get that. Our memories fade."

Will charged ahead. "Exactly! So the people with the fresh memories have a lot to trade, especially someone like you. You both remember things in great detail," he said, pointing to the chrome on the tank of his bike, "and you've picked up the knack of making it real here faster than anyone I've ever heard of."

Random cocked his head and his eyes opened wider. He understood why Will was so quick to agree to travel with him. Under these rules, he was currently a very wealthy man. This realization immediately brought to his mind a question that leapt from his mouth. "But what will someone who's been here a long time offer me in exchange if their memories are all degrading?"

Will raised his bushy eyebrows and gave a nod. "I see you've been a businessman in at least one of your lives. Those who've been here a while have discovered that they all have their own gifts, like the ear I have for music. Some are guides who know the ever-changing landscape. Tracers are good at finding other souls in the soup, if you have a loved one you want to locate. There are many other specialties that are more...exotic. Don't worry, there are plenty of shiny things to trade for."

"Are there those who can look in on the living?"

Will's enthusiasm evaporated. "Yes. Once only the orders of the Conclave could do that. Now there are those who call themselves Freebooters. Most are just con men who will tell you what you want to hear, but some are legit. If you go looking for them, you'll end up in the darker corners of Lüdertown and, before long, find yourself trying to get aboard Transit Square. My completely unsolicited advice is to let go of the concerns you have for those you left behind. I've seen that desire turn to obsession bordering on madness. It's best to leave life to the living."

This mention of madness bothered Random. "So what are some of the other services people have to trade?"

Will sat back on his seat and crossed his arms. "I told you you'd have a sack of questions. A fallback for anyone who's been here long enough is to deal in information." The silence that followed was apparent.

"I see I wasn't the only one who was a businessman. What would you like in return for some more of your knowledge, Will?"

"Well, now that you mention it, I have some things I'd like to purchase in the Lüder, and it's often hard to sell a song. However, I'm sure I could get all I need if I could trade in this fine British iron." He patted the tank of the Ariel.

Random nodded with a grin. He appreciated negotiating with someone who knew what he wanted and made an offer that was up-front.

"It's yours to trade as you wish, provided you answer the rest of my questions."

"No way; you could keep asking forever! I'll answer one more question."

Random wrinkled his face as if he'd smelled something foul. "Five questions."

"I already answered too many for free. Tell you what: three questions. That way I'll feel like a genie from a lamp!" He laughed, but Random had done enough negotiating in his life to know this was a final offer.

"Deal, O Magical One. But you have to answer them all honestly and completely."

Will unfolded his arms and feigned an offended look. "What were you, a lawyer or something? It's a deal, Counselor; I have no reason to lie to you. Ask away."

Random started with one that had been bugging him. "So how does the Conclave know what births are good for people? Do they stalk pregnant ladies?"

Will didn't expect that kind of question. "Well, technically, that's two questions. But since it's your first try, I'll ignore the second part so you still have two left. But that's the last mulligan I'm giving you." Will pulled the bike up onto its kickstand and got off. "My ass hurts."

"Why would your..." Random caught himself, narrowly avoiding wasting a question.

Will squinted at him and started pacing about. Random pushed his kickstand down; it lowered with a creak of the heavy spring. He was glad to get off the bike and stretch his legs a bit. Will kept pacing, considering his answer.

"Well, since I have to be truthful, I can say that I'm not sure on that one. I can tell you what I know, but some of it is speculation. That all right with you?"

Random nodded. "Fair enough."

Will put his hands in the small of his back and arched backward with a grunt. "Those who have the gift of being in this world and peeking in on the living are rare. Some call them Shamans. Almost all of them are either in the Conclave or on the Square. The Freebooters are the exception, but there aren't many of them either. From what I've been able to gather, there are those who are alive who can peek back this way too. They don't necessarily call them Shamans on Earth. They're more likely to be called lunatics or whack jobs. Turns out that homeless guy in the subway with the tinfoil hat may actually be hearing voices. He could also just be a drug addict. But the Shamans here do communicate with people on the Rock. I'm not sure if it's a 'Hey, how are you' sort of a conversation. I heard one Shaman talk like he'd just seen through someone else's eyes for a bit. Anyway, that's how they peek in. I don't know how they choose a good birth over a shitty one. Second question."

Random thought about inquiring into other exotic trades, but didn't know exactly how to word it into a question Will would answer. His mind kept going back to a slight hint he had heard in what Will had been telling him freely before their deal. "You said that memory was one of the ways physical 'stuff' can be made real here. What's the other way?"

"Damn! I see you were listening. Well, memory is just one of several ways. There are those who can imagine things that have never been. They can make shit up on the fly and build you something to order. The things they imagine come into being very quickly and are so detailed, they're almost as good as a first-generation memory. That is also just a gift; you either have it or you don't. These people are called Builders, and I'd bet my mother's false teeth that you are one. You could easily set up shop and live a fat life just making shit for those who can't make it themselves. OK, Counselor. Your final question."

"Well, I know what I want to ask, but the only way you could answer it would be if you knew a certain person in the Conclave. I don't want to waste a question..."

Will rolled his eyes. "I'm only going to give you this one because that bike is so damn pretty. Who are you interested in? I'll tell you if I know 'em."

"Joe."

In watching Will's reaction to the name, Random ended up getting more information than he had expected to. A wash of emotion traveled across Will's face. Random saw respect and admiration on the face of a man who did not give either lightly.

"Yeah, I know him. Most people know him. I'm not sure how much I can tell you. What do you want to know?"

Random took his time to formulate a single question that would tell him about the first man he had met in this place. He finally settled on one that was a bit of a risk. It would be up to Will how much he wanted to divulge. He was counting on Will to trust him; they were still sizing each other up, as men always do.

"What is Joe's gift, his specialty, here?"

Will's face softened and he shed at least ten years. "That is one hell of a question. Well played, sir. I don't think I'm the right person to even attempt to answer it. But we had a deal, and I never welch on a deal." He looked to the sky as a hang glider soared close enough to see that the pilot was a nude woman. "He was there nine years ago when I first woke up dead. I was a fucking mess. I had died in a pretty nasty car wreck and the scene was still playing in my head along with the rest of my lousy life. He took me to the Conclave on foot. We walked for days. By the time we got there he had talked me down and told me that my next life didn't have to be like the last. He let me stay with him in his house for weeks. When I decided to leave and seek a quicker incarnation, he let me go and honored my choice. He told me that choice was sacred to him and that he resisted the temptation to take it away from anyone. When I changed my mind and came back a year or so later, he not only welcomed me but helped me get accepted by one of the best instructors. He's been here longer than any of them in the Conclave. His skills are beyond that of a mere Builder. I've seen him create things that would take hours for me to even describe. He is one of the Five. He is an Architect."

Will stopped and walked back to the Ariel. "I believe I've paid in full for this motorcycle." He threw his leg over the bike and pulled it off the stand. "Come on; I want to get moving. Let's ride like hell all the way there. I'm sad to see her go, but I have some shopping to do." Will kicked the bike to life and revved the engine. Random went to the Indian and fired it up. He hadn't gotten all his questions answered, but he had found out that Joe held a very high position in the Conclave.

Random was not sure what it meant to be an Architect as opposed to a 'mere Builder,' but the phrase 'one of the five' told him it was not your average profession. He remembered how Joe wanted to get him back to the Conclave and offer him a job. What would Joe need from him if Joe had the kind of skill Will had described? Random thought it had to do with what Sister Del had told him about himself--that he had been a Builder gifted enough to design the Glade of Souls. He was starting to believe their story of his thousand-year sleep. He was starting to believe a lot of things that had been ridiculous to him just days ago.

He tucked his thoughts away as they rolled off the rise and back down to the flats, where they pointed the bikes north, opened the throttles, and let the engines roar.

• • • • •

The center plaza of Lüdertown was the most unlikely parking lot Random had ever seen. Every form of transportation imaginable was on display, parked haphazardly where the driver had left it. Priceless luxury cars sat caked with mud, flying carpets hovered alongside dune buggies, and a steaming tractor puffed white smoke near three small aircraft.

The bikes were perfect for weaving through the chaos of these obstacles that would, at times, fire their engines up and start moving without warning. Random gladly let Will take the lead, and tried to stay focused in the sea of distractions. The closer they got to the center of the crescent-shaped town, the more they were slowed by people on foot filling the gaps between vehicles.

Will navigated the mess with skill and determination. He found a seam of space in the chaos and they rode onto the streets of the city. The traffic on the streets was almost entirely pedestrian; the people cleared out of the way as the rumble of the bikes came up behind them. Will seemed clear where he was headed and what he wanted to trade his bike for. Random just took in the scene and tried not to hit anyone in the process.

Lüdertown was more of a camp than a town; the majority of structures were canvas tents open to the street. Some had barkers out in front trying to entice the passersby to stop. Several barkers gave them sharp looks as the noise of the motorcycles interrupted their flow. Those who walked the streets were a show unto themselves, with costuming that disregarded all boundaries of time and culture. A buxom bare-chested woman in a tutu walked with a tall man dressed in full samurai armor. A thin man with dark skin and white Bedouin robes spoke to a woman a foot taller than he in thigh-high boots and a black leather outfit with spikes on thick shoulder pads. He spotted stunning women in full-length evening gowns, a hairy naked man with a huge top hat, a group of tribesmen whose skin was bluish black, aristocratic gentlemen in Shakespearean garb, and one guy in a futuristic outfit that marked him as someone who must have spent most of his life memorizing science fiction movies.

None of them seemed disturbed by the clash of styles. Instead, they admired each other's clothing, or absence of clothing, as a stream of fellow runway models on display. All of them were annoyed by the loud bikes that disturbed the peace of their promenade. Random was glad when Will took a final turn and parked his bike in front of a two-story wooden structure.

The Indian was considerably louder than Will's bike and the thumping rattle of its engine drew people out of the building as he parked. A lean, shirtless man pushed his way through the crowd on the porch. He was muscled but not bulky, with an almost complete lack of fat on him. His features were severe and chiseled. His sparse hair hung in blond dreadlocks. For some reason, he was holding a French horn that caught the bright sun.

Before he could say a word, Will caught his attention with a friendly holler. "Hambone! How's the world treating you, you dirty hippie?"

The man with the horn shook his head and smiled. "Well, I was fine until these two assholes on loud-ass bikes pulled up in front of my shop and scared away my customers." He held his arms wide and Will gave him a bear hug that made them both laugh.

Will waved his hand. "Random, c'mere. I have a freak you need to meet." Random hung his goggles on the grip and joined them. "This is Hambone, one of the fine merchants in this metropolitan oasis. We've been friends a long time, so he's clearly someone who shouldn't be trusted." Hambone gave Will a sharp jab in the ribs with his bony elbow. "Hambone, this is Random. He's fresh off the Rock and a talented Builder. I found him screaming across the flats on that beast."

Hambone stood straight and considered Random. They were the same height, and Hambone looked him dead in the eyes when he spoke. "Any friend of Will's is clearly nothing but trouble. Pleased to meet you." He swapped the French horn to his left hand and gave Random a firm handshake. "You make that bike yourself?"

Will answered for him. "He made that one and the one I managed to talk him out of." Will motioned to the Ariel. Hambone forgot everything and walked over to get a closer look. Will gave Random a devious look, his bushy eyebrows hopping.

"Very nice! The infamous 1953 Mk2, with Anstey-link rear suspension. The last of the line! The fender plate is a nice touch." He straightened and faced Will. "So are you keeping it, or are you here to make a trade?"

"Hambone, if I wanted to keep it, I would never have shown it to you. I know you and bikes. You also know how much I want just about everything in your shop. What new treasures do you have for me?"

Hambone let out a hoot of joy. "Oh, we can set you up with something quite nice in exchange for this little scooter. Come on inside; I have plenty to show you."

As soon as Random entered the shop, he knew why Will and Hambone were friends. It was packed to overflowing with all manner of musical instruments. Drums, guitars, wind instruments and brass bristled from the walls and filled most of the floor space. Hambone walked to the back counter and set the French horn down carefully. He opened a glass case and took out what looked like a rough tribal guitar with a round body, high bridge, and twelve strings. The body was covered in animal hide.

Will rushed over to the counter. "What the hell is that?"

Hambone smiled proudly. "This, my friend, is an African kora. A very old instrument that defies definition. Some claim it's what inspired the creation of the modern banjo. The sound is--well, let's give it a go."

Hambone came out from behind the counter and took a seat on the ground. The sound of the kora was more like a harp than a banjo. He played it with ease and reverence. Random had no doubt that Hambone could play every instrument in the shop.

He stood up and looked at Will. They read each other's faces without a word. Hambone knew his customer. "But obviously you'd want more than just this in trade. Let me see what else I can add to the offer." He handed the kora to Will, who began picking on it with remarkable skill for never having seen the instrument before. Hambone was scurrying past customers to the other side of the shop. He returned with a small drum clutched under his arm.

"Now, I know what you're thinking. Why would you want another doumbek? But this, my friend, is an authentic Persian tombak. The sound is completely different. Listen to the range in its voice." Hambone crouched and put the drum diagonally across his knee. The shop filled with a rhythm of sharp high pops and a surprising amount of bass for such a small drum. The customers gathered to hear a master at play.

Hambone stopped and handed the drum to Will. He had read his customer well. Will was so pleased he didn't even bother to play it. He tucked it under his arm and smiled, still holding the neck of the kora with the other hand.

"So we have a deal?"

Will laughed. "You know what I like. Rig me up a way I can carry them on foot; I'm headed back to the Conclave. I'll come back later and pick them up. I'm going to help Random with his shopping; this is his first visit to the Lüder. Can he leave his bike here?"

Hambone put the kora back in the case and the tombak behind the counter. "No worries; I'll keep an eye on it." He turned to Random. "I'd offer you a trade for your bike, but I already have an Indian Chief."

"And I am not a musician. Thanks for watching it; looks like we're going to do some exploring on foot."

"That's the best way to shop the Lüder; you miss the details otherwise. Find me when you get back and I'll have everything ready." Random shook his hand and Will gave him a shake that turned into another hug. They left the shop and went out to the covered porch.

Random turned to Will. "I've decided to take your advice and leave life to the living. I have no desire to dwell on the life I just left." Will put his hand on Random's shoulder and gave a nod. "But I am interested in those I knew who may be here. What can you tell me about these people who find other souls?"

Will held his eyes without blinking. "A bit of a contradiction to the declaration you just made, but one I understand. We need to find a Tracer. As luck would have it, I know where to look."

"How much will that piece of information cost me?"

"For now, I'll put it on your tab; I know you're good for it. But you can start by buying us some hot food and a cold drink. Follow me, it's on the way."

• • • • •

122

The place they ended up at was a hive of activity. It had a large swath of canvas offering shade to the patrons, but no walls. Random doubted that it ever closed, so walls were unnecessary. In the center was a circular bar crowded with customers ordering drinks. Tables of all shapes and sizes were littered about. The mismatched chairs were as varied as those who sat on them.

Will had found them a small table. He gave a sharp whistle to a girl carrying drinks, but was ignored. "Damn, I guess we'll need to go up to the bar ourselves."

"No, we don't. What do you want?" Random held out his hand and an ice-cold bottle with a thick cork appeared in it. "I'm in the mood for a Belgian ale. Care to join me?"

Will sat down hard in the spindly chair. "Sounds perfect. Can you add some roast beef to my order?" Random stopped and thought for a bit. A burly glass goblet appeared. He gestured to Will. "Make yourself one of those and I'll fill it up. I did promise to help you with your homework."

Will was not pleased with the surprise manifestation lesson, but the ale beckoned him. He stared at the table and wrinkled his brow. A lumpy clay cup appeared.

"OK, I can already see your problem. You're just thinking of a cup. No. I said make one of these." Random pointed at the glass. "This is the proper way to drink good Belgian ale. I won't pour one drop into that thing. Look at the detail on this one. Notice the light on the glass. Trace the shape with your eyes and move as slowly as possible. Think of what it weighs and how the glass has some tiny bubbles down here."

Will followed the instructions impatiently. He concentrated again and produced a version of the goblet. It was cruder and a bit misshapen. Random kept himself from laughing and offered encouragement instead. "Not bad. Good enough for now. You're getting better." He filled their cups and they made a silent toast.

Will drank from his goblet and admired his handiwork. "That's some of the same crap my teacher says. How do you know all those things if you just got here?"

Random swallowed a mouthful. "I taught life drawing for five years. Drawing something is not the hard part. You can teach a monkey technique.

The hard part is slowing your eyes down. I used to tell my students that you had to learn to see in a new way. An artist has to fall in love with what he's drawing. I would guess you could give me quite a few lessons on how a musician hears."

"Wow. Thank you. No one ever described it to me that way before." Will stared at him with a slack jaw as he made new connections in his head. "That makes a big difference. You kept your part of our original bargain and helped me with the assignment I had."

Random took another swallow of ale. "What was the assignment?"

"To find out how creating objects was like creating music."

Random chuckled as he focused on the table. "You have a good teacher." A porcelain plate with a sandwich on a French roll appeared. "It isn't roast beef, but it was the best cheesesteak I ever found." He pushed the hot meal over to Will. "Eat up; I'm good with just the ale for now."

As Will polished off the sandwich, Random launched into more questions. "If you don't mind putting the answers on my tab, what can you tell me about the Tracers?"

Will answered while chewing his last bite. "Well, the one I'm taking you to is the best. Just let her do her job and let go of your expectations. If you're looking for just one person you might be out of luck. They might not be here, or maybe they aren't close enough for her to locate. But if you just let her do it her way, you'll have better results. She keys in on you and can tell you who is close by that had some connection to you when you were alive. That way, you get a list of people who are at least here and findable. If you really want to meet one, she can usually pinpoint them pretty quickly." Will pushed the plate away and finished his glass. "Damn, that was good. As a token of my appreciation, I will give you one free answer."

"What do you know about Recorders, Will?"

Will stopped moving completely, which was so uncommon for him that it stood out. "Looks like you had a busy time before we met. How'd you manage to hear about the Recorders?"

Random considered his companion. He wanted to tell him that Joe had greeted him too. He wanted to tell him that he had been snatched by Erminia. He was concerned that Will might not help him get close to the Conclave if he knew that the two sides of the conflict were fighting over him. He also knew that Will was watching him, wondering whether Random was being truthful. Lying outright at times like this was easy to spot; selectively telling the truth was a much better way to go. He decided to divulge a different truth to throw Will off the trail.

"OK, look. I met this weird old guy not long after I got here. We shared a meal and then he disappeared. He had this little silver box and he said a Recorder was inside. He talked about her like she was either a friend or a pet and it's been bugging me ever since. I find it odd that he carries another soul around in a box."

Will's eyes opened wider and he leaned in close. "You met someone who traveled with a Recorder? That is a hell of a person to stumble across. Did he tell you his name?"

Random was committed in his partial truth, so he went with it. "Barrel-chested guy in need of a shave, eyes two different colors. Said his name was Fabric."

Will sat back and looked at him incredulously. Then he leaned in and lowered his voice. "I've heard of him. Hambone met him once and is still spooked by the mention of the name. He's a Shifter. He can take on the appearance of another soul so that even their own mother would be fooled. It's a dangerous gift. He's evidently been running around the afterlife for as long as anyone can remember. My instructor at the Conclave warned me about him. She told me he's unpredictable and to be cautious if I ever ran into him." Will stroked his chin. "Crazy that he would travel with a Recorder."

Random had not expected this turn in the conversation, but he pressed on his original question. "Why is it crazy? What the hell is a Recorder, anyway? What does it record?"

Will came out of his private thoughts. "Once again, I can only tell you what I've heard from both the rumor mill and what I gathered from the instructors at the Conclave. I've never seen a Recorder, but I know there are at least three in the Conclave itself. Transit Square supposedly has two of them."

Will paused as a group at a table near them stood up to leave. "The name is misleading. They don't really record anything. The way I heard it, they're souls who have been here so long, they no longer remember being in a body.

Some say they died as children and were raised here. They became so sensitive to the activity of the Ether that they hear it all at once. An instructor at the Conclave once told me that the chatter of millions of voices never stops and drives all the Recorders insane. At the very least, they're known for being unstable. They hear thoughts, they witness creations, and births, and deaths, and reincarnations, and...well, all of it, all at the same time. They evidently speak in a long stream of babble about the things they're seeing."

Random tried to imagine it. "That sounds awful. So why are they kept like prisoners?"

"They're more like willing prisoners. They like secluded places that are as insulated from the barrage of voices as possible. The Conclave was the first to construct a way to insulate a Recorder. The story is they did it out of pure compassion for their suffering. I'm not convinced it was such a noble reason. You see, when you befriend a Recorder, you have a powerful weapon. If you're willing to protect them and weed through their ramblings, you can gain access to a lot of information. They hear it all. Evidently, the trick is getting them to focus. Some of the Recorders are more insane than others and require constant attention and a protected location. This is the first I've heard of someone traveling with one in a box."

Random was a bit overwhelmed by all the information. He looked out to the streets beyond the open-air tavern. "Can we walk a bit? I'm tired of sitting here."

"Sure thing, chief. But I don't think I'll be offering you any more free answers. Your questions pack a punch."

As soon as they stood up from the table, two young women in simple white robes scrambled over to them. "Are you leaving? May we take your seats if you're done with them?"

Will ignored them and had already started to walk away. Random stood behind his chair and offered it to the girl who had asked. "They're all yours." The girls sat down quickly, as there were other parties circling the perimeter looking for open seats.

"Thank you for your kindness! May the Truth find you, brother." They both touched their foreheads with their index fingers and bowed their heads with closed eyes. Random was suddenly uncomfortable and could feel the stares of the tables around him. He walked away without responding to their gesture and wove through the busy tavern to catch up with Will, who was waiting for him in the street.

Will only shook his head in disgust as they walked away. Random had felt this same tension in more than one church and recognized it. The girls in the white robes must be true believers, missionaries here to spread the message of the Truther rebellion right at the doorstep of the Conclave. Their message did not seem very welcome, judging by the reaction of the patrons at the Tavern.

As they walked, Random tried to get Will talking without asking a question. "It was odd to hear you say that you didn't buy the 'noble story' the Conclave gave you. I hadn't heard you say anything against them until then."

"I'm not saying say anything against the Conclave. I just think that there may be more to the story than they tell the students, that's all. I'm not a cynic, but I am a proud skeptic."

"The Truthers seem pretty skeptical of the Conclave's version of things."

Will stopped in his tracks and Random turned back to him. Will was a deeper shade of red than normal. "Look, I like you, but let me make one thing very clear. Never again compare me to the Truthers. Do you understand me?"

Random was clear he had crossed a line. His sharp tongue had pissed off enough people in his life that he knew the feeling. "I'm sorry, Will. I didn't mean it as an insult. I'm just trying to make sense of it all. The last thing I meant to do was insult or disrespect you." The apology was authentic.

Will gave a stiff nod. "Apology accepted. Come on, let's keep moving. If we head out of here in the next couple hours, we can reach the Conclave by early tomorrow morning." Will kept walking, but the air between them had changed. "You kept your part of the bargain, and I'll keep mine." Random followed behind as Will's pace quickened.

127

: : TRACE : :

They walked in silence a while. Random still followed a few steps behind, trying to give Will enough room to burn off his anger. They turned off the main street and began to weave down a thin path between tents. A thick man in a clean black suit who looked to be guarding a tent entrance puffed up a bit as they approached. Will gave him a quick nod as if to let him know they were just passing by. They continued on their way but the man continued to watch them. They ducked under some ropes that held the corner of a larger structure, and took a series of turns that made Random feel like he was backstage. Will knew the way, but it was clearly not widely known.

The narrow path between tents gave way to a small courtyard in front of a simple adobe building. Its arched entry had a bright green door. The word "Trace" was hand-painted on the door in small, simple block letters. Will turned from the door to face Random again.

"Look, I won't hold a grudge about it, but what you said really pissed me off."

"That much is clear. I spoke without thinking. Bad habit of mine."

Will smiled. "Oh, bullshit. You think more than anyone I know. You were poking around for information and you stepped on a land mine. Like I said, the apology was accepted." Will held out his hand and Random shook it. Will gave him a slap on the shoulder with his other hand and Random felt relief that he hadn't broken their new friendship.

"All right, chief, you stay here and I'll go talk to her. She's very particular about whom she accepts as a client, as you can tell by the not-so-convenient location of her shop. I'll go put in a good word for you and see what I can negotiate." He walked to the door and it opened for him before he could knock. He turned to Random and rolled his eyes. He stepped inside and the door shut behind him.

Random paced back and forth for a bit. He wasn't quite sure whom he hoped to find. He just wanted to know that he wasn't alone here in this madhouse. He trusted Will to a point, but it would be different with someone he had known in life. His thoughts were interrupted by a little girl in a pink dress and a sequined mask who came giggling into the courtyard. She appeared to be about ten years old. The mask glittered in the sun as the girl held it on a stick in front of her face. She stopped when she spotted him and gave a curtsy. Random had not seen any children here. He gave a deep formal bow. She giggled and ran off, still holding her mask in front of her.

The door opened again and Will emerged. He walked over to Random and the door closed itself. "She'll see you. I had to throw in the Indian as a down payment. I hope you don't mind."

"She likes motorcycles too?"

Will let out a short burst of laughter. "No, but she can trade it to someone who does. She'll ask you for the balance of the payment after she is done. You shouldn't have any problem sorting it out. I'm going to head back to Hambone's to pick up my instruments and the bike. I'll see you back here in a bit." Will gave him a pat on the shoulder. "You're in good hands."

Will disappeared back into the forest of canvas and Random was alone. He turned to the building and walked up to the door. Just as it had for Will, the door opened for him on its own. The little girl with the mask went giggling across the courtyard again, but Random didn't turn around. He stepped through the door into the dark space beyond. The door closed behind him.

The smell of incense was all he had as his eyes adjusted to the dim interior. The walls were covered with deep green velvet hung in flowing swags. An overstuffed couch was deep and inviting. A thick white fur rug covered most of the floor. Pillows gathered in artful little arrangements and begged him to drop to the ground and relax with them. The room had a Moroccan feel, without being too over-the-top. Two carved wooden masks hung on one wall and, though clearly African in origin, fit in just perfectly. Random had never been one to attempt interior decorating himself, but he knew the hand of a good designer when he saw it.

One of the green curtains was pulled aside and she stepped out of a veiled doorway near the back. The effect of her beauty on him was the equivalent of his being struck in the head with a blunt object. She was tall and lean with eyes that held both peace and mischief. Her skin was pale and her exposed midriff was muscled, but still womanly. Her sandy brown hair dropped almost to her waist. Glints of light winked from her as the candlelight found the many gemstones adorning the tight fabric holding her breasts. Two thin straps traced a line over her hip bones and met in a tiny junction of material that barely kept her from being naked below the waist. A glittering necklace held a red coral stone nestled in her cleavage. She knew how to make an entrance.

She didn't wait for him to find words. "Will speaks highly of you. My name is Trace. Please remove your shoes and come sit with me." She glided over to the white fur rug, gathered a few pillows, and lay down on her side, ignoring the sofa. He pulled off his boots and made his way over. He sat down cross-legged on the long, plush fur. He was glad to get off his feet, and the room was inviting.

She looked him up and down. "Were you this tall in life?"

"Yes. I've always been large." He screamed at himself in his head. Did he just say that out loud?

Her soft laugh was kind and soothing. She punctuated it by touching his arm with her warm hands. "Believe it or not, that is very apparent. You're comfortable in your skin. So do you want to tell me who you're looking for?"

"I'm not sure, very honestly. Will told me to drop my expectations and let you do it your way. He said I'd get better results."

Her smile made his face feel hot. "Dear, dear Will. You must have made quite an impression for him to bring you here. Would you care for some tea?" With a wave of her hand a simple stone pot flew in and rested on a low table near her. It was followed by two earthen cups in the same terra cotta color. She sat up on her knees in front of the table and poured the hot tea with precision and ceremony.

She handed him a cup and returned to her reclining position to sip her tea. "Will tells me you're a new arrival. How are you coping with our chaotic little afterlife?"

"As well as can be expected, I suppose. I'm still trying to learn the rules." He sipped his tea. It was delicious, warm and soothing, much like his host. He could almost feel his pulse rate drop every second he sat with her.

She placed her cup back on the table with the pot and took his from him gently. She knelt in front of him so that her knees were touching his crossed legs. She touched his face with the palms of both her hands. "You're being brave and trying to ignore the sadness and confusion you feel. You've lost your life, and everything you were told about what awaited you after death was a lie. You don't have to be heroic for my sake, sweet man. You can relax here. Take off your armor for me. I will not betray your trust."

Random felt his jaw twitching as her eyes bathed him in compassion. He'd been so wrapped up in trying to make sense of the chaos he was immersed in that he hadn't allowed himself the luxury of acknowledging his emotions. He dropped his mask a bit as he looked into her eyes. She responded by sitting in his lap and wrapping her legs around him. Her scent was intoxicating and her skin was addictively soft. She held his face and brought her full lips to his. He was hesitant to respond to her touch, and she felt it immediately. "Are you being faithful to someone? Oh, you are a precious one. You sit here in death, free from even the most puritanical of marriage contracts, and you question your integrity?"

He'd been propositioned before as a married man but had never once been unfaithful to Karen. As he had paced outside the door of this stunning creature, all he had sought was a connection to ease his isolation. This was not exactly what he'd had in mind, but he couldn't escape the logic she presented him. Death had come; he and Karen had parted.

Now he was here, not just aching to devour this woman, but longing to lose himself in her smell, her sweat, her skin. He dragged the tip of his finger from just below her earlobe down to the point on her chest where her breasts began to swell. She reacted with her back arching like a strung bow. He continued to drag his finger back up her neck and around the curve of her ear.

She removed her top and her nipples stood proud. "Let go of it all and let me show you something different. Will you allow me to be your first lover in the afterlife?" Random cupped his hand across the back of her neck and

132

kissed her hard. She wove her fingers into his hair and welcomed his lips. Her legs pulled him closer and she pushed her pelvis against him. He put his hands around her slender waist and lifted her higher to take her breast in his mouth. She put her hands on his shoulders and pushed her nipple deeper. He rolled her onto her back but she stopped him with a slight hesitation. "Wait, my sweet. I want to show you something unique to this place. Will such a divine lover let me show him something new?"

Random had reached a state too primal for words. He gave a nod as he ran his face down to her belly in a long, loud inhale of her scent. She sat them back up and once again straddled him as he sat cross-legged. She held his face so close he almost couldn't focus on her. She whispered, and her hot breath washed over him. "We're naked. You and I are naked in each other's arms...right now..."

His skin reacted as it confirmed what she had spoken. His clothes were gone. Her necklace and the scrap of fabric that had covered her crotch were no more. Her body heat had gone up and the smell of her sweat and sex was overpowering the incense in the air. She took his face in her hands again and breathed more words on him. "We are all naked here. You've just stopped pretending you're not. We are more naked than the day we'll be born." His mind swam in a haze, but he listened to her as she kissed his lips gently and stayed close. "So naked. What covers us here is truly illusion. You're here with another soul, and neither of us could be more naked. Your heart is so beautiful. I can feel you against me..."

She leaned back so that he could focus on her eyes. With a tilt of her hips, she took him inside her. He hadn't understood what she'd been saying until that very moment. Then they were one. The veil was lifted. He had glimpsed this level of connection in all the best lovers he had ever had. Their bodies remained, and the physicality of intercourse was the vehicle, but the connection ran through him like electricity. Yes, he was naked, more naked than he'd known he could be. She coiled around him but gave him room to breathe. She was everywhere but kept her shape. Time became thick and luscious. Sound became both muted and amplified. The glorious illusion of sweat rolled down them as they bucked and screamed in ecstasy.

· · · · ·

Random lay on his back, the slender woman coiled around him. The experience had been unlike any sex he'd ever had. He was at peace, but a little claustrophobic in the dark room. She had seen him unmasked and he was somewhat uneasy. She rolled up onto her side and traced her finger down his chest. Then she sat up and walked to the back of the room and disappeared through the hidden doorway.

He sat up and found that the clothes he had been wearing were neatly folded near the sofa. He went over and got dressed, but left his boots off. His shirt smelled clean, like it had just come out of the washer. He was glad she was giving him time alone. The urge to run from someone who knew him so intimately was fading as he sank into the deep sofa.

Trace returned, wearing panties and the coral necklace. She knelt at the low table and poured them tea in silence. Steaming liquid came from the pot, even though it had been ignored for over an hour as they swam in each other. She handed him his cup, but remained sitting on her heels with her full breasts displayed.

"Thank you, Random. You honor me by sharing yourself with such abandon. I'll need at least a few days to look for those who are here and have a connection to you. There's at least one who's close, but I'm still a bit too drunk from our time together to focus." Trace gave him a lazy smile over the brim of her cup as she sipped it.

Random chuckled. He had long ago forgotten the reason he had come here. He hardly cared about finding anyone now. "I can see why you're choosy about whom you will accept as a client. I am honored, Trace."

She was pleased with his words. "I don't make love to all my clients. With you, I was clear it was the only way. You have a veil over you. I can feel a few who have known you from your last life, wandering about the Ether. But there's at least one who's known you longer. Whoever it is, they seem to be hiding from me." She took another sip of her tea. "But I'll find them. Their ties to you are old, and I am very persistent."

She put down her cup and joined him on the sofa. He caressed her face, and she kissed his thumb when it reached her lips. "You've already given me what I didn't even know I needed. But I can't stay here. I need to keep moving."

"Yes, I know. You must reach the Conclave. You must get your questions answered. But you'll be back through here. When you return, I'll have information for you about those you've misplaced." She kissed him and stood up. "Will is outside waiting patiently and trying not to be jealous. We should settle your payment."

"I'm not sure what I could offer you, but I want nothing more than to give you something you desire."

She giggled and took a piece of fabric from the floor. She tied it around her breasts and over her neck. "My gift makes me very sensitive to the energy swirling around every soul. I don't go out much, as the crowds are sometimes too intense. This is my sanctuary. I've been feeling a bit cramped lately and would love some more room. Will says you're a Builder. Would you build me a small addition to my little home?"

Random stepped off the couch and into his boots. He was on his feet and looking around. "I don't have your skill in decorating, but I think I can give you more space."

She took his hand. "No, this room is perfect. I need a private space that's just for me. I've outgrown the one I have. Let me show you." She led him to the hidden door from which she had first entered. She hesitated a moment, then drew the fabric back and took him inside. The room they entered was very different from the parlor where they had made love. It was elegant in how sparse it was. The floor was teak. A bed at the back wall had soft white linens and thin, carved posts at its corners. Light spilled in from porthole windows near the high ceiling. The sky was visible, but the room still gave the effect of being isolated from the exterior. There was a plush chair near the bed and a low bookcase spanned two walls, filled with books. Off to the left was a kitchen with a small central island bathed in sun from a skylight. Everything had clean lines and simple shapes.

"I miss being outside and feeling the air. I used to garden in life, and I'd love to work the soil. This house was a gift from an old friend. I've been here a long time and I love it, but I need more room to breathe."

Random walked the room and considered it. "I don't remember having seen much space available around the structure, except for the courtyard."

"My neighbors are close on all sides. I negotiated for the courtyard but I can't build there; it's a shared space."

Random looked to the ceiling. "Well, if you can't build out, there's always up. What do you think of a second story? You could have your private bedroom up there. That would free this area up for something else--maybe a dedicated library."

Trace touched her lips. "You could do that? You could add a second floor?"

He smiled at her. "I know I could do it in life; I worked as a carpenter when I got out of art school. I was pretty good at it, too. Building stuff here is new for me, but you've made me feel invincible. Let's give it a go, shall we?"

He walked back through the curtain and into the parlor. The green door was already opening for him and he walked outside. Will was in the courtyard leaning on the Indian. Random gave him a tiny nod of acknowledgement, but was clearly on task and in no mood to chat. He walked around the building and looked at the roofline. The building was adobe. The roof was high but flat as far as he could see. He walked to the back wall and could see the high porthole windows. He needed to get up top. He needed a ladder. He focused his mind and a thick wooden ladder with rungs the size of logs shimmered into existence. He began to climb as Will turned the corner behind him.

He glanced through a porthole window as he passed it and saw Trace still standing barefoot on the teak floor looking back at him. He reached the top and stepped over the outer perimeter façade and down onto the flat roof. The view from the roof was impressive. Over the courtyard he could see the wide sweep of the crescent-shaped city embracing the barren plain. The opposite vista looked over the last few streets toward the streams of travelers on foot, making their way into the narrow pass as the sun neared the tops of the ragged, snow-crested mountains.

He could do this. He had altered the glade by focusing on what was there. He considered the view and held his fingers up to choose the best frame for a window facing west. As he looked through his boxed fingers, wooden studs began to appear. The wall built itself in his peripheral vision. He smiled and turned to the east. He framed the view and another skeleton of wood formed. His speed increased as he continued. He walked to the southeast corner and pictured a rooftop garden with a deck. Sliding doors--no, make that French doors. Windows, light, a balcony overlooking the courtyard, open beams, wide eaves. Wood, steel, stone and glass appeared around him in a flutter of sound and movement. He closed off the space, but left windows open. He matched the teak floor from her room and found himself sitting in the center of it, assessing his creation. The east window was a little off to the left and he watched with glee as it moved to exactly where he wanted it without a sound.

He added thick teak baseboards and molding to give it a polished look. He then stood and walked over to just above where he knew Trace was still standing. He looked at the floor and pictured what he wanted to see. The layer of floorboards he had just created retreated and a large circular hole appeared. His progress was slowed when he found himself looking at the existing roof. He could feel resistance from the structure, but he kept his vision locked. In a sudden burst of sound, the roof opened and the solid-teak spiral staircase he had envisioned coiled down into the room and stopped just in front of where Trace stood.

He caught her eyes and waved her up. "Come take a look. Let me know what you think."

He stood with pride waiting for her. Her head finally poked up over the floor line as she walked the last few steps with some apprehension. The look on her face was that of a child on Christmas morning. He grinned like an idiot as he watched her explore in silence.

She walked directly to the balcony overlooking the courtyard. He stood at the threshold and watched her touch the long row of empty flower boxes. "No one can see you from below. The awning acts like a giant roll-top desk. You can remove the balcony cover completely or close it as tight as a clamshell." He pointed to two red cords wrapped over a pulley system. She pulled the ropes and the bamboo roof moved effortlessly. She rolled it all the way open and the sun poured in. She did not look him directly in the eyes. She stepped back into the interior.

There were interior walls that helped segment the large space. She dragged her fingers down the walls and moved to the east side of the building. She stopped to look at the travelers entering the pass in the distance, perfectly framed in the large window.

She walked around an interior wall and found the delicate patio in the southeast corner. It was covered with an iron trellis that was not a grid but a collection of spirals. She stood with perfect posture in the middle of the space and looked at her bare feet. The shadows of the spirals fell over the stonework that covered the ground. The stones were rough and widely spaced, with thick moss growing between them--living grout lines.

She was facing away from him and he could not read her reaction. He spoke with a slight hesitation. "I wanted to give you an outdoor space that was more protected than the front balcony. The outer wall is higher. You could grow vines, all the way to the roof if you want, to control the light and the privacy. I tried not to make it feel like a cage. If you don't like it I can just make it a part of the interior..."

Trace spun toward him quickly. "It's perfect! Please don't change a thing. When I asked you for an addition, I was hoping for a rooftop garden. You have doubled the size of my home. You overwhelm me with your generosity."

"So you like it?"

She walked across the stones and put her palm on his sternum. "You've made me very happy. When you've found what you're looking for in the Conclave, remember to come back and see me. I'll have information for you, but I will also have completely redecorated and want to show it off." She kissed him and walked back inside.

Will was waiting for them in the parlor. She went to him and gave him a long hug. Will's face softened and his eyes closed. Random found his face growing hot as he watched them, and wondered how long they would hold the embrace. He had no right to be jealous, but he was. Trace and Will finally broke apart and Will reached into a bag on his hip. He pulled out a small clay shape with holes in it and handed it to her. "It's an ocarina. I made it myself." He seemed shy about his gift given the astounding act of creation he had just witnessed. She immediately took it to her lips and blew a few notes. The sound was crisp and enchanting. She touched his face and kissed him tenderly.

There was an awkward moment between the three of them. Will broke the silence and looked at Trace. "The bike's outside. Hambone said there've been a few inquiries on it already. But I wasn't sure what you were looking for."

"Well, given recent developments, I believe I'll see if I can trade it for a very large bathtub, maybe one that's solid copper. I have a lot of decorating to do." She flashed a look at Random, then went to sit on the sofa. "I'm not much for goodbyes; I save all my energy for hellos. You need to get moving or you'll miss the last ferry. Off with you." Will walked out first. Random stopped at the door. She held her hands together in prayer position and bowed to him. The door closed behind him on its own as he left.

Will was by the Indian lifting an awkward backpack that held the kora. Random rushed over to help him pull it onto his shoulders. Once it was on, the long neck of the instrument reached a foot or two above Will's head. The many tuner knobs stuck out along the length of the neck and made it look like he was carrying the spine of an animal. The drum hung from his hip on a strap.

As Random helped Will balance the weight, they locked eyes. Will brought a smile and put his hand on Random's shoulder. "That was an impressive thing you did for her. I knew you were a Builder, but I had no idea you were that good." They looked at each other in silence a moment. "Come on, she's right; we need to get our asses in gear. The last ferry won't wait for us."

"Ferry?" Random asked Will's back as the musician turned and walked away from him.

Will didn't look back. "Come on, Chief; less talking, more walking." Random allowed himself a final look back at the second story of the adobe building. He thought he saw Trace's shadow moving, but wasn't sure. Will was walking fast. Random felt the map, still rolled in the inner pocket of his light jacket, and jogged a bit to catch up with Will.

The big Indian cast long shadows in the courtyard as the sun sank toward the horizon. The little girl in the pink dress ran up just in time to see Random and Will disappear in the maze of tents. She dropped her mask and looked to the west. The sun caught her one hazel eye and made it glow yellow, while her other eye remained a grayish-blue. She giggled and ran after them.

: : THE PASSAGE : :

The sun came to rest in the crook that marked the only pass in the sheer range, its last rays filling the pass with golden light. Random and Will walked toward it, eyes squinting, until it dropped past the horizon and painted the clouds a spectrum of orange and violet. The path became narrow and steep. Soon they and the others who raced the sun were climbing steps carved in the rock. Sometimes the path would widen before snaking sharply in another curve that climbed abruptly. There was no idle chatter. The obstacles were challenging and required everyone to look to their footing.

Random followed the spiny neck of the kora on Will's back. Will was surefooted, and hiked the incline with surprising speed. They used the wider spots to pass as many travelers as they could. Will was clearly tracking their progress against a timetable in his head. Random saw his face only when he turned his eyes to the sky to judge the amount of time they would still have light.

The other travelers were as varied as those he had seen on the streets of the Lüder, but their garb was more utilitarian. Many had items strapped to them, but few were inclined to carry anything as large as the kora. Some of their fellow travelers fit the stereotype he had constructed in his head before he had seen Lüdertown, with staves and simple robes. Others wore bright colors and festive adornments. A few played simple instruments as they hiked. The tones of flutes, the ringing of bells and the banging of drums didn't entice Will to slow. They passed several large groups at a pace just short of a jog to get ahead of them before the path narrowed and forced them back into another single-file stair climb.

Random didn't question his guide; he simply tried to keep up with him. He knew conceptually that any physical limitation was only in his mind, but that knowledge didn't stop his muscles from burning. He was glad to have the challenge of the trail to quiet his mind. He would get carnal flashes of his time with Trace. A memory of her naked body in a position that pleased him would intoxicate him for a moment. He reluctantly shook the visions off to keep from falling too far behind the man with the bare red chest and all the crap strapped to him.

Will reached the top of a very steep staircase by jumping two steps at a time. Random lost sight of him, having gotten caught behind a man in a jester hat who was more concerned with the dirty limerick he was singing than his progress. Random felt a small sense of panic and forced his way around the man in his way, knocking him aside and ignoring the protests. He took to the stairs the way Will had, two at a stride. He came to the top and was relieved to see the silhouette of the kora, motionless in the decaying light. He jogged up alongside Will, who was standing at a ridge looking over the edge.

For the first time in over an hour they were looking downhill. The last bit of the trail wound down to the shore of a vast lake that filled the valley below and stretched to the horizon. The trail widened at the shore to a small beach dotted with thirty or so people and three campfires. A vessel was anchored at the end of a narrow pier. Will put his hand on Random's shoulder and turned to him. "We made it just in time. Come on."

Random laughed to himself as they sprinted down the hill. He had misinterpreted the wide-open space on the map as a plain. Now he was excited at the prospect of sailing the rest of the distance to the Conclave rather than walking.

The ferry was large enough to hold a few hundred people on its three levels of decks. A paddleboat with a large red wheel in the middle of each side, it was not as extravagant as those that still steamed down the Mississippi. Its lines were simple, devoid of the filigree ironwork and ornamentation of a tourist boat used to stir nostalgia. This was a working vessel. As they raced down the slope to board it, strings of lanterns with open flames flared to life on the railings. The crowds on deck and those still on the shore let out subdued hollers.

As they approached, Random noticed they were moving through an encampment of sorts on the shore. Everyone seemed very aware that the ferry was leaving, but some were warming themselves around the fires with no intention of moving. He saw some boarding the vessel, but many seemed to just be seeing the boat off. He and Will wove through the bystanders and reached the simple dock. It was just wide enough for the two men to walk side by side. Will slowed his sprint to a brisk walk. Random matched it. When they reached the end of the pier, a wiry man with mocha brown skin, crisp pants and a collarless striped shirt was helping a woman come aboard. When he saw Will, his face lit up, his smile full of bone-white teeth.

"Will! So good to see you again!" His eyes spotted the neck of the kora strapped to Will's back. "And what new prize have you brought back this time?"

"Oh, just a little something I talked Hambone out of." Will gave him a sturdy handshake. "This is Random. A new arrival on his first visit to the Conclave. Random, this salty dog is Saul, our captain on this voyage." Random shook Saul's hand.

"Welcome, Random. I must ask you both to board; we're just about to depart."

Will looked at the lower deck, then up at the souls leaning over the upper railings. There was more than enough room to accommodate all those who waited on the shore. He gestured to Saul. "Quite a few staying behind tonight. Do they question your skills as a skipper?"

Saul's eyes flared a bit, but he relaxed when he saw the mischief in Will's grin. "Get on board before I change my mind." He poked Will in the ribs like a tolerant older brother and set to untying the rope from the cleat on the pier. Will jumped aboard and turned back to look at Random.

Random hesitated a moment as he looked at the space between the pier and the deck. Will watched him closely and remained silent. Random found his head filled with questions as he considered the gap. He was not sure what the Conclave was, or whether he should trust them. He looked at the still water of the lake as it lapped against the hull in a lazy rhythm. The air was beginning to chill and he thought of the warmth of the fires they had passed. Was it wise to deliver himself to the Conclave? Would he be able to maintain his anonymity once they docked at the opposite shore?

Random looked up and met Will's eyes. He took a breath and stepped down onto the bobbing deck. Will nodded and began to walk with a look over his shoulder and a motion to follow. They made for the stern and climbed up two sets of stairs to the topmost deck of the three. The top deck was slightly more crowded. Most of the passengers looked to the west and the last dances of the sunset painting the thin lines of clouds an imperial violet that was fading to the blue-black of night. They made their way forward as the deep hoot of a steam whistle announced their departure in a long, resounding note.

They found a patch of open railing on the starboard side, facing those on the shore rather than the sunset. From this height, Random studied the details of the shoreline. The small beach ended after a hundred feet or so on either side of the landing. The lake met ragged rock that rose to become the sheer walls of the bowl the lake filled. There was no walking around the water on either side. The only way to reach the Conclave was by boat. It was a very effective defense. It made him wonder what they were hiding.

The huge red paddle wheels began to churn the ferry forward. No one waved farewell. No final passengers rushed to catch them. Random looked down and watched the faces in the makeshift camp lit by firelight. They were filled with a mix of strange emotion he could not name.

"Why did they come all this way if they're not getting on board?" Random asked regarding the eyes that watched them pull away.

Will also watched the eyes of those on the shore as he answered. "There's an ancient Chinese curse that my teacher always reminds me of: 'Everyone gets everything they ask for.'" The faces on the shore continued to watch the ferry depart in silence. "No matter how long the road has been that led them here, that final hesitation you had as you boarded is a moment they must all step through. They may wait for days, weeks or even years until they're ready. Some will change their minds, turn back and choose another path. I camped there for two months until I was sure this was what I wanted, until I was ready." Will turned to him. "For a moment back there, I thought I might be making this crossing alone."

Random turned to meet the kind eyes. "We had a deal. You kept up your part of the bargain. I wasn't going to back out at the last second. By the way, what's the damage on my tab with you? Am I going to find myself owing you a six-room mansion when we reach the Conclave?"

Will chuckled deeply. "It's been interesting traveling with you, Mr. Random. I have new toys for noise, some progress to report to my instructor, and a new friend. You were very generous to Trace. She holds a special place in my heart. Consider us even...for now."

The ferry made a wide turn to port and pointed west. The fires of those on the shore were behind them. Random turned his eyes forward. The lake stretched wide, a rippling mirror locked between sheer rock walls. Will slapped him on the back. "No point looking for our destination. The water weaves through the mountains for miles. We won't be in sight of it 'til morning. If we're lucky, we'll arrive at sunrise. Come on, I have a good spot for us to bunk. It pays to be friends with the Captain."

The passengers were silent. The splashes of the red wheels and the sputter of the gas lamps were the only sounds to be heard. The ferry churned toward the dying glow of the sun and the dark open waters that would bear them to the Conclave.

BALANCING

: : ESCAPE : :

Chains sprouted from both the walls and the floor to end in heavy manacles that encircled his arms and legs and attached to the brutal collar around his neck. The room that had been Erminia's peaceful bedchamber was now a cell for his imprisonment and torture.

She had left hours ago, after riddling him with questions about Random. He had remained silent save for the screams she tore from him with the sadistic visions she had concocted to cause him pain. He sat wearily, weighed down by the chains binding him. She had replaced the door with a heavy iron portal that had taken her almost an hour to create. Given the force of will she had poured into it, there was no way to breach it even if he escaped the chains. Now and again, he could hear the footsteps of the guard, pacing the stone hall outside the door.

He heard a latch move, but it was not the latch of the metal door. The sound was a precise movement of gears and springs, followed by a tiny pop. His attention was drawn by the debris on a portion of the floor jumping slightly. A floor tile hinged upward slightly for a moment, then dropped back down. Then the hidden trapdoor swung open all the way, deftly guided by a hand from below opening it silently, precisely. He could see the brass latch on the underside, along with the sliding rod that then snapped into position to prop the hatch open.

He felt a glow of warm, flickering firelight coming from the secret passage under the floor. He watched as a bright red bowler hat emerged, perched on the head of a man with warm olive skin.

149

Otto unfolded himself into the room without a sound. He crept over to the prisoner and squatted down, his forearms resting on his legs. Joe's face looked up at the man with the tiny tuft of white hair on his chin. Otto tipped his red bowler hat back and gave a small shake of his head.

"Well, this is a fine mess you've gotten yourself into, old friend," he whispered. "Luckily, you still have a favor on account with me. Let's get you out of here." Otto began to examine the manacles but the look on Joe's face stopped him. Joe's skin began to ripple and flow like liquid. His body became smaller and his features younger. In a matter of moments, he had transformed into a small boy, no more than a year old. Otto helped lift the neck manacle over his head and slide the bindings off his wrists and ankles, careful to make as little noise as possible. Otto took the exhausted child into his arms and carried him back to the trapdoor. Lowering them both into the passage, Otto closed the hatch behind him, sealing it flat with a click.

· · · · ·

A fire roared in the stone hearth flanked by two Ming Dynasty vases so big a man could stand inside them. Otto carried the naked child to one of the opulent, overstuffed couches and laid him down gently. The boy's skin began to ripple, like liquid. Otto watched the long serpentine scar, raised high above the boy's smooth flesh, which ran from the base of his neck down his right arm and stopped at the crook of his elbow. The old wound glowed golden as the boy's skin darkened to black with a blue iridescence. As the tiny form darkened, it grew in size. Within five minutes, the pale infant had been replaced by the muscled form of an African warrior woman.

Otto sat in silence until the scar stopped glowing and she opened her dark eyes to look at him. "Now I know why you kept the identity of your mysterious client from me. What the hell were you thinking, Tazir?"

She attempted to sit up but Otto stopped her. He waved his hand in the air and a warm blanket coiled over her naked body. "Thank you, Otto. Thank you for finding me. I wasn't sure I could take much more.

"You're welcome, you crazy bitch. Stay still and I'll make you something hot to drink."

He focused on his hands and a small gourd set with silver on the rim and base appeared, filled with steaming liquid. He produced a silver straw with a bent mouthpiece and a flat filter on the other end, which he submerged in the liquid and then brought to her mouth. "It's Mate. It's hot and very strong, so sip it carefully." She allowed him to nurse her, and sipped from the silver straw.

Tazir stopped and looked into the hearth at the crackling fire. "The worst part is that I don't know why she hates me so...I don't know what I did to foster such bitterness..." The serpentine scar down her right arm began to flow like liquid.

Otto put the Mate down and grabbed her arm forcefully. He dug his fingers into the raised scar until she winced and locked her eyes on it, then on his face. "YOU did not do anything. That was Joe. Remember yourself. Your name is Tazir. You're a Shifter, and Joe hired you to take on his image." His eyes danced with the firelight, but the flame came from within him. The tuft of hair below his bottom lip glowed a brighter white as he spoke. Her anger at the way he clutched her arm cooled. Her scar faded back to match the deep black of her skin. He released his hold on her, and touched her face gently.

She nodded to him and reached up to touch his bald head with her ebony fingers. "Thank you again, brother."

He gave her another sip through the silver straw. "We may not know the details, Tazir, but everyone knows she hates the Conclave and carries some grudge against him personally. Why would Joe send you into her custody disguised as him?"

Tazir did manage to sit up this time. "I don't normally discuss the deals I make with clients, but in this case I must. I need your word, Otto. I need you to promise that what I'm about to tell you will remain between us."

He paused for a moment but then took her hand. "I promise."

She sat back, accepting his word. "He told me that he needed her to believe that she'd caught him. He told me her wrath would be severe. When she first attacked me, he was under our feet, in this very room; I could feel him deflecting some of the objects she was throwing at me. I was to let her subdue me."

"To what purpose? What was the trick meant to accomplish?"

Tazir's face became stern. "He had given me a key to wear around my neck." She pointed to the amulet Otto wore. "It was much like this one, but very heavy and with a simpler design. He needed her to know that the key was authentic..."

Otto nodded and interrupted. "And if she ripped it right off his neck with her own hands, she would believe it was the real deal. Go on."

"Joe warned me that she would be very cruel and that she would imprison me. He apologized many times for asking me to do this. He needed me to take his place so that he'd be free to go back to the Conclave to prepare..."

Otto stood and paced as he spoke. "What's the fake key he gave her? What is the trap he's luring her into?"

"The key's not a fake. Joe told me it's real, but not what it's for. But when she had me in chains and spent hours ranting at me, I found out what it was. Otto, it's the master key. He gave her the master key."

He stopped pacing abruptly. "There's no such thing. The master key is a fairy tale constructed by charlatans here on the Square to dupe fools." They looked hard at each other. It had been rumored to exist and both of them had secretly looked for it. "Even if this mythical object existed, he would never give it to her. He was lying to you."

Tazir shook her head. "I had to become him, Otto. You know what that takes. I was with him in this room and allowed myself to fall in love with him, to know him so completely that I could fool her. You know there's no way to lie during that process. The master key is not a myth. It's real, and now she has it."

"But that would mean she could bypass all of the Conclave's defenses. She could fly the Square across the lake and right to their doorstep..." His eyes darted back and forth and he resumed his pacing. He was looking at nothing, but his mind was churning in an attempt to see the strategy. "Why would he do that? Why would he open the door and invite her in?"

Tazir's energy waned and she lay back. "He said it would bring an end to this war."

Otto froze. "He's going to have a final battle. Instead of chasing the Square around, as he has for years, he's going to fight her openly. He's going to do it on his terms and on the battlefield of his choice. He is willing to risk the very balance of the Ether to bring it to an end."

She put her hand on her forehead. "I need to get off the Square. I need to get to the Conclave before it begins." She took a deep breath. "But I think it's too dangerous for me to alter my form again for a while. I might truly forget myself."

He stood up and walked over to the large ebony desk. "Rest for now. You're safe from discovery here. I've run my business on this boat for at least seventy years, and this room remained hidden even from me. She won't find you here." He sat down and began to look over the papers organized in neat stacks. "Turns out your client left some interesting reading material for me. Someone as clever as our friend Joe wouldn't do that by accident." Otto held up a sheet of paper with a hand-drawn diagram. "This rather detailed little map showing me how to find the secret entrance to Erminia's room was right on top of the stack. I've spent many hours piecing together what I found here. I have a whole new set of tools to work with. There may be a way to get you off the Square undetected."

Tazir pulled the blanket up over her and stared at the fire. Within a few minutes her eyes became heavy. Otto spoke to her in a gentle tone. "Tazir, what payment did Joe offer you that had you agree to take such a risk?"

She fought to keep her eyes open as she answered. "He promised he'd help me let go of the loss I carry with me. He told me he could get me a very high birth without any wait. I'm tired of this place. I want to move on... I want to live a life where I don't miss Sarah every day..."

Her breathing changed; she was asleep. If Joe was really planning a final confrontation between the Conclave and the Truthers, Otto wasn't sure how Tazir would receive her payment. A battle on that scale could destabilize everything they took for granted. The more he had read through the contents of Joe's desk, the more he realized just how fragile the Ether was. He set to scribbling notes and diagrams on clean sheets as he examined a fresh stack of paper that Joe had left behind. As he read and schemed, he absentmindedly fingered the key that hung from the cord around his neck.

: : RETURNING HOME : :

Night shrouded the circular buildings of the Conclave that perched on the terraced shoreline of the rippling lake. The full moon illuminated the layer of mist rolling off the water. The buildings on the higher terraces stood proudly above the vapor in the cold night air. Those on lower ground could only be seen when the slow-moving fog revealed them hiding below the cloud-veil.

The size and placement of the structures varied, but they all shared a similar design. They were three to five stories high, and perfect circles. The center of each structure was open and served as a communal space for all who occupied the structure. The courtyard had a single entrance on the ground floor, and windows were only present at the second floor and higher. It was a very old design that made for both a vibrant community of neighbors and a strong defense against any who would seek to harm the occupants.

Joe stood on a precipice. The steep, thin trail he had walked for hours widened here at the apex and provided a stunning view of the Conclave he hadn't seen for a lifetime. He had kept the mountain trail open even though it was a slight hole in the Conclave's security. It was a narrow back door that only four other people knew of, and even some of them had forgotten it.

He reached into Tazir's satchel and took out the golden cylinder. He held it to his forehead for a moment and determined that the Recorder was dormant. It made sense, given that this was one of the most insulated places in the Ether. A Recorder who had never been here would be overcome by the silence even in the most active part of the day. At this time of night, the silence was thicker than the mist off the lake. Tazir's Recorder had been in the chaos of the open Ether for a long time. Joe guessed it would sleep for as long as it was here. He would keep it safe as he had promised Tazir.

From here, a short downhill hike could have him in his own bed soon, but he would resist that luxury. He needed to get to the temple and warn the others. Things had been set in motion. She was coming; it was just a matter of time. Their world was about to be torn apart. The silence that draped over the Conclave would soon be ripped by the clamor of war.

He adjusted the satchel on his hip, took a deep breath and closed his eyes. Wind rose up around him and his hair blew in all directions. His feet lifted from the ground. His eyes snapped open and he soared into the open sky above the Conclave. His body tipped forward and he went into a steep dive. He pulled up as he passed the small circular building that was his home, piercing the lazy fog as he rose higher. He remained on course for the temple on the highest terrace, but banked and rolled in an aerial dance over the slumbering hamlet.

He took a final turn and approached the temple from the east at high speed. It shared the same turret design as the other structures, but was seven stories high, with a slender tower that rose from its central courtyard and looked out over the Conclave. The temple housed eight hundred souls, while still accommodating study rooms, lecture halls and gardens. He shot over the exterior wall and angled straight up, climbing the last hundred feet to the flickering light at the top of the tower. A domed roof hung over it like a mushroom cap, supported by a ring of stone columns. He slowed as he neared the top, gliding through the columns and over the polished stone floor.

In the center of the open space was the bonfire that never ceased burning. The moment his full weight was on his feet, he knew he was not alone. The voice of the woman that addressed him was full, clear, and sharp with annoyance. "Were you trying to set off every alarm we have as you approached? Because if that was your intention, I believe you've succeeded."

He smiled at the darkness. "It is good to see you again, Alma. I figured it would be the easiest way to assemble everyone. Where are the others?"

Alma stepped from behind the bonfire. She was barefoot, and wore a simple green dress that draped over her wide hips. Her hair hung in bright red ringlets on her pale shoulders and her eyes sparkled blue-green like the Caribbean. "They're on their way. It was my watch." Her eyes stayed locked on him as she approached, her gaze unyielding, but somehow inviting. He never grew tired of looking at her. "Did you find him?"

Joe breathed a sigh and dropped his eyes. "Not exactly. I have much to share, but I will wait for the others to arrive."

The rushing of wind drew their attention northward. A man in orange robes floated between the columns with the moonlight illuminating him. He sat with his legs crossed in lotus position. He had short-cropped black hair and a peaceful face. He hovered four feet from the floor as he glided toward them.

A second rush of wind from the south was followed by a man in a business suit with a crisp, collarless shirt buttoned high on his neck. He stepped out of the air and onto the stone floor as if he had just arrived in a high-speed elevator. His shoes clicked with authority as he approached the other three waiting for him.

As they assembled, three plush red chairs appeared. The man in the orange robes continued to hover and the other three sat in the chairs. The fire crackled behind them.

Joe removed the satchel and placed it on the floor beside his chair. "The last I heard, Random was leaving Lüdertown for the pass. He should be crossing the lake now, as long as they made the last ferry."

The man in the suit re-crossed his legs. "'They.' So he's not alone?"

Joe nodded. "Correct, Harris. He is traveling with one of Alma's students. It was a fortunate coincidence that Random happened to run into Will."

"If you believe in that sort of thing." The man in orange robes spoke in a lyrical voice that almost sounded like singing. He followed his words with a slight chuckle.

Harris turned quickly to the hovering monk. "I'm surprised you find this all so amusing, Cho."

The monk's eyes widened and fixed on Harris. "I am surprised you take it all so seriously. I would think you have been here long enough to see beyond the illusion of control."

Alma broke in firmly but calmly. "Stop it, both of you." She turned back to Joe. "Please, continue."

Joe stood and walked to the edge of the fire. He traced the flames from the fury of immolation near the embers to the tops of their dancing tongues where the spark diminished to lines of smoke. He drew a heavy breath. "I have made the choice that I have been avoiding for a long time. Despite all the objections you presented me, I have put my plan in motion." Joe turned to face them. "Erminia now has the master key."

The moment was thick. Cho broke the silence with a deep hum as he pressed his hands together in prayer position. Alma sat motionless.

Harris uncrossed his legs and leaned forward to place his arms on his knees. He drew a deep breath and cast his eyes to the polished stone floor. "Your so-called 'choice' puts the future of everything into question."

Joe responded without hesitation. "The future is not a question. It is always an immediate answer to the choices we make. I created the master key as a way for me to move freely through the maze of locked doors that were also my creation. The locks themselves were a mistake. They were built from the fears of a much younger soul. As deeply as I cherish this sanctuary, it is, by its very nature, arrogant and hypocritical. I see now what my teacher was trying to tell me before she ascended into the mystery--"

"A good door needs no locks?" Cho opened his eyes and interrupted with impish mischief.

Joe smiled at the monk. "That which is built from fear will forever be a monument to fear, no matter how noble the intention. It is time to open the door."

Cho unfolded his legs and lowered his feet to the ground. He grasped Joe's hands in his and pressed them to his forehead. "You honor your teacher."

Harris had stood and was pacing the floor in a methodical gait. He looked out at the three hundred sixty-degree vista that was broken only by the stone columns supporting the roof. "How much time do you think we have?"

Joe gave a small bow to the monk before he answered. "The Square just set down. The jump crew will need some time to recover before they move the city again. They will have to stop in the Lüder and use the key. My guess is that they will rally as many supporters as they can and then fly the city over the lake. We will have some warning, but we can expect them in a matter of days, a week at most."

Harris walked over to face Joe at close quarters. "And what role does Random play in your scheme? Where will his loyalty lie when the time comes for him to choose?"

The fire crackled loudly.

Harris threw his arms up and walked away. He turned and faced Joe again. "You have no idea! That's quite a wild card to throw into the mix, isn't it? This is why I've opposed this idiotic plan from the moment you proposed it!" Harris was almost screaming and his face had flushed red. "So you've decided to simply roll the dice and hope? What kind of a plan is that?"

Joe stood firm, his feet planted flat. "One that leaves room for free will. Random must choose freely. No matter what, the world we know will change. I will not continue to fear that change. I will not sacrifice what we stand for just to maintain comfort and stability. What we have built no longer serves the souls here or those who wander the open Ether."

Cho stepped forward and spoke to Harris. "The stakes are high and the outcome is uncertain. Yet Will brings him to us as we speak. I believe that there will be time to speak with Random and reacquaint him with who he is." Cho touched Harris softly on the chest. "I also agree with you that, once the battle begins, our friend is going to live up to his name."

Alma finally moved. She walked to Harris and put her hand on his shoulder. "Erminia's been waiting a long time for this. She's not foolish enough to waste the opportunity by acting hastily. We will prepare our students and ourselves. When she arrives..." Alma paused and turned her eyes to Joe. "...we'll welcome her home."

: : HOUSEKEEPING : :

The wooden door opened and Joe entered the courtyard of his home. He stood for a moment in the doorway looking at his shadow, cast on the flagstones by the moonlight behind him. His first few steps were that of an intruder, hesitant and careful not to wake the owners. He noticed what he was doing and shook his head. He crossed the center of the courtyard and began climbing the spiral staircase.

As he ascended, he took in the sanctuary he had created for himself. The flagstones covering the inner yard were rough-hewn and varied in size. They were spaced four inches apart, the space between filled with thick green moss. The stones had been matched with precision. As he reached the landing at the top of the spiral stair, he paused to view the larger pattern. It always reminded him of a shattered mirror.

The round landing was a hub; five elevated catwalks led from it like spokes. He walked the wooden planks of the north spoke and watched the fire flicker to life as he approached the dark archway. The red clay hearth was central to the room. Its light reflected off the highly polished wood floor. The main exterior wall was a wooden grid covered in rice paper that diffused the light of the moon over the sparse furnishings. Three pillows lay upon a round Persian rug. Spaced evenly on the perimeter of the rug were five wooden chests. Joe removed his shoes and crossed the floor to the rug. He bowed and stepped onto the opulent carpet. He went to one of the chests and opened the heavy lid. The chest was lined in red velvet, but was otherwise empty. He reached into the satchel and removed the golden cylinder that had been put in his care. He placed it gently in the chest and coiled the fabric of the satchel around it like a nest. He closed the lid and gave a small bow. He stood and went back across the room, leaving the way he came in.

He left his shoes and went back onto the catwalks barefoot. When he reached the hub, he chose another spoke, heading southeast. Another fire flared to life as he approached. The hearth in this room was black marble and against the outer wall. The room had no windows or paper screens to let in light. It was smaller than the first room. Several plush sofas huddled around the blazing fire. He ignored the call of comfort and turned to a heavy oak desk with gold fittings at the corners. Light pooled around it as he pulled out the overstuffed leather chair. He sat down with a loud exhale and opened the drawer. He withdrew three metal keys and placed them on the deep green desk blotter. Each key was distinct, but they shared a heritage of design, both with each other and with the master key he had hung around Tazir's neck.

Tazir. He hoped she had not suffered too greatly. He hoped the breadcrumbs he had left for Otto had enabled him to rescue her from the wrath that was not hers to bear. Joe sat back in the chair and steepled his hands in front of his mouth.

The voice that flowed across the room brought him out of his thoughts. "No rest for the wicked, I see." Alma stood in the arched doorway, her long red hair spilling down over her green dress in a waterfall of ringlets.

Joe kept his hands steepled and moved only his eyes to her. "Should you not be rousing your students and getting them prepared?"

She smiled and walked toward the fire. "You and I both know that there's little I could say to prepare them for a flying city loaded with zealots crashing into their world. Besides, let 'em sleep the night without worry. Dawn will come soon enough." She had reached the plush sofa in front of the fire and poured herself into it. "Come sit with me a moment."

Joe stood up, feigning the reluctance of a man who wanted to work at his desk. He was glad she had come; he longed to curl up with her in front of the fire. She sat up straight and proper as he came near and gave a formal pat to the cushion next to her. He stood smiling at her and shaking his head. He coiled down into the sofa like a panther and pushed her over slowly as he positioned himself on top of her. She giggled and welcomed him with her arms wide. Her pale legs wrapped around his waist. He kissed her gently and then laid his head on her shoulder. She put her arms around him lovingly and kissed his forehead.

"Welcome home, dear one. How long has it been since you relaxed in your own home? Months? Years?"

Joe sighed and melted into her bosom. "Too long. I have been waiting on a blade's edge for almost a year to make sure I was the first one to greet Random. I was lucky that he switched direction so quickly and managed to speed up the process. I have learned to expect the unexpected from him."

She stroked his hair. "You also know him better than anyone. Erminia didn't know him before we put him to sleep, did she?"

He shook his head. "No, she arrived some time after he walked among us and wove his magic. She only heard my stories about it. Even when she managed to snatch him away from me, I knew she would not be able to hold him. She thinks she can manipulate him the way she does the poor souls that follow her. She has no idea what he is capable of."

Alma sat them up. "Can we trust him? When he awoke he was refreshed and joyous...but we put him back in a body before he could remember the demons that drove him to madness. Do you think his time on Earth healed his heart?"

Alma saw a great heaviness come over Joe's face. "He had quite a life. The beauty and innovation he brought to the world of the living was significant, and beyond what we could have predicted. I can only hope that the old wounds have healed, or at least scarred over. Our time together was short, but he knows I have an offer for him. In many ways, it is perfect that she stole him away before I could present it." Joe forced a smile. "If I know my old friend, he will not rest until he finds out for himself what job I wish him to consider."

Her eyes sparkled as the firelight danced in them. "Do you believe he'll accept the offer?"

"That remains to be seen. But I don't think he will be inclined to listen to Erminia when he sees the wrath she will bring in her wake. The bitterness she has carried since we banished her from the Conclave has festered over these hundreds of years. The city is a decrepit ghost of what she and I built together. The beauty has been replaced by decay and greed."

He stood and paced. "What I found, Alma, was the nightmare realized. Some good incarnations are possible, but the feeling of the place is hostile and it is devoid of guidance. I can only assume that Erminia still sits in judgment of those souls she finds irredeemable, saving the lowest births in the cruelest conditions for them. She never understood the depth of that transgression, even though it led to her fall from grace with all of you...and especially with me."

Alma sat up and crossed her legs under her. "We're as much to blame as she is. We took a kind soul and vilified her in the eyes of many, even though she would secretly come back here and have dinner with us."

Joe joined her again on the couch. "I am the one who deserves the most blame. I let my love for her blind me to what Harris told me a million times. He was her teacher; he knew her better than anyone. He warned me that she had not reconciled her lifetime in a culture of death bent on conquering enemies and applying force of will. I should have listened to him. I was young and flush with the power I had to shape this world, convinced that I could just as easily shape the world of the living. I was arrogant and stupid."

Alma took his face in her hands. "You were also in love. You would have painted the Ether any color she named to see her smile. She was the one who squandered that loyalty. I heard the evidence the day you brought her before us. We listened to what you both had to say and we all agreed: the experiment had failed. If she'd accepted our ruling, she could have come back here and resumed her own path."

Joe's eyes dropped. "I did worse to her that day than present her for judgment. I humiliated her in front of all of you, the souls she held in the highest regard. That shame is what drove her to rip the city from its very foundations and take it with her." He looked at Alma again. "She tore down the fountain, Alma."

Alma stroked his face with the tenderness of a mother. "That's the difference between you and she. For all she's done, you see the suffering she continues to inflict on herself and you only wish to make it stop. You knew you could no longer be her lover, but you still wish her soul a peaceful path." Alma kissed him on the forehead, then stood. He watched her cross the room and pause at the door. "That's why I've always supported this crazy plan of yours. I know that it's born of love." She blew him a kiss and disappeared into the night.

The fire crackled loudly and he sat in silence. He cherished Alma and felt her warmth linger, though she had left. For the moment, his doubts were banished. He knew this was the correct path. He closed his eyes to breathe in a steady rhythm.

His gentle meditation was stirred by the click of heels on the catwalks. He stayed still, monitoring his breathing as the sound drew closer until the clicking heels entered the room. They were followed by the whisper of fabric as his guest sat down in the plush sofa opposite him. Joe took a final breath in and opened his eyes.

"I am glad you stopped by, Harris."

Harris sat with his legs crossed, the firelight reflecting off his highly polished shoes. The pleats of his pants were sharp and perfect. He no longer wore his matching jacket, but his collarless white shirt was still buttoned high on his neck, giving him a formal air. "I still think you're wasting your time with her and putting everything at risk for a plan that won't work."

"I know. But I will not abandon her as irredeemable. That would be the worst form of hypocrisy on my part, don't you think?"

The impeccable clothes didn't keep Harris from looking tired and somewhat defeated. "I know you're right. I just...I just don't want to look into her eyes again..."

Joe saw the opportunity to broach the one subject he always avoided with Harris, and took it. "You cannot keep blaming yourself. She was your student, but her choices are hers alone. You were the most conservative and vocal of all of us. You saw the dangers I overlooked and tried to warn us all. I wish I had listened to you instead of my ego. You are a fine teacher, Harris. Do not let the actions of one student make you question that."

Harris partially covered his face with his hand. Joe expected him to launch into a tirade; he was pleasantly surprised when Harris said softly, "Thank you, Joseph. That means a lot coming from you."

They sat in silence. Joe monitored his breath. The space of his own personal sanctuary was nourishing.

Harris stood quickly and straightened his shirt. "Well, what's done is done. I'll station some students in the Lüder to wait for the arrival. She'll have to stop at the obelisk to unlock the barrier, that much is certain."

"Thank you, Harris. Let me know if there is anything you need from me."

Harris gave a small tip of his head and walked out the door. Joe listened to his heels descend the staircase and cross the courtyard.

He knew this was the right path. He also knew that the person he wanted to confirm that most would not be paying him a visit. If he wanted to speak with Cho, he would need to seek him out. Joe smiled and gave a slight snort. He knew that Cho would never say one path was better than another. He would laugh at him and send him away for even making such a plea for justification.

He stood and walked back to the desk. The three keys sat waiting on the green blotter. He left them there and walked out of the study. He took a sleepy walk in the moonlight once more, to the spoke that would take him to his bed. Alma was right. Dawn would come soon enough. He would rest his soul in a dreamless sleep until the morning came.

: : INCARNATION STATION : :

Crowds streamed around the dormant smokestack that rose a hundred feet from the main plaza of Transit Square. The rusted cylinder was the nexus of the oversized plumbing system that sprawled over the limestone plaza. It was also the tallest structure on the mobile city.

The second tallest structure was at the corner of the square and had just recently been completed. The shining new building at the edge of the plaza, an octagonal tower seven stories high with a golden spire at its peak, dwarfed the buildings around it. Each level of the tower had a Chinese-style roof with blood-red timbers under the eaves, covered with stacked shingles in a saturated yellow ochre color. The whole thing was iced with elaborate gold ornamentation. In many ways, it resembled a towering birthday cake.

It was visible from anywhere on the plaza; its sheer scale made it hard to look at anything else. Even those exiting Genseric's at the opposite corner of the square could see the tower rising above the tangle of pipes that snaked over the limestone. Adding to its demand for attention was a sign on the railings of the fifth level that read "Jared's Incarnation Station" in bright red neon. The building narrowly managed to be more ostentatious than the man who had ordered its construction.

Otto stood in front of the tower, squinting up at the neon sign in disbelief. He shook his head and adjusted his red bowler before wading into the crowds that packed the entrance of the ridiculous building. When he managed to get inside, he was greeted by an interior design born of the high-speed collision of Asian stereotypes and the Arabian Nights. The ground floor was a single open room. A sculpture of a Chinese dragon holding an Aladdin-style lamp hung above his head, circling the main hall. Crowds were pushing toward counters at the back to haggle with the staff who stood behind them. The staff all wore Japanese kimonos, but for some unknown reason also sported colorful turbans. The open floor was a sea of mingling and chatter, with several plush, round booths wrapped around tables full of patrons puffing on hookahs and watching belly dancers. A beautiful Indian woman sat in lotus position on a raised platform in the very center of the large room. She was mostly naked save the glittering jewels covering her nipples and crotch. She wore a tall, golden tiara with a large Yin-Yang symbol in it. As she waved her arms in a strange seated dance, soap bubbles flowed from her hands and over the crowd.

When he had managed to recover from the initial visual assault, Otto located the stairway that led to the upper levels. It wasn't hard to spot, given the thick-necked man who guarded it. The guard spotted the bright red bowler and his eyes darted to the tuft of white hair below Otto's lower lip. Otto grinned knowingly and nodded. "Glad to see you found honest work, Jules. Quite a spread your new boss has here. He must be a much more...entertaining employer than I ever was."

Jules looked down at Otto and unhooked the velvet rope stretched across the stairway. "Jared is waiting for you. Someone on the second level will show you up."

Otto began to climb the stairs. He spoke over his shoulder as Jules replaced the velvet rope. "Nice turban, by the way."

• • • • •

Jared stood on the top balcony looking through a telescope mounted on the railing. He scanned the front of Genseric's in the hope that he would spot Erminia looking back. She had not been too happy about fulfilling the terms of their deal, but had admitted that his information had been accurate, even though Random was gone by the time she arrived at the location. Jared had looked for her since he had completed his masterpiece, but had not yet had the pleasure of seeing the look on her face.

The penthouse suite of his tower was furnished in the same garish style as the rest of the building, but with more care toward showcasing the opulence of each item. The showpiece of this room was a massive cherry wood desk carved in the shape of a crouching tiger. The desktop balanced on the tiger's back held a neat stack of papers and an inkwell in which a long peacock feather quill rested. Jared's signature red turban sat perched on a stone bust of himself in the corner.

There was a knock at the door and Jared walked away from the telescope. He considered the turban for a moment, but ran his fingers through his jet-black hair instead. He positioned himself in a few practiced poses before choosing to place his hands on the desk and look down at the papers, deep in thought. He waited a beat and called out. "Enter!"

The door opened and a stunning young woman in a tight dress addressed him. "Mr. Otto here to see you, sir."

Jared didn't look up. "I see. Give me just a moment and then you can show him..."

Otto walked past the woman and into the room. He went straight to the crystal decanter sitting on a side table and poured himself a glass of scotch. The young woman shot a glance at Jared for instructions. Jared waved her away and she closed the door behind her.

Otto took a drink from his glass and turned to Jared with raised eyebrows and a satisfied nod. "Well, at least you have good taste in scotch."

Jared was not happy with how this was going. "Yes...do be conservative with that. It's a rare batch that I traded for a while back..."

Otto looked Jared in the eye as he refilled the glass generously, even splashing a bit on the table. He took his drink and walked past Jared to the balcony, where he put his eye to the telescope.

Jared gestured to the view. "It's a fine place to watch the dance of souls in our little circus of death!" Jared spoke too loudly. He was not happy that he didn't have Otto's full attention. "I'm very excited about the valuable services that the Incarnation Station will be providing to the Square. Some promise to be quite lucrative." Jared shuffled some papers on his desk. "I have three new employees who've become very gifted at entering Glory Bubbles. Within a week we'll be launching Bubble Tourism! Imagine it, Otto! Step inside the private heavens of others! Of course, the tourists would need experienced guides to help them navigate once inside. A whole new industry will be born!"

Otto stayed focused on the eyepiece and moved the telescope slightly. "Gosh, that is a great idea Jared. You could also offer tours into the private damnation of the Hellocked."

Jared scoffed. "I hardly think anyone would be interested in touring such places."

Otto straightened up and looked the taller man in the eye. "You seem rather interested in your reluctant neighbor at the far corner of the square." He took a sip from his scotch as he once again locked his disquieting stare on Jared.

"You know, I believe I will join you in a drink!" Jared turned away from Otto's eyes and went to the crystal decanter. He poured a tiny bit in a glass and dabbed what Otto had spilled with a cloth. He turned with a flourish to propose a toast but was instantly deflated when he saw Otto sitting in his chair behind the tiger desk. His legs were crossed and his red bowler hung on his foot.

"Jared, I need to get someone off the square undetected."

Jared gave an incredulous huff. "Impossible! The city is completely locked down ever since--" He caught himself.

"Ever since the queen's prisoner escaped? Yes, Jared, I know all about it. You're not the only person who deals in information. Erminia's thugs have been combing every dark corner looking for him. Most of the darkest are in the quarters of the city that belong to me. However, I still have a client who wishes to disembark. She has rather pressing business at the Conclave that requires her attention."

Jared's eyes darted back and forth as he processed the information Otto had given him for free. "Well, your client is out of luck. There's no way on or off the square...at the moment." Jared took a sip of his scotch and his eyebrows gave a small hop.

Otto smiled broadly and gave a hearty laugh. "But you have a rather juicy little rumor you want to sell, don't you?"

Jared walked to his desk and gestured for Otto to kindly get out of his chair. Otto stood slowly and dusted off the seat. "By all means..."

Jared sat with renewed authority and re-stacked the papers that were already neatly stacked. "I may have a bit of information that would be useful to your client. I also believe it would be extremely enlightening to someone in your position, given the network of people who rely on you."

Otto took a gulp of his scotch and set the wet glass on the bare wood of the desk. Jared's eyes tracked from the glass to the black pinholes of Otto's eyes. "Here's the deal, you little gossip whore. If your tidbit is as juicy as you're pretending it is, I'll consider it partial payment for what you already owe me."

Jared calmly opened a drawer and took out a delicate cloth. He picked up Otto's glass and wiped the condensation off the wood. He put a stone coaster down and put the crystal tumbler on top of it. "Actually, let me tell you what the deal is: I give you the heads-up on some of the most guarded information I have ever acquired and you wipe my debt clean." Jared sat back in his chair and finished his own scotch. He tossed his glass into the empty marble fireplace, where it shattered. "This is a non-negotiable price. Given the quality of the information, it's a bargain."

Otto held Jared in his stare, looking for a tell that would let him know Jared was bluffing. Jared had never had the stones to be so cavalier with him, given the sizable debt that he carried. Whatever it was that he knew, it was big enough to lend real confidence to this noisy rooster of a man. Otto considered the weight of the events unfolding. "Very well. But you'd better tell me something I don't already know."

Jared sat up. "And my debt to you will be paid in full?"

"If the information is as good as the smug look on your face, yes."

Jared sat back with relief. "Erminia will not find Joe hiding in some corner of the Square. You know that, I know that, and even she knows it. The bad news is that, despite the futility of it, the lockdown will remain in force until we depart." Jared sat forward. "The good news is that we will be departing in two days' time. She's landing the city right in front of the Lüder. She's declaring open war. If your client wants to reach the Conclave in a hurry, she only needs to sit tight. My source tells me that all the Truthers in the open Ether are being summoned to Lüdertown. Whatever they're planning, there'll be no way to keep the lockdown in place once we arrive. Your client will be able to step off the Square unchallenged in the chaos."

Otto stroked the tiny tuft of white hair below his lip. "Two days?"

"Two days."

Otto placed his red bowler on his bald head. "Your debt to me is paid in full. I look forward to all the extra time I will now have, since I won't have to balance the intricacies of your account any longer." Otto opened the door to leave. "Oh, and Jared? You have your little castle now. Enjoy it. But stay out of my side of the city."

The door closed and Jared sat alone behind the wooden tiger.

:: DAWN ::

The morning sun laid a soft glow on the edge of her cheek. He watched her sleep. He had no desire to wake her, but he had promised he would. He traced the curve under her chin and down her neck. She stirred as he made his way to her collarbone. The opening of her eyes signaled the end of her dreamless sleep and the beginning of the last day he would see her.

Her heavy eyelids popped open with a snap. "Today's the day...isn't it? Has it really arrived?"

He rested his chin on the pillow. "Yes, Dawn. Your day is here. And, before you ask, yes, I woke you early enough to see the sun rise over the lake, one last time."

Dawn sat up with a bounce and sprang out of the bed. Her bare feet slapped across the floor until she reached the ladder. She pushed the hatch open and scampered onto the simple rooftop balcony she had built her second year. The lake was glass, and Dawn stood naked in the cold air, eager to witness the moment. The purple glow of the lake brightened and the sky warmed to an orange hue. He climbed up and wrapped his arms around her waist just as the sun crested the horizon and set the lake ablaze with golden light. She gasped as the full impact of the beauty filled her eyes. He kissed her shoulder and she tightened his arms around her. "Thank you. I'll miss our mornings." She turned and kissed him, but then pulled away and dropped her eyes.

"I know. I promised you no long goodbyes." He kissed her forehead. "I'll see you soon, kid. Keep an eye out for me."

She perked back up and met his eyes again. "I'll see you soon!" She turned back to the glorious sunrise and he knew their time together was over. As he reached the bottom of the ladder, clothing materialized and wrapped around him. By the time he turned the knob he was fully clothed, but still barefoot. He took a straw hat off the hook by the door and left with nothing more than a click of the latch.

She heard the click and spoke to the absence. "I'll keep an eye out." She looked down from her perch to the courtyard below. The great common space she shared with her neighbors held a few early risers, braving the cold. She needed to get moving; she didn't want to have her last day be a sea of goodbyes.

Within a few minutes she had chosen her final outfit. She paused at the door and gazed at the room she had lived in for six years. She scanned all the items she had created, the colors she had chosen, the place that had been her home. She left it all there for the next student. There was no need to take anything with her. Whoever the next occupant was, they would go through her things the way she had gone through what had been here six years ago. She had constructed a whole story about the former occupant by examining what had been left behind, then had gotten to work making the place her own. She wondered who would be lucky enough to get the only room with a rooftop balcony.

She held out her hand and a small piece of parchment unrolled in her palm. She laid it down in the entryway and closed the bright yellow door behind her. Handwritten on the parchment were the words 'Welcome Home' in loving script.

The curving hall ran the circumference of the building. Rows of doors to little rooms like hers lined the inside curve. The outside curve of the hall was mostly windows, looking down from the third floor to the forest below. She could see five other round buildings on higher terraces and could just glimpse the temple tower between the trees. She took a deep breath and headed down the hall. She took the stairs down and, with a quick turn at the bottom of two flights, cut across the courtyard and out the main door.

She walked briskly away from the turret-shaped building with tears in her eyes. She did not allow herself to look back. The day had come; there was nothing left to say. Her instructor had warned her that final goodbyes were often just grasping at what we did not want to let go. She had taken the coaching and scheduled time with everyone who was dear to her. She had spent the last month getting complete with all her friends and family here. She had ignored the advice to spend the final night alone, however. She just had to have him one more time.

She walked to the edge of the terrace on which her dormitory sat. It was near the top of the stepped mountainside. She looked out over the hundreds of other round buildings nested on the steep shore of the lake. Each had hundreds of stories unfolding, thousands of souls who walked their own path before returning to Earth. She adjusted her dress and walked down the earthen stairs to the cobblestone avenue that wound through the terraces.

The simple road widened, and she came upon an old friend warming up for his daily practice. The short, unassuming man was adjusting a music stand and singing scales as he prepared to start his morning song. She was glad to get to see him one last time. She called out to him in Chinese. "Hello, Ping! Another day of singing?"

The man was at first startled by her voice and cowered a bit. He gave a shy smile and answered in halting English. "Few months...to go." He fiddled with his music stand self-consciously. She maintained her pace and heard his song begin as she walked away. His teacher studied under Cho's house. Cho himself had prescribed Ping's practice. At first she had thought it cruel that such a shy soul should be instructed to sing on the street every day, but she had seen his confidence grow during the practice. When she had first passed by over a year before, Ping hadn't even been able to look her in the eyes.

The avenue began to climb uphill as it snaked between the terraces. Rounding a bend, Dawn was able to see the whole Temple instead of just the tower. A deep reverberation found her ears as the Temple horn sounded. She turned toward the lake, shading her eyes from the bright sun as she scanned the waters. She spotted the ferry at the very edge of the horizon just as it blew its horn in answer to the Temple's call. Someone on that ferry might be the one to take up residence in her old room. She grinned and skipped up the trail.

The cobblestone street joined the four other paths that converged on a circular slab of granite. Classes had started earlier than usual for the twenty students that were gathered, practicing the art of moving. The instructor hovered around them barking instructions as they moved massive stone statues in a complex aerial dance. "The size of the object only exists in your mind! Moving a mountain is the same as moving a pebble! Now up and...hold!" Most of the stone statues rose to a height of roughly fifty feet and froze in various angles of rotation. Two hovered much lower than the rest.

The instructor flew over to the two students who were struggling to move them with only the force of their will. "You fight only with your mind! Breathe. Relax." Dawn walked confidently under the tons of hovering stone as the last two students managed to make their burdens rise. She stepped off the slab and onto a cobblestone spur that led southwest.

There was more activity this morning than usual. Classes of fliers zoomed overhead on almost every street. A line of at least forty students chasing their instructor zipped over her head, fast and low in the direction of the Temple. She looked down toward the shore. The lake water rose and fell in long, arching bands woven together like threads in fabric, the work of a large group of Water Movers practicing vigorously. The sharp, tearing pop of students transporting from one spot to the next echoed like popcorn popping. It was becoming more frequent.

The sounds and activity would be normal if it were midday, but there was a feeling of rushed urgency. Such movement so soon after the sun rose struck her as odd. She closed her eyes and took a breath. She was stalling. Today was the day. She needed to stay focused and keep moving.

She came to a fork with three signs on a single post. Two signs pointed left: 'Ferry Landing' and 'Petition Hall.' Dawn smiled and thought of her arrival here, years ago. She thought of all the time she had spent in the last few years at Petition Hall, competing with others for the perfect set of parents. She was happy with her choice of parents and couldn't wait to meet them; she had petitioned aggressively to get them.

The third sign pointed to the right and read 'Windmear's Portal' in simple text. Dawn stepped close and traced the O with her finger. The path narrowed and climbed gently. She picked up her skirt a bit and took the right fork at a brisk pace.

A loud, tearing pop close behind her made her grab her ears. "Dawn! Wait up!" She turned around to see her friend Erin running up to her.

"Erin! I told you, no long goodbyes! Leaving is hard enough as it is."

But there was something else in Erin's eyes. "No, that's not why I came. The instructors woke us all early and had us assemble in the courtyard of our building." Erin was talking fast. "Next thing we know, Alma teleports in. Alma! Right there in the courtyard of my building!"

Dawn grabbed the smaller girl by the shoulders gently but firmly. "Erin, that's great. I know how long you've wanted to meet her. I only saw the head of my house once in six years. But I'm going back today. I'll miss your friendship but you're making it harder for me to leave by coming here. I need to get to the portal."

Erin shook off Dawn's hands. "I didn't break my promise to you just to tell you that! Listen to me! Alma told us that the barrier that protects the Conclave has been breached. The Council is not sure when, but they expect Erminia to arrive any day. They think she's going to fly the Square right to our doorstep!"

Dawn shook her head. "That's impossible. Even if she could, why would she fly the city to us? The Council is the one that has been chasing her for hundreds of years."

Erin took Dawn's hands in hers. "The Council thinks she may try to take control of the Conclave by force. Alma told us that she's coming...and that we should be prepared for war."

"War? Alma used the word war?" Dawn was visibly shaken. Alma was known for her empathy and calm; peace was a driving force in all who studied under her house. "I still need to get to the portal; they're expecting me. I can talk to the Priestess and see how much time I have left before they need to place me in my new body." Dawn touched Erin's shoulders gently. "I'm glad you came to find me. Can you transport us both to the portal directly?"

Erin nodded and squeezed her hands. Dawn hated teleporting; she had never gotten used to it. She had always been glad that her gifts lay in other areas. She relaxed and let out a deep breath. She gave Erin a nod and was sucked into the tight embrace of the world collapsing on her. Her mind pinched, then the sensation of being thrown from a moving vehicle made her stomach jump. The tearing sound was loud but not unbearable. Erin was very good at her art and one of the few souls Dawn trusted enough to hitch a ride with. They now stood in front of a simple adobe building shaded by a thick canopy of trees. The night's chill still lurked here in the shade, not yet warmed by the light of the new day.

"I'll go in and speak with her. Get back to your house; I'll find you later." Dawn approached the massive wooden door and turned the heavy iron handle. The latch resisted at first, then released with a sliding of metal. Dawn put her weight against the door. It swung inward slowly.

She walked into a small anteroom and was immediately greeted by the eyes of a young woman in a simple blue dress. She knelt sitting on her heels, her posture perfect. She smiled broadly and gave a small shake of her head. "She said you'd be early. Welcome." Behind the woman was a heavy red curtain that led to the main room.

Dawn was overcome with emotion. She tried to form words, but found herself mute. The woman gestured to a cushion on the floor next to her. Dawn dropped down to kneel with her.

The young woman pressed her palms together in prayer position in front of her lips. Her eyes sparkled with joy. "She also said you'd want to speak with her. You can go right in, but don't interrupt just yet; there's a soul just about to depart. As soon as he's through, you can speak with her."

Dawn nodded and stood with care. She walked to the curtain and gently pulled it aside. Her eyes adjusted as it closed behind her. The windowless room was partially lit by torches mounted on the wall, but the majority of the light came from a glowing pool of liquid in the center of the dirt floor. The soil was dark and rich, like fresh ground coffee.

An old woman in thick, layered robes of deep blue sat on a red pillow near the boundary between the glowing liquid and the rich soil, her legs crossed. She was old, but beautiful. Dawn recognized the man beside her. She couldn't quite place his name, but she had seen him around. He studied under Harris's house. He was naked, and knelt just behind the old woman.

Thirty or so students sat with their backs against the walls. Some looked up at her when she entered, but the blue-robed woman kept her eyes on the liquid and the room stayed silent. Dawn took a seat along the wall with the others. The glow from the pool was yellow, and pulsed like a heartbeat.

The old woman looked deep into the liquid and moved her palms just above the surface. The glow faded and the pulsing stopped. The room went dark save the torches, but then the liquid turned a brilliant blue. The old woman sat back and gestured to the naked man. He stood up and walked to the edge. With a small hop, he entered the water feet first. The glow brightened to pure white as he disappeared below the surface, then dimmed, returning to the slowly pulsing yellow.

The old woman put her palms together in front of her forehead and bowed to the pool. She then sat up and looked Dawn directly in the eyes. The old woman's eyes were deep, calm, and ancient, the knowledge within them vast, and Dawn found she could not maintain eye contact. The woman continued to look at Dawn and spoke with authority and stillness to the room.

"This one comes with worry in her heart. The weight is one of love, but it is not yours to carry, Dawn."

At the sound of her name Dawn brought her eyes from the ground and met the old woman's kind, intense stare. "Then it is true? The barrier has been breached and Transit Square travels here to wage war?"

A flurry of whispers rippled around the room. The old woman held up her hand and the whispers stopped abruptly. "You have all traveled a long path to get here. You need only take the final step. Those who remain will face whatever change is brewing. The souls you wish to protect are precious, but they are not as fragile as you perceive them to be." The whispers erupted again as a hushed panic overtook the students. The old woman shook her head and spoke loudly toward a dark corner of the room. "They won't listen to me. You will need to tell them yourself."

Dawn looked into the darkness and saw the head of her house emerge from the shadows. He was striking to look at, but somehow put her at ease. He was so comfortable in his skin that the whole room relaxed at the sight of him.

Joe looked Dawn in the eyes but spoke to the room the way the old woman had. "There is a change coming to our little corner of the Ether. Even I cannot say what will emerge on the other side. But I urge you all to leave the path of the dead today. You have families waiting to fall in love with you. They need your spirit as much as you need theirs. Take the lessons you have learned here back to the world. They are needed more than ever."

The old woman once again waved her palms over the liquid and it pulsed. Joe walked over to Dawn and held out his hand. She took it and he helped her stand. The pool glowed blue and the old woman nodded to Joe.

Joe stopped addressing the room and made his tone more personal as he looked at her. "Dawn, the choice is yours. I will honor whatever path you choose. But I urge you not to pass up this birth lightly."

Dawn straightened her spine. "I don't take it lightly. I have studied for years to be ready for this day, to be ready for my new family. But in the process, I have found a family here. I need to know they are alright before I leave." Dawn took in a deep breath. "I choose to stay and make sure they are safe."

Joe nodded and dropped his eyes. "If that is your choice, I will honor it. If you plan on staying, I would ask you to come with me. I could use your help organizing a special team."

Dawn looked back at the central pool and watched the blue glow fade. She straightened her dress and turned back to Joe. "I am glad to help in whatever way I can. Lead the way."

Joe turned to the room. "I advise you all to continue on your path to the births you worked so hard for, but the choice is yours to make alone." He touched the old woman on the shoulder and she patted his hand. He stepped away from the pulsing glow of the portal and held the heavy red curtain open for Dawn. He gave a worried sigh as he followed her out of the room. It was going to be a busy day.

: : ARRIVAL : :

The sound of the ferry's horn stirred Random from his dreamless sleep. Will had found them a nice place to bunk down near the wheelhouse on the top deck. It was a small room with a single porthole window, but it had cots and a stack of warm blankets. Random had tried to stay up for a while, but he was mentally exhausted and there was little to see as the paddle wheels churned in the darkness. Not even Will plucking at the kora could keep him from sleep.

The brilliant light of dawn streamed through the small porthole and made the room glow. Random sat up quickly and realized he was alone in the room. The massive kora leaned in the corner, but the cot where Will had bedded down was empty save a wadded blanket. Random pulled on his boots and opened the door to the deck. The light made him squint and the crisp air made him shiver.

The water was a blue-black, highlighted with the gold light of morning on the lazy ripples they left in their wake. Random walked toward the bow to catch his first view of their destination across the glassy surface of the water.

The Conclave was much larger than he had expected. Hundreds of cylindrical buildings were nested in every available space of the steep shore for miles up and down the westernmost coast.

A firm slap on his right shoulder startled him. "Well, there it is. I kept my part of the bargain." Will sniffed the air. "Damn, I love the smell of the air this early." He leaned against the railing next to Random. They watched as the light of the sun filled the darker shadows of the city.

181

"I didn't expect it to be so...big." Random's eyes kept scanning up and down the shore.

Will chuckled. "Surprisingly, a far greater number find their next body on the Square. A few deals there and you can be crying in your new mother's arms inside a month, or even a few days if you aren't picky." Will gestured to the shore. "This takes a lot more time and not many have the patience for it, but with seven billion people stomping around on the Rock, there are still quite a few who find their way here."

They were silent for a while. Other passengers stirred and found their way to the railings on all decks. Random tore his eyes from the Conclave and looked at Will's profile. He seemed at peace. "Are you still happy you chose this path, Will?"

"Damn straight." Will answered quickly and fell silent. His eyes drank in the sight of the Conclave. He had the look of a man returning home.

Random joined him in witnessing their approach. It was a stunning city to behold. At the top of the steepest hill was a large building with a tower rising from it, capped with what reminded him of the wide straw hats worn by Chinese peasants. The steep slope had been cut into a thousand times and reformed into grassy steps. The man-made terraces did not mar the natural beauty. Instead, they danced with it, honoring rock formations and providing more room for the thick trees and grass to flourish. The buildings all allowed the wild growth of trees to take center stage. It was a village that had grown large, but somehow maintained the intimacy of tribal community in its circular dwellings.

Will gave a nod to the coast and delivered another slap to Random's shoulder. "I'm going to pack up my instruments. We'll be docking before you know it." He left Random alone with his thoughts.

As the ferry churned closer, he saw strange ribbons of water dancing at the shoreline. They stood out sharply, as the rest of the water was smooth as glass. Great arcs of water rose and fell, weaving between each other like a sweater knitting itself. He looked around for Will but he was already out of sight. He considered asking one of the many passengers on the deck about this, but headed to the wheelhouse instead.

Random found Saul at the wheel, looking as crisp and tailored as he had the night before. A wave through the window and Saul opened the door to the wheelhouse. "Good morning to you! You're Will's friend... Sorry, what was your name again?"

"Random. It's Captain Saul, right?"

The brown face gave a hearty smile, revealing the bone-white teeth. "Just Saul; no need for titles. What can I help you with, son?"

"I was wondering if you could tell me what that is." Random pointed to the ribbons of water near the shore. "The water's doing something odd there in that one section. Is that normal?"

Saul followed the sight line with the gravity of a sailor watching for a hidden reef. When he spotted it he relaxed. "Ah! Well, I don't know if I would classify it as normal, but it's nothing to be alarmed about. Looks like some Water Movers are playing around."

At Random's blank look Saul continued the explanation. "Movers are just what they sound like. They have a special gift for moving things in the Ether." Saul locked off the wheel with a loop of rope. He leaned against the wall, letting the ferry continue on course without his guidance. "It's been a long, quiet night; I wouldn't mind chatting for a while. You see, things here have a certain permanence depending on how much intent was used by whoever created them. If you want to move something, you have to use an equal or greater intent than the soul who created it. Water is a tricky one to move. There's a whole school of study at the Conclave devoted to it. A beautiful woman, who also happens to be the love of my life, is the master of that particular art. You may be lucky enough to be placed in her house, if your gifts lie there."

"Her house?"

"If you're here to study, you'll be placed in one of four houses once you arrive at the Conclave. Each one has its own specialization, so it depends on your talents. Do you have anything that seems to come naturally to you since you arrived?"

Random shrugged. "I can make stuff pretty easily. Will said he thought I was a Builder."

Saul crossed his arms. "I see! A fine talent, that one. If he's right, you'll join a very prestigious house."

"So you're in love with one of the masters?"

The captain's face looked younger as he grinned. "Aye, and I'm proud that she returns my affections. I worshipped her from afar for years before I could get her attention. She had many lovers at the time and was not impressed with me. But I'm a patient man. Most of her lovers eventually longed to return to a body on Earth. The day she realized I was here to stay was the day she agreed to meet me." Saul stood proud and tall. "Once I had her in my arms, she never wanted to leave."

Random knew a taste of the love Saul spoke of. "How long have you been married?"

Saul laughed. "My sweet Alma has not yet agreed to that! I propose to her every day; she always replies that she'll think about it." Saul saw the confusion on Random's face. "Son, forever here is not just a concept. In many ways it's a beautiful game we play. Every day I think of new ways to profess my love to her. Every day I am a man preparing to propose to the woman he loves."

There was a slight awkwardness. Random was not sure how he felt about this arrangement, and found himself judging it.

Saul's eyes went back to the bow. He scanned the water and spoke without looking at Random. "Now, if you don't mind, I need to get back to the business of steering us to the correct dock. A small adjustment at this distance can save us a lot of time." He turned back to the wheel and flipped the loop of rope off.

"Yes, of course. Thanks for talking with me, Captain." Random found himself giving a small salute as he left, inspired by Saul's crisp uniform and military bearing.

The deck was more animated now, the passengers milling about and crowding the railings for a better view of the rapidly approaching coast. Halfway back to the room in which they had bunked, Random spotted Will with his prized instruments strapped to him. Will motioned for him to follow. They met at the stairs near the stern, then descended all the way to the bottom level, taking a seat on a bench. Will handed Random the small bag he had forgotten in the room. Inside was the map he had taken from the crater, tucked away in the scroll case he had imagined for it. He hadn't looked at the map again since he had studied it at the fire while Will slept. That morning seemed so long ago.

"You know, I never did ask why you wanted to come to the Conclave so soon after arriving. It's usually a pretty personal question to ask someone you just met. Now that I know you better, I don't mind being nosy." Will sat forward to keep from damaging the kora strapped to his back. Hambone's rig was cumbersome to sit in. "What do you plan to do now that you're here, Mr. Random?"

Random looked at the big red man with the wild eyebrows. Will had been nothing but kind to him. He had taken him to see Trace even though he was clear that it might mean sharing her intimately. He had answered all his questions and been a fine companion to travel with in a land of chaos. Random suddenly felt guilt at the prospect of looking into Will's eyes and telling him anything but the truth.

"I'm here to find Joe. He met me when I first arrived and said he wanted to offer me a job...but Erminia managed to snatch me away from him before he could tell me what it was. She seemed to want me to work for her instead. Then Fabric showed up and got me away from both of them." Random paused and let out a deep breath. It felt good to finally come clean with his friend. He then carefully considered the complex expressions traveling over Will's face. "Look, I would've told you sooner but...well, honestly, Will, I wasn't sure whether I could trust you." He looked at the bay that was closing around them as they came closer to the shore. "I wasn't sure whom I could trust. Until Fabric dropped me in the wastes alone...I tried to convince myself I wasn't really dead." Random looked back into Will's eyes with a gaze that made Will stop breathing. "But I remember my death, Will. As much as I would love to forget it, I know exactly how I died. Now I'm here. I don't know why, but there are some very powerful people who know more about me and my past than I remember."

Will allowed himself to resume breathing. He looked at Random as if he were looking into a cave.

Random knew the look from business deals and poker games. He dropped the shields he would normally have in place. He had nothing to hide. He was tired of trying to make sense of this mess by himself.

Will finally spoke after long minutes. "Anything else happen you haven't bothered to mention?"

Random sat up a bit. "Yeah, I ran into two old women in a forest who told me I had gone so insane the last time I was here that they had to put me to sleep for a thousand years."

Will started to crack a smile, but then his face dropped as he saw the frightened look and the raw fear that gripped Random. "You're not making this up, are you?"

Random fought the tears he felt welling in his eyes. "I wish to God or whatever sadist built this place that I were, Will." He shook his head and stood up in an attempt to hold his composure. The last thing he needed now was to give in to the despair. He went to the railing, where he focused on the boat's wake. "I'm not sure whom to believe. But I've been running logic circles in my head ever since I got here." He had regained enough composure to look at Will again. "Now I'm going to listen to my gut. My gut tells me, even though I haven't known you that long, that I can trust you."

The sloshing of the wheels driving the boat was the only sound that filled the space between them.

Will pulled his arms out of the straps that held the kora and the drum. He left the rig on the bench and stood to look Random in the eyes. "Trust like that is not something I find granted often, nor is it something I take lightly." Will put his hand on Random's shoulder. "I also trust my gut. I knew you were different the moment I met you. At first I thought you were just an easy mark, fresh off the Rock and dumb as a post. But when I saw you create those bikes...and what you built for Trace...well, I knew you were not just anybody."

Random's body relaxed as he felt a little less alone. "I'm not sure what I'm going to end up saying to Joe, but I was glad to hear you speak highly of him."

Will steered him back to the bench and got him to sit down. "I feel indebted to Joe for all he's given me, so my opinion is biased. Trust your own gut, not mine. This is definitely not your first spin of the wheel."

"I would have to agree with you on that theory. A few places have seemed familiar. The trees where I met the old women, the place we camped, even my first sight of the Conclave. But they're not full memories. They're more like echoes that have lost their original voice. I can't remember anything about being here before. If I can't remember who I was, how can I make a choice?"

"The same way we all do, my friend. By listening to your heart." Will looked over the railings and gauged how close the ferry was to its destination by the landmarks he saw on the shore. "Look, we have at least another half hour before we dock. What else can you tell me? Who were these two old women who told you you were crazy?"

• • • • •

The ferry slid quietly into the slip with practiced grace. Men and women on the dock grabbed the mooring lines and tied them to cleats. Random and Will had prime seats to disembark first, but they let the other passengers go past them as they finished discussing the details of the map they had rolled open on the bench.

As the last of the passengers left the ferry, Random rolled up the map and stowed it back in the scroll case. Will sat down in front of the rig that Hambone had made for him and pulled the straps over his shoulders. They stood together and stopped for a moment to consider each other.

Will spoke with enthusiasm. "Well, looks like this day will not be boring! After you, you crazy son of a bitch!"

Random laughed easily. He was so relieved to have someone he really considered a friend. He jumped the small gap between the ferry and the dock and headed to shore, Will close behind him. He had told Will everything. Many of the things that had been haunting him seemed lighter when he spoke them out loud. The greatest weight had been lifted when he expressed his deep concern for his own sanity. Will had dismissed it as nonsense. Random was glad it wasn't just he, alone with dark thoughts.

As they got closer to the end of the dock that was anchored to the shore, Random slowed, distracted by the scene around him. Many docks had boats moored. Some boats had people aboard, preparing to launch.

Will caught up to him and took the lead. "Come on, sport, let's keep moving." Will reached the end of the dock and hopped the two small steps to the ground.

When Random got to the steps he took them slowly, one at a time. When he dropped his foot onto the dark soil, his head filled with a reverberating sound, like he had stepped on the taut head of an immense drum. The sound shook him to the bone. He dropped to one knee. As his hands hit the dirt, two more deep notes thrummed in his consciousness.

His mind filled with flashes of events, waves of memories. He grabbed his temple as the flood of moving pictures came at him with unrelenting force. He felt submerged in them, struggling with their enormity like a tiny fish trying to comprehend the ocean. He was finally able to ground himself again in his body by focusing on his breathing. His blurred vision cleared and he found himself staring at the dark soil between his fingers.

Will was kneeling beside him, his hand on the middle of his back. As Random managed to find himself again, he became aware of the sound of Will's voice. The volume of the world around him rose as an invisible knob was turned so he could hear again.

"...you need to answer me! Are you OK? What's wrong? Look at me. What's happening?"

Random looked up and found Will's eyes with his. "I'm OK... I don't know what just... there was a sound like a drum...and pictures...so many pictures..." He dropped his eyes back to the ground and focused on his breathing again.

Will spoke with worry in his voice. "Can you stand?"

"I think so." Working together, they got Random to his feet. Will steered him and Random just focused on moving his legs. Will walked him to a large rock and sat him down. Random felt a flush of heat in his face and a break in his equilibrium. He was glad that Will had a firm grip on his upper arm.

Will sat patiently. Random finally straightened his back as he felt more stable. Will released his grip but stayed close. "What just happened? You went down like a sack of hammers."

"There was a sound. Did you hear anything?"

Will shook his head.

Random continued. "It was deep...I could feel it, like a wave hitting me. I saw images, so many images flashing in front of my eyes. Faces, thoughts, movement...they were all so familiar..."

"Like a memory." Will finished the thought. Random's head snapped up. He locked his eyes on Will and gave a wide-eyed nod. Will put his hand on Random's shoulder. "It's like that sometimes. There's a trigger, a circuit fires and the memories come rushing back. Looks like you got what you asked for:

some recollection of who you were before. I've seen memories stop people in their tracks, but I've never seen anyone fall to their knees. What was it that you remembered?"

Random looked around. His vision had changed to high-definition. Colors were intensified; everything looked sharper and more vibrant. "I remember this spot. I remember the smell of the air..." His eyes tracked along the ground and followed the path the other passengers had taken. He could still pick out a few he recognized from the ferry, even though they were hundreds of feet away. They joined crowds of people assembled in a wide, circular plaza ringed by a wall at its perimeter. "I remember that there's an arched gate at the far side of that plaza. The road on the other side of the gate is paved with red brick and leads to the steps of the Hall. The building is round, with seventy-two columns that are a pale yellow limestone. Each column is cut in a spiral that diminishes slightly as it rises to the top, ending at exactly twenty-two feet, six inches. The columns hold a domed roof that's three hundred and eighty-seven feet in diameter, with an oculus at the crown."

Will offered nothing but a blank stare. "Well, yes...but how do you know such exact dimensions of Petition Hall?"

Random stood and stretched to his full height. "Because I built it."

: : PETITION HALL : :

The morning sun streamed through the oculus at the very crown of the great dome, casting a golden circle of sunlight that wrapped around the western columns and spilled onto the inlaid marble floors.

Thirteen steps led from the red brick roads to the great marble slab that held the seventy-two twisting limestone columns. Every step brought more clarity to the memories flooding Random's mind. Will followed a few steps behind, watching the change in the way Random carried himself. Random did not stop and admire the views that were designed to be admired. He did not stop and look up the twist of one of the columns from the foot of it. He walked with purpose, dodging the clusters of people to reach the top of the stairs. When they got there, he did not marvel at the designs inlaid in marble across the vast space. He gave a glance to the oculus at the apex, but he did not stop to appreciate the curve of the massive dome.

Instead, he immediately made a beeline across the floor toward one of the stone sculptures that resided under the dome. It was a likeness of a Chinese woman holding a bowl in front of her. She stood twenty-five feet high, her eyes focused on the opening at the top of the dome. Other sculptures stood in the great open space as well, many more grand and dynamic than this smaller one near the perimeter. Random walked at such a brisk pace that Will fell behind.

When Random reached the great stone curves of the sculpture's robes, he stopped and waited for Will. He smiled as Will dodged past a group of people who had slowed his progress.

191

"Where the heck are you headed in such a hurry?" Will adjusted the rig that held his instruments.

Random turned to the statue and ran his hand over one of its many stone curves. A latch clicked and he swung open a hidden door in the statue. He turned back to Will with a smirk. "Right here. Come inside; I want to show you something."

Inside, a small room had a ladder on one wall. Random closed the door behind them. The room was lit with strategically placed openings, not noticeable from the exterior, that allowed just enough light in to define the space. Will stood, nodding. "Interesting."

"Drop your stuff here; let's head up." Random gestured to the ladder and began to climb. Will followed. They emerged at an opening that was invisible from the ground. They walked the top of the statue's outstretched arms to stand in the stone bowl that she held aloft. It was a view of the Hall that few had the privilege of enjoying.

From their private balcony they could see the full scope of the designs in the marble floor, woven knots of stone inlaid with precision. The other statues stood before them, most of them rising higher as the increasing height of the dome allowed. The statues were not of gods or heroes. They were ordinary people from all walks of life and all corners of the world. Each one stood in celebration, some dancing, others playing instruments, all turning their eyes toward the round opening at the peak of the dome where the golden light of morning poured in.

Will had been in Petition Hall a million times, but he had never seen it from this vantage point. Souls milled about below, traversing the floor of the great hall and crossing paths with others en route to their destinations. The scope of the dome was even more pronounced from this height. Random crossed his arms on the rim of the stone bowl and put his chin on his wrists, a shine of wonder in his eyes, like a child seeing his first snowfall.

"I made this spot just for me. I could always come here to collect my thoughts without being bothered. In the afternoon, the light comes down right here and warms the stone. It's a good place for a nap."

Will was craning his neck to survey the space. "It's a helluva view! I never would have thought of coming up here. I know a lot of people fly up to the top of the dome to watch the sunset. I can't say I've ever seen anyone perched up here."

Random sat down with his back against the bowl's rim. He closed his eyes and relaxed in a way he hadn't in lifetimes. He looked at home. "This was my spot. I made it easy to miss."

Will sat down next to him. The curve of the bowl provided a comfortable support to his back. "So you remember making this place? You actually remember when this wasn't here?"

Random's eyes opened. "I remember designing it as we sat in the Temple tower. There was a lot more open space back then. We wanted a common area where people could gather. We didn't have a name for it then."

Will hung on Random's simply stated words. "Who's 'we?'"

Random sat up and scanned the memories in his head. It took concentration to look into the vast maze of memories to answer a specific question. "Joe was there, pointing at the paper as I drew...Alma was dancing and laughing...I think someone else was there but it's all kind of fuzzy." Random looked Will in the eyes. "It was also a very long time ago."

"Do you remember anything about what the Sisters told you? Do you believe that you were asleep for a thousand years?"

Random shook his head with a bit of confusion. "I don't remember anything about that. But I do remember coming up with the idea of the Glade." He slapped the stone on either side of him. "I was sitting right here when it finally hit me! I jumped up and flew to find a bald man in orange robes so I could share the idea with him. We talked for days about it in his house. We were good friends...but for some reason, I can't remember his name..."

"That would be Cho. He's one of the masters."

Random chuckled. "Cho...nice. That's not the name I knew him by, but Cho is a good fit for him."

Will threw his hands out in disbelief. "Wow, so you were there with Alma, dreaming this place up from nothing? I can't wait to take you to see her! She's my teacher, the one who leads my house of study."

Random wrinkled his brow. "I spoke with Saul on the ferry. He talked about these 'houses,' but I can't say the concept is familiar to me at all. They've broken the place up into divisions based on individual gifts?"

Will gave a nod. "Well, sort of, but each master also has a slightly different approach. Cho's house tends to get those who are in the biggest hurry. Given that his approach takes the most time and patience, I always thought it was a bit cruel. Alma tends to get most of the Movers, but there are people with all manner of talents. She's a brilliant teacher. She gets the people who are overly serious. Within a few years she has them all dancing like idiots."

"I have a hard time seeing you as too serious!"

Will's face went slack. "You didn't know me when I first got here. I was not the most pleasant person to be around. At first, I wanted to study under Harris. Most of the people who fly around like superman end up there. But from what I've heard, the study in his house can be a real of a son-of-a-bitch."

Random scanned his freshly recovered memories. "I don't recall knowing anyone named Harris."

Will laughed. "Are you telling me that you were here before Harris was even around? Wow, that's rich. If you had known him, I don't think you'd have a hard time pulling up a memory. I've met him a few times; he's pretty hard to forget."

"I guess they had to start dividing things up as it grew. I don't know if I would've been supportive of that approach; reminds me of sorting people into little boxes."

There was a sharp crack, followed by a tearing sound. Will grabbed his ears. Random looked across the stone bowl to the source of the sound. A barrel-chested man stood holding a walking stick, looking back at him.

The ruddy-faced man spoke with a sarcastic tone in his voice. "You would think dying would free you from the burden of bureaucracy, but it seems it even follows us beyond the grave."

Will sprang to his feet and planted himself in a firm stance. Random kept his eyes locked on the man and stood slowly, not allowing himself to blink. "Hello, Fabric. Good to see you again."

"And it's good to see you! You have more pep in your step than the last time I saw you. You seem to be making yourself at home." He gestured to the private balcony they stood in.

Will shot his eyes to Random, then back to Fabric. He relaxed slightly but stayed on guard. He remembered Alma's warnings about how unpredictable Fabric could be.

"I'm still getting my bearings, but I'm not as lost as I was when I arrived. Once again, thanks for getting me off the Square and sharing a meal with me."

Fabric's walking stick evaporated and he held his hands wide. "It was the least I could do. You were always a nice kid, ever since the first moment you stepped off the Rock into this carnival of madness. In many ways, I always liked you better than the rest of 'em." He reached into the inner pocket of his coat. Will tensed visibly, and Fabric froze. "And I see you found yourself a bodyguard along the way. Relax, son; I was just going to offer my old friend a drink." He took the silver flask from his pocket and extended it to Random.

Random stood very still as he spoke. "What do you want, Fabric? You never do anything without a reason. You helped me off the Square to settle a score with Erminia, that much I believe. What are you after now?"

Fabric shrugged and uncapped his flask. He took a swig and put it back in his pocket. "Everyone is so damn suspicious these days! I help you out of a jam, drop you off right near the Glade to get you started right, and I even go so far as to lead you right to the place where Vandal Square used to be before it went on the run. Even after all I've done for you, here you stand still assuming I'm up to something." He shook his head.

Random remembered the strong pull he had to choose the campsite and the drumming that had drawn him to the crater. "I've started to remember a lot of things, Fabric. One thing I remember about you is that you don't believe in favors."

Fabric nodded, not disputing the statement. "You also might remember that I love to watch chaos unfold for no other reason than that it amuses me. You, sir, are at the very center of a big swath of chaos headed this way!"

Random walked past Will and approached Fabric cautiously. "And what chaos is that, old man?"

Fabric smiled widely. "The very best kind of chaos, son. The kind with multiple layers, an uncertain outcome, and enough variables to make a bookie scream trying to figure out the odds!" Fabric put his hand on Random's shoulder. "Why don't I just let that rascal Joe fill you in on the details?"

With a sharp ripping snap that threw Will off his feet, Random and Fabric were gone.

: : BRIDGES : :

Joe sat behind the desk in his study trying to stay focused. He knew the ferry had landed by now and that Random was somewhere in the Conclave, but he would not allow himself to leave his house. The three keys were still on the blotter in front of him, strung on a simple leather cord. He absentmindedly pushed them around with his finger as he wrote with the other hand.

The tearing sound echoed through the courtyard and made him stop writing. He stood and quickly walked out to the catwalks to see who had decided to pop in unannounced.

Fabric stood in the courtyard with his hand on another man's shoulder. The tall man struck the hand away and stepped back. Fabric was looking up at Joe. The tall man followed his eyes and turned around to look up.

In many ways, Joe was glad to see Random's face. He was glad he didn't have to spend any more time locked in his study wondering what was happening. He was not pleased that Fabric had brought him here. From the looks of it, it had been against Random's will.

Fabric broke the silence with a voice that was altogether too loud. "You wanted me to keep an eye on him and let you know where he was. Well..." Fabric held his palm out in presentation. "...he's right here."

Joe really hated dealing with Fabric. He kept his eyes on Random. "Since you are here, why don't you come on up. I am sure you have some questions." Joe turned and went back into his study. He went to the desk and swept the keys into a drawer. He put the paper on which he had been writing on top of them and closed it.

He went to the couches in front of the hearth and stood looking at the door. The footsteps up the spiral staircase were not hurried. The fire had long gone out and only ashes remained. Finally, Random appeared in the doorway. Joe had forgotten how tall he was. Their last interactions had been in unfamiliar territory and mostly outdoors. Here, in a room they had both been in many times, he could see him in relation to items he saw every day.

Random crossed the threshold and moved toward the couches. Fabric came in behind, looking around at the items in the room. "Say, nice little hacienda you have here. If I weren't hopelessly addicted to wandering, I might consider spending a lifetime or so here." The two other men ignored him as they closed the distance between each other.

"Welcome to my home, Random. Please have a seat. We have much to talk about."

Fabric sped up his walk and came between them. "As fascinating as this discussion will be, I have more important things to do than listen to you two reminisce. I kept up my side of the bargain; I do hope you intend to keep your word."

Joe breathed a sigh. He was more concerned about how this looked to Random. "Very well; just a moment." Joe held his palm toward the door and focused his energy. After a few moments, a heavy wooden chest came floating into the room and settled at Joe's feet. He knelt down and opened the lid with a creak. He stood up holding the golden cylinder he had carried back from the Square for Tazir.

Fabric held his palms out and allowed Joe to place the object in them. He cradled it gently and brought the cylinder to his lips, where he gave it a delicate kiss. "So good to finally recover what was stolen from me." He placed the cylinder in the buckskin sack on his hip and turned back to Joe. "Pleasure doing business with you, kid. You two have a good time catching up." Fabric disappeared with little more than a pop.

Joe waved his hand and the wooden chest closed and hovered back out the way it came. Random held his palms out and focused on them. Two highball glasses with iced amber liquid shimmered into being. He offered one to Joe. "Scotch?"

Joe smiled and accepted the glass. "Thank you." They toasted silently and each took a sip. Wordlessly, they sat down on the two couches, facing each other.

Random took another sip and then spoke. "I remembered a lot the moment I stepped foot on the shore. In some ways too much. It was a mass of memories, in no particular order. I'm still sorting through them all."

Joe took a sip of his scotch. "I hope you remembered our friendship."

"Yes, some of it. I remember building this place with you. I remember the high hopes we had for all the good we could accomplish in the world." He paused. "I'm having the easiest time with the earliest memories, back when we first started. The rest of them are still hazy, like a camera that won't focus." Random put his glass down on the table. "So you made a deal with Fabric. Does Alma know about that? I know she never trusted him."

"No, she didn't, and no, she does not know I was in contact with him."

"What did you give him? If it's what I think it is, that's a pretty high price to pay him to babysit me."

Joe finished the scotch in one gulp and set the glass down. "The Recorder was originally his to begin with. One of his so-called 'students' managed to run off with it when she felt she had learned all she could from him. He taught her very well--so well that even he couldn't find her to get it back."

"Was it your idea to have him steal me away from Erminia?"

Joe shook his head. "That was his idea and definitely not part of my plan. Once I realized what he had done, I contacted him and struck a bargain. I had found his student and promised him the Recorder once you were here safely. As usual, no deal with him goes unpunished. He was not supposed to bring you to me like this. I guess he got impatient for his reward--also something I didn't predict."

Random picked up his scotch and sipped it. "And how does his former student feel about losing her Recorder?"

Joe smiled. "She was done hiding from him. She will be entering a body soon and starting over. Her only wish was that the Recorder be kept safe. I can think of no safer place than with him."

"So you didn't mention to her that you were returning it to Fabric's care? That's quite an omission on your part." Random finished his scotch in a large gulp.

Joe sat forward. "Random, none of this is important right now. What is important is that Erminia is on her way here. Knowing her flair for drama, she will fly Transit Square across the lake for maximum effect. There are events unfolding that will change the very nature of this world. I need you, Random. I need everything to be settled between you and me and, most importantly, I need you to stand back and not interfere with whatever wrath Erminia brings with her."

Random shook his head in disbelief. "Wait, how will she manage that? I thought you'd made it so that nothing could fly into the Conclave? Will told me you locked it down-- Oh, God! Will! He's in Petition Hall!"

Joe shook his head. "No he is probably on his way to find Alma. Don't worry about Will, he is fine. He is also correct; we locked down the entire Conclave long ago. But that barrier is no longer in Erminia's way."

"Why? What's changed?"

Joe sat back. "I gave her the master key."

Random stood and began pacing. He was confused and annoyed. "Who is this woman? Why the hell would you give her a key and invite her in?"

Joe put his feet up on the table and went into a full recline. "She was a talented student who arrived here and took the Conclave by storm. She threw herself into life here with joy and love for everything and everyone. Her life on Earth had been one of violence and bloodshed. She had no desire to return. The freedom of creation she found here was the life she wished to lead. In less than fifty years, she was an instructor with students of her own. She was Harris' star pupil. Before I knew it, she had captured my heart. For a time she lived here with me and helped design many of the programs we still offer to our students." Joe paused and looked at the hearth. The fire roared to life once more.

Random sat down again and put his arms on his thighs. "Something must've gone very wrong."

Joe took in a deep breath and let it out in a long huff. "Yes: my own arrogance. You often spoke of leaving souls at peace. It is why you created the Glade for all the soldiers and those who arrived here in pain from what they had lived through. I took it upon myself to see if I could cure what I saw as the problem, rather than just treat the symptoms."

Now it was Joe who stood and began to pace. His normal air of confidence was gone. He did not relish telling the tale. "Long before Erminia arrived, I started a project we called the Reshaping. If we could build anything we wanted here, why couldn't we build a better world to incarnate into? I sent souls back with specific missions. I looked beyond what was the best path for them as individuals. I sent them back with seed ideas, things that would inspire changes in the world, ideas to end conflicts and create innovations. I trained them hard here in the hopes that they would remember even a shred of it on Earth. I wasn't sure whether it would work, but I soon found that it was effective beyond what I could have imagined. However, the results were...mixed."

Joe had paced to the desk. He leaned on it with both hands. "When Erminia became my lover, she encouraged me to continue the Reshaping and expand it. With her help, we were able to design new programs to send back. The changes began to accelerate. We had some great successes...but also horrific failures. We justified every failure by telling ourselves that we were just not thinking large enough. I fueled the fire and one night..." He sat down behind the desk. "...one night, Erminia and I came up with an idea. We needed to generate a critical mass. We needed more than just the fraction of souls who found their way to the Conclave. We needed to reach those in the open Ether who would jump into any portal they might find in the wilderness and take their chances."

Random sat silently, his brow wrinkled as he listened.

"We came up with the idea of creating a black market, a place of fast incarnations to take the place of the open portals that are found in the wilds of the Ether. It would be a farce, a construct that we controlled. If we could just slow down those souls, seed them with ideas and send them back...if we could convince them, even in a small way, to listen to the leaders we were creating here in the Conclave, then we could cause changes on a global scale!"

Random finally found his voice. "You knew there was no God here, so you decided to appoint yourself as one?"

Joe sat up in his chair. "No, it was not like that; it was not a cult of personality centering on me. It was a group effort to make a difference. Everyone was involved. Alma and Cho, then Harris. It was an exciting time.

We presented the idea for the Square to the Council and they all agreed. The only dissent came from Harris. He liked the idea but he disagreed with my suggestion to have Erminia be the puppet master of our fake black market. He was her teacher. He warned me that she had never come to peace with the violent life she'd led, that she was not ready for such a role. I ignored his warnings. I thought I knew her better than he did."

Random shook his head in utter disbelief. "So you created Transit Square?"

Alma walked into the room followed closely by Will. "It was originally called Vandal Square, and it used to stay in one spot." Both men stood as she entered.

Will raced to Random and gave him a bear hug. "Glad to see you're OK. Where's that Fabric guy?"

"Long gone." Random turned to Alma. "So you agreed to this plan?"

Alma took a seat on the couch across from Random. He sat down, and Will sat down next to him. "Yes. I admit it was naïve. We didn't quite know what we were doing at first. But once we got it up and running, we started to see results immediately. Experiments we concocted here launched the Renaissance--"

"But they may also have accelerated at least one World War." All heads turned as Cho floated into the room, his legs folded in lotus position and his robes almost touching the ground. "We all acted with arrogance; what we view as our triumphs do not cancel out the other, negative consequences we unleashed." Cho took a moment to smile at Random and place his palms in prayer position.

Random mirrored his actions and gave a reverent bow. "Namaste, old friend. So they call you Cho now?"

Cho chuckled and gave a nod.

Will's head snapped back and forth as if he were at a tennis match. He was overwhelmed to be in this room with the leaders of the houses, and he was trying desperately to track what was being said.

Random turned back to Alma. "When did Vandal Square become...mobile?"

"It's good to see you again, too." She smiled. "We set Vandal Square up with portals, Shamans, everything that was needed. Erminia was supposed to be a figurehead. We sold everyone on the idea that she had defected from the Conclave because she had a better way. We demonized her publicly while still loving her privately. The ruse worked. She became our double agent, shepherding those who had no interest in growth without their knowing. The illusion was perfect...but we were all blind to the danger."

The room was silent. Will's head kept pivoting as he waited for the next person to speak. Finally he couldn't take it any longer. "What danger? What happened next?"

Alma smiled at him like a doting mother. "Erminia had come from a violent people during a violent time. She had been a princess and had regularly granted life or death on her whim alone since her teens. We discovered that old habits of sitting in judgment of another's fate are hard to break."

Joe spoke loudly from behind the desk. "I discovered it, quite by accident. I had full access to the Square through the secret tunnels. I decided to surprise her one day with an unannounced visit." Joe opened the desk drawer and pulled out the string of keys. "She was proceeding with the plan and offering gentle instruction to most of those on the Square. But she was also sitting in judgment of those she viewed as 'irredeemable.' I watched in secret as she instructed her Shaman to send these souls into the most tragic of circumstances. Souls already on the brink were born into horrific conditions as some sort of punishment for being inadequate, in her eyes." He dropped the keys on the desk. "I knew then that it had to stop. Even the woman I loved had become corrupted. I brought Erminia before the Council to answer for her actions."

Alma spoke to Random. "Joe refused to sit in judgment. He knew he couldn't be impartial. He left it to the three of us, and we agreed to dismantle the Square and end the entire experiment. Erminia was embarrassed and shamed in front of all of us. She couldn't even look at Joe. She left in tears. She felt she'd been betrayed by the man she loved. We didn't see the rage lurking just below the surface. By the next morning she'd convinced her followers in Vandal Square that the Conclave would move to attack them. In an extraordinary act of coordination, she had them rip the city from its foundations and take it on the run. That was the day Transit Square was born."

Will spoke in a whisper. "No shit?"

Random remembered the cold bitterness of the tiny woman on Transit Square, and her thinly veiled sadness. "And how long ago did you end this 'Reshaping' experiment?"

The room was silent. Cho giggled and drew Random's attention. "The Reshaping didn't end. It goes on to this very day. We tried to stop it, but it carries on under its own momentum even without our guidance, no longer under our control. We had already taught everyone here how to do it; they didn't need our approval to continue. Souls now Reshape with their own agendas. If you can think it, you can make it real."

Random was barely able to comprehend it all. "Wait just a second." He stood and walked over to Joe's desk. "Why the hell would you give this bitch the key?"

Joe sat up straight in a slow, controlled movement. His eyes were locked on Random and his voice had a menacing undertone. "Please do not call her that again." He let the silence hang and his stare let Random know he had reached a boundary. Joe took a breath and then answered the question. "I gave Erminia the key because this has to end. It's time for her to come settle her score. Her latest invention is this ridiculous 'Truther' rebellion that has people think we are hiding God from them. It was just a way for her to manipulate those who would rather have some divine being to guide them than face the void the rest of us do. Even though it has no basis in fact, the very question is turning souls against each other. Let her come. Let her bring all her followers to search for the god we are supposedly hiding. Let her take her vengeance on me. I won't have everyone else continue to pay for my mistakes." Joe sat back. "That is why it is important for you to stay out of it. You have to let her tear the entire Conclave to the ground, if that's what it takes."

Random stood very still. "This was the job you had for me? You fought to be the first one to meet me after my death so you could get me to come here and do nothing but watch the Conclave fall?"

Joe smiled widely and stood with a formal stiffness. "No, Random. The job I have for you is much more important. When the destruction is complete and the dust all settles, that is when your job begins. The canvas will be clean. I need you to build it again."

: : GUESTS : :

Erminia entered the main engine room of Transit Square wearing a skintight red skirt and a white linen blouse with an oversized collar. A matching red vest accentuated her breasts and framed the master key she wore as a pendant.

It had come to be called the 'engine room,' given its function in moving the city, but it was a dark mix of mysticism and mechanics. Great geared flywheels turned in lazy circuits as the massive iron rods connected to them converted the radial motion to the linear movement of pistons. The steam of industry mixed with the sweet smell of incense that rose from the many elaborate shrines nested among the forest of iron. The shrines held a collection of idols from every flavor of belief. Erminia ducked under the arm of a god with a monkey head and made a quick step to the right to avoid the small pool of black liquid that was leaking from a high-pressure pipe. Her heels echoed across the room as she navigated the knotted catwalks that wove through the pipes and valves of the engine room. She descended several sets of grimy stairs without slowing her brisk pace, despite her skirt and heels. She wound ever downward into the subterranean chamber, stepping over junction boxes, to be confronted by the eyes of yet another stone deity staring down at her.

She reached the bottom-most landing. The pipes continued to snake downward, but this was the lowest point that could be reached on foot. She straightened her skirt and walked up to the enormous man who sat on an immense purple cushion in the middle of the iron platform. He was truly a giant; he would easily pass thirteen feet if he ever stood at his full height. But he sat here in the engine room with his legs perpetually folded under him like one of the many stone Buddhas Erminia had passed. Even seated, he towered over her. His belly was round, his head bald. The flickering orange glow of the room showed her that his eyes were firmly closed. Her heels stopped clicking as she stood in front of him and craned her neck up to speak.

"Are you ready to fly me home, old friend?"

The giant remained silent. A tiny, spindly man came scurrying out from behind him and approached her like a dog in fear of being hit. "You said we had more time! He's gathering strength. We've never had so little time between jumps. You ask too much of him!"

Erminia kept her focus on the giant's closed eyes and ignored the man's protests. "We're ahead of schedule. All activity at the portals has been stopped, despite the protests of the Shamans and the whining of my dear citizens. The gates are sealed and those who'd wished to board are already moving away from the city."

The thin man kept bending over as he spoke. "But you said we had another day to prepare! We will still need to assemble the rest of the Movers here. He'll need every one of them for such a task!"

Erminia turned to the groveling being, and he winced as her eyes found him. "Every Mover on the Square has been summoned; they make their way here as we speak. He will have more help than he has ever needed in the past."

The frail man gathered the shreds of his confidence. "But it's still too soon! He needs more time to rest."

The opening of the giant's eyes was audible enough to draw their attention. The darkness of his skin made the solid white orbs in his sockets seem to glow by contrast. He continued to look forward with his blank, unfocused stare. His voice exploded across the hall, echoing off every surface. "I am ready."

Erminia nodded simply. "Thank you. Your support staff will be here momentarily." She turned back to the thin man cowering just out of arm's reach. "He will have a short time to rest once we arrive at the Lüder, but the Movers will stay here with him. Then we will simply be making a short flight rather than a full jump." She turned gracefully and headed back to the stairs to leave.

The man found another scrap of courage. "Do you know where we'll set down once we arrive at the Conclave? Those who have scouted ahead don't believe there's enough land to accommodate us..."

Erminia paused on a stair and spoke over her shoulder. "Then we will land in the lake itself. Once we arrive in the Lüder, seal off the passages below deck." She allowed herself a tiny smile. "We will be an island of change off the coast of their depraved little village." She continued up the stairs.

The tiny man straightened his spine as she disappeared around a corner and mouthed silent curses at her. He touched the giant's knee gently and started rushing around, making the space ready for the Movers who would be cluttering the deck soon.

• • • • •

As some of the massive pipes that snaked across the limestone began to groan and shake, customers came out of Genseric's to see clouds of steam begin to pour from the great central tower of the Square. Jared went to his balcony and cursed at the delays being caused for his new business. The open Square emptied as the crowds moved to the perimeter, clustering on the front stoops of buildings.

The crowds usually in the shadow of the city were gone and the gangplank had long been folded up. Jets of hot gas shot from the great inverted pyramid of iron that angled down from the main deck. With a deep rumble, the city began to rise. The joints of the landing gear rotated with the angry protests of tons of steel rubbing, accented by high squeals. The noise quieted for a moment as the city broke free of gravity and the gear hung limp from the now hovering mass. A deep bass rumble filled the air. The sharp hiss of steam and hydraulics echoed off the dark spheres of the private hells that towered around them. The landing mechanisms retracted, each at their own pace, folding into the rusted root structure of the floating city.

The sharp edges of the main decks pushed deep dents in the dark, swirling bubbles of the Hellocked worlds on all sides. They looked to be holding the city in a sticky embrace, either begging it to stay or holding it down by the throat.

Glimmers of light began to appear, silent bursts that danced from every point of the city. The number and frequency increased and the iron hulk was soon a flickering mass of flashing lights.

Then came the sound. As the lights collapsed together into a central flare, the ripping of the fabric of the Ether sent ripples over the surface of the private hells. In a sucking implosion of light, Transit Square departed. The dismal bubbles jostled slightly in the void it left as they rebounded from the violence and found their shape again.

The space between the bubbles rang with deathly silence.

· · · · ·

Erminia sat in the tower above the Truther control room. Several levels below, her staff scurried around the bubble that insulated her most volatile Recorder. Thankfully, he had been docile in the past few days, allowing her time to finalize the plan. The tower was near the edge of the deck and high enough to take in a good view of the Ether when they were at speed. She liked seeing the Ether streaming by when they were in mid-jump. It was a cloudy soup, but the points of light and incandescent pools of activity speeding past them loosely indicated their direction and speed.

Footsteps sounded behind her, climbing the spiral staircase. She swiveled in the large chair and saw Salvo enter the room.

"Everything is running smoothly. We're moving a bit slower than usual, but as far as I can tell--" he consulted the notepad hanging from his neck, "we should be arriving at Lüdertown within a few hours, our time."

"Good. Did we get any word from our people in the Lüder before we departed?"

Salvo consulted his notes. "They've set up an encampment on the southern arm of the city. That'll place them on the very edge of the city closest to where we will set down."

Erminia sat in thought for a moment. "Send word to the engine room. Ask them whether it is possible to simply hold altitude without dropping the landing gear. Once we arrive, we can just drop the gangplank to welcome the faithful. I will not need much time to unlock the gate."

Salvo raised his eyebrows at the request, but followed it with a nod. "I'll send word. Not having to set down and then take off again from a standstill may actually require less effort, as long as they don't have to wait long."

Erminia spun her chair gently and faced the windows looking out on the Ether. "I'll be quick. I have no desire to linger in the Lüder. I'm anxious to see my old home once more."

Salvo turned back to the stairs. He had become very familiar with Erminia's non-verbal cues over the years. He knew that she was done speaking to him.

"Salvo, just a moment." He turned back to her. She stood and walked over to face him. "Thank you for all your hard work recently. I couldn't have done this without you. I know it can be difficult to work with me at times. I hope you know that any unkindness you experienced at my hand was not...well, personal."

Salvo was stunned by the acknowledgement; he had never heard one from her lips before. "Well...I don't know what to say. Thank you."

She gave a rare smile. "It is I who owe you gratitude. After so many lifetimes, I finally have my chance. Much of that is thanks to you."

Salvo grew a few inches as pride found him. "We'll show everyone the truth they've kept from us! We will not be denied communion with the Divine any longer!"

She touched his arm. "The truth will be revealed. But they will deny it to the very end."

A flash of something remembered crossed Salvo's face. "I'll make sure that strike teams are ready to accompany you when we arrive. I just realized that all the Movers are in the engine room. I'll have them pulled from duty. They'll be well rested when we arrive at the Conclave."

Erminia turned away and walked back to her chair. She stood behind it and looked out the window into the Ether. Salvo touched the middle of his forehead with his index finger and gave her the traditional parting of the rebellion. "May the Truth find you!" He then bounded down the stairs to return to his duties.

Erminia spoke to the empty room and the open Ether. "The Truth...is about to be rewritten."

• • • • •

Trace relaxed in her new copper bathtub. It had taken only a few trades to convert Random's motorcycle into this elegant vessel. Its hammered sides were covered with the wonderfully flawed strokes of a master of metalwork. She had placed it on the private outdoor balcony Random had built for her. Delicate vines covered the trelliswork overhead and mottled light lay gently on her skin. The balcony had become her favorite sanctuary.

When the awful noise hit Lüdertown, the force of the sound threw her against one side of the tub and water spilled over the edge onto the cobblestones. She lay stunned for a moment, then jumped out, grabbed a towel and ran to the front balcony, leaving a trail of wet footprints across the wooden floors.

She pulled hard on the red cord and the pulleys spun easily. The roll-top awning opened completely, revealing the floating city that cast its shadow over the south arm of the Lüder. Trace had seen Transit Square once, but that had been over seventy years ago. She had forgotten how huge it was. It was much larger than Lüdertown, and its presence here right at their doorstep accentuated the difference.

Trace was overcome by the waves of emotion that radiated from the city. They hit her like aftershocks of the sound wave. She pulled on the red cords desperately to close the awning tight, hoping to insulate herself. It helped, but she remained crouching naked on the floor, taking deep breaths to regain her composure.

$$\bullet \ \bullet \ \bullet \ \bullet \ \bullet$$

Patrons lay sprawled out on the porch of the music store. The motorcycle parked in front had been knocked over in the blast and all the windows of the storefront had shattered. Hambone rushed out holding a flute in one hand to find the sun eclipsed by the shadow of the floating city looming over his little corner of the Lüder. The patrons stood one by one and joined him in silent awe of the mass of iron that hovered in silence.

A thin woman with short-cropped hair rushed out of the store and ran up to Hambone, a screech of panic in her voice. "What the hell was that! Look at the windows! Was there an explosion? Hambone! Answer me!" She had not lifted her eyes skyward, but soon followed the collective gaze of the crowd.

Hambone turned to her and grabbed her hand. He put the flute in her open palm and lowered his voice as he spoke. "Stay here. Mind the store and keep people calm. I'll be back soon." Hambone ran to the fallen motorcycle and lifted it back up on its wheels. With his swift kick, the motor roared to life. He spun the back wheel as he laid into the throttle. He sped through the streets of Lüdertown away from the hulking city. Pedestrians flinched as the bike roared past. He dodged the crowds with the skill of an expert rider.

When he intersected with the central road that ran like a spoke from city center to the mouth of the pass through the mountains, he took a hard left and the rear wheel broke loose into a slide. He regained control and accelerated, heading due west. He glanced to his left and saw a long ramp unfolding from the belly of Transit Square. Hambone shifted to a higher gear and added more speed.

Within moments he saw his destination approaching. He let off the throttle and dropped down a gear. The engine spun loudly as he wove through denser foot traffic. Soon he had brought the bike down to a crawl. He popped the clutch hard and the bike stalled. He jumped off it while it was still rolling, letting it fall unceremoniously to the ground. He left it where it lay and continued on foot, angling his lean frame past most, pushing some out of his way, without apology.

Hambone spotted the squat granite obelisk and found it already guarded by a stocky man with more tattoos than neck. The man wore a black kilt and held a long spear. Seeing Hambone approach, he gave a flip of his chin in recognition. Hambone slid up next to him and took up a matching position. They stood at the ready, shoulder to shoulder, their backs to the obelisk, eyes locked on Transit Square. Hambone spoke to the man without looking at him. "Just the two of us, Kanake?"

The thick-necked Samoan grunted. "Looks that way."

The obelisk was no more than four feet in height, its once sharp lines rounded and worn. It was the last marker souls passed as they made the trek to the Conclave. It was an unwritten ritual to touch it three times for luck.

The pilgrims in the area were confused and frightened. Some ran toward the Conclave while others sprinted back to the Lüder as they kept shooting quick looks skyward. Only Hambone and Kanake held their ground. The round plaza around the worn piece of stone became quiet, save the spinning of the motorcycle's front wheel as it lay where Hambone had dumped it. Kanake pointed the tip of his spear at the hovering city. Hambone struck a wide stance. His lean form showed deeply cut muscle across his back and bare chest. They scanned the sky meticulously.

"There!" Kanake pointed his spear at a tiny dot that launched from the deck of the Square and began to arc in their direction. It moved with banking turns and clear purpose. As the dark shape approached, they began to make out its nature. It was a flat rectangle. Waves rolled over its surface, but the corners were less mobile, pinned to globes the size of bowling balls that hung like weighted tassels. Three figures were visible atop the thing, and they bobbed as the shape moved toward Hambone and Kanake. The shape dove into the city and they lost sight of it for a moment. Then it reappeared above the central road, twenty feet above the deck and closing fast. The flying carpet made a final bank in front of them and descended with grace to hover just a foot from the ground.

Erminia stood between two kneeling, muscular women, using them as support. She wore a simple white robe that moved in the wind. Her long, dark hair, released from any binding, flowed behind her. When the carpet came to rest, her two muscled assistants sprang from it like cats and flanked either side. Erminia walked to the edge and jumped off with a girlish squeal. When she stood on the ground, she lifted her robe and looked down at her bare feet. She moved her toes in a grasping motion, digging them into the loose dirt. She looked to the sky, let out a laugh and spun around with her arms out.

"Oh, my! I never thought I would ever be so happy to return to this dusty little camp!" She stopped spinning and looked at the two men. "And what do we have here? Brave warriors defending the castle walls? I expected more of a force to be assembled."

Hambone spoke loudly as he watched the two amazons begin to circle him and Kanake. "Others are coming. You won't be disappointed with the welcome!"

She smiled wickedly. "They will not arrive in time. I only need a moment." She nodded to one of her guards and they both rushed in. Kanake swung his spear but his attacker jumped over it and locked her legs over his head, pulling him to the ground in a heap. Hambone waited patiently for his attacker and let out a booming yell when she was close, a blast of sound that sent the woman tumbling. Erminia was walking slowly toward the obelisk. She held her palm out and focused on a tent near the perimeter. It ripped from its stakes and flew toward Hambone. He turned to deliver another yell but the canvas wrapped him tight and took him off his feet, the ropes coiling and snapping like tentacles. Kanake had dropped his spear and was on his back trying to pry his attacker's legs off his head.

Erminia reached the obelisk. She lifted the necklace off her neck and held the master key in her left hand. She knelt down and pressed it against the stone that had been worn by the touch of countless hands. The point of contact with the stone glowed with a brilliant gold light. Fissures of light shot across the surface of the obelisk. Soon it was covered with a network of glowing cracks. Erminia turned the key counterclockwise and the integrity of the stone gave way. The obelisk crumbled into a pile of hissing rubble.

She stood and looked to the pass, smirking. "Knock, knock..."

Hambone still struggled with the canvas and ropes wound around him. Erminia walked back to the carpet and climbed aboard. The guard who had attacked Hambone staggered to join her. The woman wrestling with Kanake managed to flip him over on his stomach before releasing him and vaulting back to the carpet with the dexterity of a gymnast. The carpet rose quickly and sped away.

The mass of canvas stopped restraining Hambone and he finally broke free. He stood to watch the carpet ascend in a wide arc and make a beeline for the deck of the Square. He looked around for Kanake. The massive man knelt in front of the remains of the stone obelisk. Hambone walked over and put his hand on Kanake's shoulder. The tattooed face turned to him. Kanake's eyes were wet. "I thought we had more time to wait for backup. She had a key, Hambone! Where the hell did she get a key?"

Hambone looked at the pile of rubble. "It doesn't matter. Door's open now and there's no way to shut it again."

Kanake stood and they looked back to the sky. Transit Square was already moving. The gangplank dragged behind and lines of true believers in white robes clamored to get aboard. The Square hovered slowly around the outskirts of Lüdertown and made its way toward the pass, staying low, carving a line in the sand with the gangplank.

Hambone slapped Kanake on the shoulder to get his attention. "But that means anyone can fly into the Conclave! Come on, we can get there faster than that beast!"

Kanake retrieved his spear and ran after Hambone as the shadow of Transit Square continued to swallow the sun.

RESHAPING

: : CASTING STONES : :

Random stood at the top of the Temple tower, looking out over the lake. The early afternoon sun danced on the choppy surface of the water. The non-stop schedule he had kept since he arrived had made him miss the morning sunrise; however, the view from the tower was still impressive. He found himself once again in that strange, halfway place between the present moment and the echo of memory. He looked out over the Conclave with the eyes of a novice, yet in the same instant he had recollections of having stood here countless times before. The net result of these two sensations colliding was a slightly groggy dream state.

"They told me I'd find you here." The voice was resonant without being startling. Random turned to find a man in a starched, collarless shirt ascending the stairs. "It must be very satisfying to enjoy a vista you helped create. I figured it was time for us to meet. My name is Harris." Harris offered his hand in greeting.

Random accepted it in a warm handshake. "Good to finally meet you."

"The honor is mine. I have lived for lifetimes among so many of the structures you built, not the least of which is this very tower." Random still held the other man's hand in a handshake that should already have ended. His attention had strayed and he was looking past Harris to the lake. Harris was not used to being ignored. He spoke louder and tried to regain Random's eyes. "Of course, I've been an instructor here for a very long time. I was awarded an entire house of study..."

Random's attention locked back onto Harris and he gave the smaller man's hand a tight squeeze. Looking him directly in the eyes, Random spoke with intensity. "Your house of study focuses mainly on flying, correct?"

Random's face was much too close for polite conversation. "Well, it's broader than just that, but yes, most of the gifted fliers end up with me." Harris extracted his hand and managed to gain some distance. "What's the matter with you?"

Random pointed out to the horizon. "I believe we have guests." Harris followed the direction Random's finger indicated, to the farthest visible point of the lake. It was the spot where the ferry would round the corner and blow its horn to be answered by the tower.

Harris tracked his eyes back and forth until he spotted it. The distant buzz of a plane flying a few hundred feet off the surface of the water reached them as it banked hard and headed directly for the tower. It was still too far off to make out details other than that it was a biplane with bright yellow wings and a big radial engine, but the important part was that it was airborne over the lake.

The plane began to bank and waggle its wings in an obvious attempt to call more attention to itself. Harris shook his head. "Why would she have a plane buzzing in front to warn us?"

Random slapped Harris on the shoulder. "She wouldn't! Why don't you go see who's flying that crate? I'll let the others know!"

Harris leapt off the edge of the tower with ease and directed his flight into a perfect intercept course. Random ran to the stairs and met Joe running up them.

"We have incoming guests." Random led Joe to the edge of the tower and pointed at the plane. Harris had reached it and was flying alongside.

Will came up behind both Joe and Random. He squinted at the biplane and let out a laugh. "That's Hambone's plane! He's been fiddlin' with that damn thing for years! I never thought he'd get the stones to put it in the air."

Joe looked at Will. "You would be surprised what people are capable of when the times call for it." Joe turned to Random. "Will's friend has given us some advance warning, but I doubt the Square is far behind."

Alma came up the stairs. She watched the biplane circle around the tower. Hambone waved joyously at Will from the back seat. Kanake sat in the front, his tattooed face stoic and somewhat pale. Three of Harris's students had joined him in flying alongside the plane. They stayed with it as Harris peeled off to land expertly next to Alma. "The Square is right on their heels. They tried to protect the lock...but they didn't expect her to have a key."

Will watched the plane make a lazy curve along the line of the mountain. He turned to Alma. "How much time do we have?"

Joe walked away from all of them. He leaned on one of the coiling columns that held the roof over their heads. His voice rumbled deeply as he spoke to the horizon. "She is here..."

The sharp edge of Transit Square rounded the corner and the city cast its dark shadow on the water. It took several minutes for the large shape to fully reveal itself. Dark clouds traveled with it as it hovered near the horizon. Those on the shores of the Conclave yelled and pointed in disbelief. Those crowding the decks of the Square let out cheers of triumph and waved their arms. After a short burst, all sounds died down to silence. The two cities considered each other in a long stare. Joe scanned the spires of the Square, wondering where she stood. He could feel her eyes focused on the Temple Tower. He ran past the others with a devilish grin on his face. He raced over to a stone podium on the east edge and pulled the long bronze handle mounted to its side. With a deep reverberating note that shook the silence, the Temple horn sounded. Joe waited for a response from the floating city.

Joe pulled the handle again and let the Temple horn blow once more. Harris flew over to Joe and pushed him away from the handle. "What the hell are you doing?"

Transit Square began to move, Joe's eyes taunting it. It was still far off but it approached with surprising speed. Joe turned to Harris with a disturbing gleam in his eye. He jumped backwards off the tower and rolled into a steep dive. Joe pulled up and cut a wide arc as he flew over the Conclave and away from shore.

Harris snatched Alma off the top of the tower and went into a steep dive. He had lost sight of Joe but it didn't matter. He was behind Alma with his arms under hers and his chin over her shoulder. She barked directions to him over the sound of the wind. "To the right! Take me over the Hall!" She turned and watched the Square charging over the lake. She scanned the terrain below them and spotted her students taking positions along the tops

219

of the walls that surrounded Petition Hall. "Best of luck to you, Harris! Drop me! Now!"

He kissed her cheek and let her body fall away from him. She scanned below her as she fell, then, with a ripping pop, she vanished. He saw another flash of light on the ground and knew that she had joined her students. Harris looked out to the harbor and the angry city bearing down on them. He banked hard and headed down to the docks.

• • • • •

Random and Will stood alone on the tower and watched the Square steam toward them, floating just above the waves. Angry clouds of white smoke poured from the central stack. Will pointed down at the Conclave. Hundreds of souls soared over the streets like a swarm of insects while the ripping pops of teleportation echoed like fireworks.

Transit Square was picking up speed as it approached. Random was sure that it was going to ram into the Conclave in an impact that would assure the devastation of both cities. As it reached the mouth of the harbor, the leading edge of the Square rose and Random found himself looking at the twisted pipes on its belly. Then there was a great absence of sound. All the will that held the city aloft ceased. The engines had been cut, and Transit Square fell. Its mass dropped into the water, sending a tidal wave rushing toward the shores of the Conclave.

Hundreds of boats became either tumbling flotsam or airborne missiles. Docks unzipped and coiled into the air like whips. Much of the immense wave did not complete its final crashing impact, however. Random watched as huge sections of water came down but then arched back up and away from the shore before they could pummel the coast. Sprays of water arced hundreds of feet into the air and fell back onto the decks of Transit Square like hard rain. Some boats continued to careen into structures on shore, but many were deflected and cast back into the harbor. The remainder of the crashing wave headed for Petition Hall.

The Hall sat in the center of a vast plaza. The high stone walls around the perimeter had stood for thousands of years. The wave of water and debris was corralled into the space by the hundreds of Water Movers who had rushed to their posts when the Temple horn had blown, thereby deflecting the force of the wave and protecting the bulk of the city. However, Petition Hall itself was the necessary sacrifice. The seventy-two limestone columns snapped one by one and the great dome broke like a heavy eggshell. The great mass of the statues was no match for the water. They were ripped from their footings as the water overtook them.

Soon the great plaza where Petition Hall had stood was a sloshing basin of water. Then, almost as quickly as it had advanced, the water started retreating toward the lake. Some structures held their ground and collected flotsam as the great basin drained. Random turned his attention back to the harbor. Transit Square was now a great iron island bobbing just off the coast. Luckily, the efforts of the Conclave's Water Movers had lessened the devastation, but much of the coast was in ruins. Alma had warned the Movers to be alert in the event that Erminia attempted to 'use the water' against them, but of all the possible scenarios they had gone over in the past day, causing a tidal wave by belly-flopping the entire city had not been one for which they had prepared.

• • • • •

The lower Harris flew, the thicker the air traffic became. Thousands of his students buzzed the streets, picking up others and heading off to higher ground as they watched Transit Square fly in. The students had practiced hard; he swelled with pride as they performed flawlessly. He saw a woman run out of a building right near the shore and shuffle back and forth in the middle of the street, looking at the sky in utter confusion. He dropped down next to her and she jumped at his sudden arrival. "We need to move!" She nodded and he stepped behind her, scooping her up by her arms and launching them both into the sky. They saw Transit Square drop its full weight into the quiet harbor just as they cleared the rooftops.

"No!" The woman screamed so loudly it made Harris flinch, but he gripped her to him more tightly and accelerated. The water displaced by the metal city launched a wave over a hundred feet high.

Harris watched the line of Water Movers who stood bravely on the coastline to greet it deflect the bulk of the wave, curling the water skyward, redirecting its energy rather than fighting against it.

He raced to gain more altitude, but they were too close. The vertical spray of water hit them with merciless force. He lost his grip on the woman as the wave slapped them and launched them another fifty feet into the air. Harris searched for her as he tumbled, but could not spot her. He tried to gain altitude but had lost track of the horizon. By the time he realized he was shooting down instead of up, the curl of the wave had caught him. Tons of water folded over his tiny body in a cataclysm of sound followed by silence and darkness.

• • • • •

Harris saw light in front of his eyes and felt his cheek pressed against cold steel. The world was soft and out of focus. He rolled to his side, spitting up water, his body racked with pain. His vision starting to clear, he rolled onto his back to see a thick-muscled man in white looking down at him. His face was a study in severe angles. The man looked off to his left and called out to someone. "Here! One fell from the sky!"

Harris could hardly move. He had bounced hard against a solid object. Dazed, he tried unsuccessfully to turn his head. When he couldn't move his arms, either, he realized that the man in white was restraining him.

A woman appeared in his field of vision. She had dark hair, pale skin and sharp features. The bridge of her nose was kissed with a hint of freckles. His eyes widened as the wave of recognition hit him harder than the water had. He only managed to force one word past his lips. "Erminia...!"

"Well, Harris! How lovely it is to be greeted in person by my former teacher. You have saved me the trouble of looking for you. I have a very special gift for you, a special thank-you for the kindness you extended to me, so many lifetimes ago." She nodded and Harris found himself lifted to his feet. Pain shot through him. He attempted to struggle but he was having problems even holding his head up. His sagging head watched the ground; the iron deck he was being dragged across suddenly changed to a pure, glowing white.

When he saw the shimmering liquid, he realized what Erminia had planned for him. He used the last of his strength to lock his arms around his captor. The muscular man attempted to peel him away but Harris had him in a true death grip.

Erminia walked up to the struggling pair with a look of disgust. "I am sorry, my brother; sometimes sacrifices need to be made." With a swift kick she knocked both Harris and the muscular man into the shimmering pool, where they vanished in a blue flash of light.

The other disciples gathering on the deck stood frozen. Erminia turned to them, her head bowed. She raised her voice to be heard by the hundreds of true believers in white robes who had witnessed her action. "The sacrifice our brother has made is an important one." She spun slowly and looked them in the eyes. "We have eliminated a member of the Council before even touching the shore of the Conclave! That he was delivered to us is a good omen, a sign! Our brave brother's sacrifice shall not be in vain! Fly now and let the truth be revealed!"

A great chorus of shouts came up from the Truthers as they climbed aboard the white discs and began to float off the deck and toward the Conclave.

Erminia sat on the edge of her disc as the five members of her personal strike team boarded and positioned themselves around the central vessel of glowing liquid Ether. She spoke to herself with glee. "Let's see now, where would I find Alma's little boy-toy..." She scanned the devastated shoreline. "Ah! There's his boat!"

She kicked her feet playfully and the white disc began to move toward the ferry. Soon they were being buzzed by the Fliers of the Conclave. Erminia navigated the disc and would point at them as they soared over. Heavy weights would appear, chained to their ankles, and the Fliers would plummet. As they fell, the closest white disc would rush underneath to catch them. One moment the souls would be airborne, and the next they would be falling into a shimmering pool of liquid, bound for a birth they did not have the luxury of choosing.

: : RETRIBUTION : :

Random and Will finally turned from the scenes of destruction to face each other. Will opened his mouth to speak, but the sound of a large structure collapsing made both of them turn to find the source. "There!" Will pointed down the shore. The massive ferry that had transported them and countless others across the lake lay on its side over three hundred feet inland. It had landed on one of the lower terraces and shattered the outer wall of a round dormitory. It shifted again, emitting another loud groan. Near the edge of the terrace, it was in danger of sliding down to the next one below it.

"Dammit!" Will paced back and forth and bounced on his heels. "Saul is in that thing! Why can't I teleport or fly like so many others!" Will turned to Random in desperation. "Can you fly us down there?"

Random's eyes shot back and forth rapidly. "I never had the knack for flying..." The ferry was nearly half a mile away. Random set his feet and unfolded his arms in a purposeful motion. "...but I can get us down there."

Will stepped back as thick bars of steel grew from the stone deck like vines. The sprouting metal wove together into an arch of truss work. Thick steel plates formed like feet and bolted themselves violently into the stone, releasing clouds of dust. Will saw two small glimmers of light two feet in front of Random, where his eyes were focused. Thin strands of metal wire were moving, folding, and braiding themselves into thick cables. Will saw Random's mouth move and his head nod as he counted silently. The cables grew to three feet long, weaving themselves ever longer. Random reached out and took hold of the two hovering cables. In a burst of sound and light, the braided metal lines shot out from the tower. Random's feet stayed planted

225

firmly as he held the ends of the cables, which shot like bullets toward the ferry. As the length of the metal lines passed hundreds of feet, they began to sag under their own weight. Great iron towers sprang from the ground to meet the cables, supporting them as they continued to race to their destination. Tower after tower sprang up. After the fifth tower rose, the cables made a steep dive to the ground near the ferry. A flash of blue light announced their arrival.

Random stepped back and gently released the ends he'd been holding. In flashes of blue-white light, steel supports quickly coiled down to grip them and lock them into place. Above each cable, complex mechanisms began to form: wheels, gears, pulleys and hooks. The light faded and Will saw two rolling trolleys resting on top of the cables. Random walked over with purpose. He waved his hand and body harnesses appeared on both Will and himself. He walked over to one of the trolleys and clipped in, using a large carabiner attached to the chest point of his harness. He nodded for Will to do the same.

Will scampered up to his trolley and copied Random's actions. Random stopped him once and untwisted a line. "OK, so this handle is your brake. Gravity takes care of the rest." He rolled the trolley back and forth. "I did this in Costa Rica once. Ever ridden a zip-line before?"

Will gave a deep laugh. "Nope! Race you to the bottom!" Will and Random ran to the edge and lifted their legs, dropping their full weight into the harnesses. The wheels of the trolleys spun and hummed loudly as they shot down the zip-lines. They tested the brakes but then allowed their speed to increase. Before long, Will had a considerable lead.

As they sped down the lines, Random looked out into the harbor. Hundreds of white discs were hovering off the deck of the Square and floating over the Conclave. The discs each held five to ten Truthers in their signature white robes. There were shimmers of light in the center of the discs. Random was disgusted to see them floating in like self-proclaimed angels even before the water had finished retreating. He released his brake completely and tried to catch up to Will.

Within moments, they had passed the fifth tower and were angling sharply downward. Random pulled hard on the brake as the ground came closer. Will had unclipped his harness at about ten feet and jumped the rest of the distance, finishing in a forward roll as his trolley slammed hard into the ground. Within moments he was on his feet and running to the ferry. "Saul! Can you hear me?! Saul!"

Random brought his trolley to a full stop and unclipped only after his feet were both on the ground. The ferry lay on its starboard side. Out of the water, its great mass was even more apparent. Its shallow keel had a large weight at the base that had acted like a wrecking ball when it had impacted the outer wall of the round dormitory. Random could hear Will shouting Saul's name but had lost sight of him. As he walked around he found himself stepping in sinkholes that left him knee deep in the wet muck. He followed Will's voice.

The top two decks of the ferry were cantilevered over the edge of the wet terrace. The only thing keeping the vessel from dropping the remaining fifty feet and crushing the dormitory on the lower step was the weight of its keel lodged in the rubble. The waterfall that cascaded underneath it was not helping. The muddy ground was eroding fast, falling off in great chunks.

Random spotted Will climbing out of the wheelhouse on the top level of the ferry. He had Saul over his shoulder in a fireman's carry. The boat shifted sharply and dropped Will to his knees.

Random looked around in a panic and began to talk to himself. "It won't hold...the edge is too unstable... Rock. I need solid bedrock." He focused on the lower terrace. All of his hair stood on end. He held his palms out and a rectangle of granite the size of school bus appeared floating in midair. He dropped it at the base of the waterfall and had conjured a second one before it came to rest. Block after block, Random laid three rough courses of huge bricks to form a rough wall that rose to meet the ferry. In a final stroke, he created a granite wedge that drove itself into the remaining space between the ferry and the top of his improvised wall. The wet ground gave way but when the craft fell, it was a distance less than a foot. A few of its banisters splintered against the granite, but it came to rest.

Will had regained his footing. He climbed down the ferry, Saul unconscious over his shoulder. Random helped them reach the ground safely. He and Will carried Saul to a raised patch of muddy grass to lay him down. Random looked to Will. "Is he...well..."

"Dead? Well, yes, but aren't we all?" Will gave him a slap on the shoulder. "We may all be dead, but pain still hurts. Looks like he took a heavy smack to the head. He's just out of it." Will shook Saul a bit. "Saul! Can you hear me, brother? Wake up, buddy!"

Saul stirred somewhat and moaned, but his eyes remained closed.

A quivering hum filled the air, the sound deep and traveling in waves. It was unpleasant and made them wince. The white disc crested the ridge and hovered over to them. On board, five muscled Truthers stood encircling a shimmering pool of liquid. Erminia sat on the edge, her legs dangling off the edge like a precocious child.

"Oh, would you look at this! This day just keeps getting better!" Erminia cackled and held her palms out. Chains shot out of her hands and encircled Random and Will, knocking them back twenty feet.

Two of the Truthers sprang from the disc and landed near Saul. He was still stunned but had rolled onto his side. The Truthers took hold of him under his arms and started hauling him back to the white disc, dragging his legs through the mud.

Will struggled against the chains holding him. He watched, powerless to help, as his injured friend was dragged away. Then Will opened his mouth. He released a sound; it started as a yell but then focused into a noise that was shocking and alien. The burst of sonic energy was targeted at Erminia. She rolled to her side instinctively and it struck the four remaining members of her strike team still standing aboard the disc. All four were knocked backwards, off the disc and over the side of the terrace.

Erminia laughed and pointed at Will. A red cloth appeared and wrapped itself over Will's mouth. "You are a noisy little sheep, aren't you?" She nodded to her men to continue. They dragged Saul to the edge of her disc's glowing pool. Erminia looked at Random. "Now watch closely, because I need you to be able to recreate every detail for my dear friend Alma. Let her know she should not have played so hard to get with the ferryman. You never know when you will run out of time." She nodded to the muscled Truther, who twisted Saul's arm behind him savagely and pushed him head first into the shimmering pool of liquid.

Erminia laughed. "And there he goes! Back to Mother Earth to make a fine young son for...someone."

Random screamed. "What have you done?! Where have you sent him?!"

Erminia giggled. "That is the best part: I have no idea! It is just like the old days! I just opened up some portals and let Lady Luck do her worst! I would think you would approve, Mr. Bridges. It is completely random."

The disc rose as Random and Will struggled against the chains. Erminia pointed at Will, whose face was as red as the cloth that bound his mouth. "Remember to tell Alma all the details, especially the look on the ferryman's face when I tossed him back to the Rock. As for you, Mr. Bridges, you may want to reconsider coming to work for me. I will have so many new positions to fill once I take over."

The disc accelerated away from them and headed toward the temple. The chains relaxed and they fought their way to their feet. Will ripped the red cloth off his face and released a scream that scattered some of the debris littering the ground. It echoed off the mountains, then faded to silence.

Random shrugged his chains off and watched the disk bearing Erminia join the many others headed toward the Temple. Will was shouting something, but Random had become deaf as his mind became deathly quiet and his other senses sharpened. He turned his attention to the hull of the broken ferry that had crossed this lake for over three thousand years.

"That will do." He said softly to himself. His own voice reverberated in his ears, but he was still oblivious to the rest of the world around him. He planted his feet firmly and focused the full force of his concentration on the ancient ferry. He could feel its resistance to changing. The permanence of its form had been reinforced by every passenger who had ridden it. But Random's mind was set in its vision and his purpose was driven by the rage that filled him.

The ferry began to shake. The wooden slats and rails tore away. The debris from the ground raced back to join the mass of wood and iron that was twisting, tearing, and ripping itself apart. The ferry became a swirl of movement and sound as the hull split down the keel. Swarms of smaller debris started clumping into larger masses. The new assemblages knitted themselves together with purpose and speed. Precision didn't seem to be their goal.

Will had stopped trying to gain Random's attention. He backed away from what had formerly been the wrecked ferry and joined students from the dormitory it had hit to watch the dance of materials reform themselves under the raw determination of Random's rage. Pieces of broken stonework from the dormitory joined the dance as the construction accelerated.

The mass began to move as a single entity. Debris continued to race to find its place in the new form as two large, jointed pillars got underneath the main center of gravity and lifted it skyward. The pillars straightened, forming legs that supported what had been the main hull but was now the torso of a human shape, a giant formed from the wreckage. Its head was the former wheelhouse that Saul had manned for so many lifetimes. Some of its windows were traced with spiderweb cracks in the glass. A bright orange glow came from within the head, as if a star had been trapped inside. The swirl of debris slowed as all the pieces found a place on the monstrous body. It stretched its new arms out wide. The cracked glass eyes of the wheelhouse head looked down on its crude hands and arms in a moment of quiet self-awareness.

"Here!" Random screamed loudly and held his arm high. The wood-and-iron golem's attention was drawn to the ground. It struck the wide stance of a man prepared to fight, the dropping of its huge feet making the ground shake. The giant lowered its hand to the ground. Random stepped aboard his creation to stand in the center of its palm. Random scanned the crowd of students watching and found Will's face among them. He motioned Will to join him.

Will only hesitated for a moment before running to join his friend in giant's palm. The golem stood in a fluid motion and lifted the two men to a section of deck that was now its shoulder. Random moved confidently to a staircase that led to a railed observation deck atop the wheelhouse. Will followed him and tried not to look down, as he was now very far from the ground. He was happy to reach the observation deck and held tightly to the sturdy, iron railings.

The look in Random's eyes was distant and intense as he finally addressed Will directly. "I don't care what this grand strategy of Joe's is. I will not stand here and watch her hurt so many."

Will nodded but said nothing. Random turned his eyes forward just as three white discs loaded with Truther soldiers approached the terrace where his creation now stood. The golem's arms swung with impressive speed and immediately began swatting the hovering discs from the sky. The Truthers were launched into the air. The liquid that had formed the portals at their centers was ejected from the vessels that had held it. Some Truthers took flight, some teleported, but several were swallowed by the liquid as it fell to the ground and simply ceased to be.

The golem stepped off the terrace with a stride that crossed a small ravine. Random guided his new pet toward the Temple, making small detours to knock more discs out of the air when the opportunity to do so presented itself.

: : PUPPETS : :

Salvo had coordinated the landing of most of the white discs in a perimeter, about a hundred feet from the outer walls of the Temple. The first part of Erminia's plan had worked flawlessly. They had pulled hundreds of Conclave students out of the fight by casting them into life. But the initial shock of the Square's arrival was wearing off. The students of the Conclave had organized and fallen back to the Temple. Salvo had commanded the troops to land after several of them had been knocked out of the air by Conclave Movers throwing large objects at them.

He was glad to see Erminia join them and assume command. He quickly touched his earpiece. "Raven, she just arrived at the east wall." He walked over to meet his General.

Erminia stood on her disc and spoke to the crowds of Truthers that cheered her arrival. "You have fought well, my friends. Now we will strike at the heart of our enemy!" She spotted Salvo approaching and hopped off her disc to the ground.

Salvo instinctively touched the notepad hanging from his neck as he approached Erminia. "There are groups holed up in some of the surrounding buildings, but the bulk of them retreated to the Temple, just as you predicted. We spotted large numbers moving toward the mountains, but we're not sure where they're headed."

Erminia shook her head as she looked to the sheer mountains. "Knowing their leader, I am sure he has a secret back door they are running for. No matter. That leaves fewer to oppose us."

231

Raven pushed through the faithful to join Salvo and Erminia. "We have the Temple surrounded, but they have sentries on the walls keeping us from getting any closer."

Erminia smiled at the young woman. "Thank you, Raven. Don't worry, they won't be able to keep us from the Truth. We must move quickly, before they have a chance to organize any type of--" The crashing sound of a white disc hitting the ground less than fifty feet from them interrupted her.

They turned away from the Temple to see the towering golem that had once been the ferry moving up the hill in their direction. Two white discs buzzed around it but kept their distance to avoid being swatted out of the sky.

Salvo jumped between Erminia and the giant. He kept his eyes on it but spoke to Erminia over his shoulder. "This is a problem! We won't be able to concentrate our forces on the Temple with this behind us!"

Erminia nodded slowly and looked to Raven. "He's right. I need to focus all my energy on a king defending his keep. You always told me that Mr. Bridges was not necessary to our plans. You claimed your talents were equal to or greater than his. Now's your chance to prove it, my dear. You need to slow him down."

Raven straightened her spine and held her head proudly. "I'll do more than that."

She turned to leave but Erminia caught her arm. "Be aware that he has a Screamer with him. Do not let a well-timed blast of sound catch you off guard." Erminia called to the short, muscled man still aboard her disc. "David! Take Raven where she needs to go. Follow her orders as if they were my own."

"Yes, Ma'am!"

Erminia touched Raven's shoulder gently and moved in close. "Do not underestimate Mr. Bridges. He may be out of practice, but if half the stories I have heard about him are true, he is both unstable and unpredictable. Strike hard and show him no mercy."

Raven nodded and began moving with purpose to the disc on which Erminia had arrived. It began to ascend the moment she and David were aboard. Raven stood tall in the center. David squatted near her feet and piloted the craft.

As Raven's disc approached the other two groups that had been harassing Random's golem, they broke off to join her. A thin man with dark skin addressed Raven as his disc hovered near hers. "It's faster than it looks! We don't know how to stop it!"

Raven kept her eyes focused on Random. "That's because you're not thinking big enough. Hold this position and follow my lead." Raven's craft moved to intercept the golem.

• • • • •

When the Truthers who had been buzzing around them broke off and joined the new arrival, Random could see a woman standing confidently on it. At first he assumed it was Erminia, but as it moved closer he began to make out the slim girl he had seen in the Truther control room so long ago. A white flag appeared in her hand and she raised it high above her head. "Stop, please." Random's voice was calm and low as he gave the order to the golem. It still managed to hear its master and come to a shuddering halt.

Will stood at Random's shoulder, gripping the rail tightly. "She's almost close enough. Give me the word and I can knock her out of the sky."

"I want to know what she has to say. They've staged most of their forces around the Temple. I rarely believe what an opponent offers up by choice, but I'll be able to get other information, no matter what she tells us."

Raven held the white flag high. Her stout companion held her legs, to anchor her thin body to the disc. She held her head proudly and kept her eyes locked on Random as they approached. The disc stopped just out of the giant's reach.

The golem shifted its weight in anticipation of slapping the disc out of the air. Random spoke to it again. "Hold...Hold...Stand your ground." It had been over a thousand years since he had brought one of his creations to life. He knew that whatever intention he had when he created it would drive its rudimentary personality and govern its choices. He knew that this creation had a core of rage and revenge. It was powerful...and dangerous.

When Raven spoke, her voice was close to them, an intimate whisper in their ears, despite the distance between their bodies. "That is quite a pet you've created, Mr. Bridges." The trick of sound made Will nervous. The man holding Raven's legs stood up, his eyes on Will. The moment Will released his grip on the iron railing, a sharp pop rang out. David appeared behind Will and wrapped his arms around Will's waist. With a second tearing sound, he and Will were gone. Raven laughed. "Now let's see how resilient your creation is!"

Raven raised her arms and all the loose debris from the ground at the golem's feet rose up and began to hurl itself at the giant's body. Rubble from a broken wall struck the giant's left knee hard. An overturned wooden cart flung itself against its head, showering Random with splinters. Several trees ripped themselves out of the ground and hit the golem's chest, pushing it down the hill slightly and almost knocking it off its feet. The golem adjusted its footing against the attack, dropping its back foot onto a section of roof that had been torn off a dormitory and now lay flat on the ground. Raven moved her arms back swiftly and yanked the roof section out from under the giant's foot. The golem stumbled and only kept itself from falling by catching its weight on a nearby building, sending up clouds of dust as the stone wall crumbled under its weight.

Raven laughed and her disc began to move north, down the slope and away from the Temple. "Your juggernaut's not too smart, is he?"

The golem regained its balance and began to chase the white disc with the laughing girl. Random screamed out orders for it to stop, but they were ignored by the enraged giant. Random held tight to the railing and scanned for Will. He could hear him using his sonic weapon, but couldn't see him. Will was locked in combat somewhere but would have to take care of himself for the moment. Random was cursing himself for losing control of this fight. The girl was using the golem's rage against it, luring it away from the Temple. For now, all he could do was hold on.

Raven led them into a rock basin at the foot of the sheer mountains. Her disc hovered out of the golem's reach. Once the chase stopped, Random was able to gain some measure of control over his giant, but it still paced, swatting skyward at the girl on the disc. Raven laughed and pointed. "Your lapdog seems frustrated! Maybe he's just lonely. Let's give him someone to play with!"

Raven brought her disc close to a rock ledge and jumped. She landed nimbly, then got down on all fours, pressing her hands against the rock of the ancient mountains. She mouthed words under her breath as her body went rigid. Small tremors began to shake the ground. The loose, scattered boulders in the rock basin began to move slowly, gathering into five groups.

Raven increased her concentration until veins began to stand out on her neck and across her left temple. The groups of rock stood as five misshapen soldiers, only slightly larger than an average man.

Random looked down from his high perch. He was not happy to see that she, too, could animate the material of the Ether. He was secretly impressed that she had managed to use the rock of the mountains. It was very old and extremely resistant to change. He made his body take a confident stance and laughed at her creations. "They seem a bit vertically challenged! Maybe they could stand on each other's shoulders!"

Raven's body relaxed and she sat back, exhausted by the effort it took to re-form the rock of the mountain. Her stone soldiers looked to her, high on the rock ledge. She summoned the last of her energy to speak to them. "Tear it...apart..."

The rock soldiers moved together and attacked the giant's left leg. Their granite hands tore into the wood and steel of the former ferry, shredding it into smaller pieces. Random's golem struck at them, but more debris broke off the giant's hands upon impact with the stone attackers.

Within a few minutes, they had reached the giant's knee and focused all their hatred on it. The golem managed to knock one of them off but was pinned in place by the sheer weight of the others. Random could hear the groaning of the steel and wood far below, but he could not focus on the stone attackers as his creation flailed violently. He caught sight of Raven once more as the other two discs arrived to pluck her limp body from the rock ledge. Then he heard the sound that haunts the dreams of any Builder. It was a tearing, groaning sound followed by a chorus of a thousand snapping twigs. It was the sound of structural failure. The giant's knee broke and Random rode the remains of his towering creation down as it came crashing to the ground.

: : THE TEMPLE WALLS : :

Joe stood on the top of the great round wall of the main Temple structure. The shadow of the tower above him had begun to point toward the battered shore as the day wore on into the late afternoon. Joe walked the rampart, watching the long line of white discs that surrounded his outpost.

He had watched the golem storm up the hill and then get lured off. Joe knew it was Random's work. Animating the objects he built had been a signature trait of his a thousand years ago. Joe was not pleased to see Random so quickly take up his former hobby. He hoped it would not rekindle Random's obsession. He wanted to speak with his old friend and remind him of the dangers of this practice, and how his obsession with it had ultimately driven him mad.

For the moment he could only focus on the Truthers organizing at the eastern wall. The mass of white-robes was gathering together into two large groups. They had abandoned their floating discs and taken to foot. About twenty of the Conclave's most gifted students had stayed to defend the Temple. The Truther air attack had been stopped when his students began knocking them out of the sky. He strained to find his former lover in the masses, but was not able to locate her from this distance.

Then the masses began to move. They did not attempt to mask their intentions. They simply began walking toward the Temple walls. They didn't march in formations like dutiful soldiers. They simply started walking.

The students on the wall with him began to run back and forth. His small team gathered around him, seeking instructions. Joe ignored their pleading stares and watched the mob of Truthers approach. The single door in the great round wall was on the south, but the two loosely organized groups were headed to the face of the east wall. What did they plan on doing when they got there? Why this wall? Why here?

The students gathered around Dawn and started shouting their questions at her as their panic rose. Dawn raised her voice with authority. "Enough!" Dawn walked over to Joe and touched him on the arm. "Sir, what do we do? Should we stop them?"

Joe knew that even the newest of these students could slow the crowd using rolling boulders, flying objects, or the classic defense of boiling oil down the Temple walls. Joe hesitated. What was Erminia doing?

Dawn grabbed Joe by the shoulders as if to shake him from sleep. "What do we do? They're about to reach the wall!" Joe shrugged her off and ran to the edge of the rampart. He looked down the wall as if to make sure there was not a door he had forgotten.

Dawn stopped waiting for permission and addressed the others. "All right, let's show them that we can defend our home! I want every Builder to have a Mover with them. Start by dispersing the main group and getting them to scatter. I'll be on the right flank. I need four…"

Joe turned around suddenly and his voice boomed with authority. "No! I need half of you to come with me. We need to get to Rechter Hall! They are coming directly through the wall where it is thinnest. They are ignoring the gate because, even if they breached it, they would be in the central courtyard. We would still have the higher ground atop this wall. If they break in there, they will be in the heart of the main complex." Joe turned to Dawn. "You are in charge up here. Try to slow them down as much as you can and then join us below. Remember, we just need to buy time." Joe ran for the stairs with a group of students on his heels.

Rechter Hall was a hub for the main hallways and chambers of the Temple. The sheer numbers of those faithful to Erminia's cause would find a way to knock a hole in the wall before long. She was exploiting her knowledge of the complex. She was also exploiting her knowledge about Joe's nature. She had commanded her followers to simply walk like lambs to the slaughter. She knew Joe's past lives, especially the one that haunted his dreams. She was betting that he would not be willing to stand on a castle wall and rain down destruction. She was right.

Time. All he needed was a little more time. He knew the Temple would ultimately fall. He was losing this battle by choice. Ultimately, he was choosing to also lose the war. It had torn so many things apart; now was the time to end it. The cost of opposing the Truthers any more would be paid by everyone over lifetimes. Laying down his sword and letting Erminia have her victory only required two things. He had to let go of the kingdom he had grown to love and he had to swallow his pride.

By the time Joe and the handful of students with him reached Rechter Hall, the outer wall was already shaking as unknown objects assailed it from the other side. The students with him took up positions behind the heavy furnishings adorning the large hall. The room was often used to settle disputes in town hall-style meetings. Sometimes instructors would meet with the Council here to go over the students they felt were ready to incarnate and the best families for those candidates. As the wall shook with another impact, Joe remembered a day lifetimes ago when he brought Erminia before the council and asked them to judge her for her actions. This was the room in which they had passed judgment. Joe realized that Erminia may be breaking into this very room for what it symbolized to her, rather than its strategic placement in the complex.

The large stones in the wall began to jump and move independently, breaking its smooth plane. Whatever was striking the wall would soon breach its integrity. The students tensed as they anticipated the final blow. Instead, a thick blanket of quiet fell over the hall. They waited.

Just as they began to relax, the wall exploded inward, showering the room in a thick hail of rubble as the stones of the Temple wall gave up their fight. Clouds of pulverized stone, illuminated by the late afternoon sun, obscured the view of both the invaders and the defenders. Pebbles fell like hail as the cheers of the Truthers outside rose up in a roar.

One of the students in the hall broke cover and stood up defiantly to greet whatever might enter. She held her hands out in front of her and focused her energy. A mass of water shot from her hands and washed across the floor. It was a wave of liquid that carried loose debris with it as it filled the opening and drenched the battlefield beyond. The student continued to create the water until her strength waned. Her body became limp and the powerful flow became a trickle. Another student was there to catch her weight and keep her from falling. Joe guessed that the girl had never before attempted to create so much water at once. She had given all she had.

The triumphant cheers of the invaders had been replaced by screams from outside. Another of the defending students stood up and began re-forming the rubble into rough stones, working to replace the masonry to fill the massive hole. Before the new wall could gather itself into a significant barrier, it was blown apart again as one of the white discs came crashing into the room like a battering ram.

Truthers spilled in around the disc. The first invaders were knocked back, but their numbers were too great. Soon they were in the room, filling it with the sound of teleportations and crashing objects. Joe saw Dawn leading her group down the stairs to join the battle. She was forming chunks of granite out of thin air. The young Mover with her was launching the rocks she created at the invaders as fast as she could imagine them.

He turned to the opening and saw a more organized force entering in the wake of the initial wave, including a lanky man with a note pad swinging from a chain around his neck. Despite his awkward appearance, he moved as a captain of troops. Joe heard a brutal rip of a teleport followed by a horrified scream. He watched as Dawn was dropped from high in the room and fell into the pool of liquid Ether in the center of the white disc. Her scream was silenced as she left the world of the dead for an unknown birth.

Joe stood up and spoke in a voice that shook the room. "Enough! I am here! Come for me!" All action stopped as the booming voice echoed inside the heads of even those outside the wall. Joe pointed at Salvo. "Tell her to come find me and face me alone! She will know where to look!"

A ripple of electricity danced through the hall. Bolts of energy sparked off the Conclave students defending the room and traced their way to the students rushing down the stairs to provide reinforcements.

The sound that followed was nothing short of an explosion. Salvo and his entire team were blown away from the building and their bodies launched skyward. The hole that had been knocked inward doubled in size as the force from within the hall sent stones hurling through the air to join the bodies of the Truthers.

Joe had grown tired of stalling. He had grown tired of watching the students they had taught peace in the midst of a battle. In a single blast of raw focus, he had teleported them all away with him, sending shockwaves across the Ether with the force of his intention. The blast had knocked the army to its knees. The quiet that followed lingered like mist.

: : REUNION : :

Joe sat with his legs crossed in the courtyard of his home and waited. He was facing the lone wooden door and controlling his breath. The door began to shake, jumping on its hinges and rattling against the latch. The wall shook and puffs of dust shot from the mortar between the bricks. In a single violent burst, the door and several feet of stonework on all sides of it broke loose and flew away from the building, leaving nothing but a ragged hole. Joe sat quietly, watching his front door tumble down the slope in front of his sanctuary. The bright light of the day streamed through the cloud of dust and across the flagstones of the courtyard. He waited.

The silhouette that walked into the space was petite and shapely. The light behind her made the white robe all but transparent. She walked in with the grace of a queen, stepping over the rubble. She stopped twenty feet from him and put her hands on her hips. Her toes hung off the edge of a large flagstone and wiggled in the moss that surrounded it.

"Hello, Erminia. Come right in. Make yourself at home." Joe sat very still as he spoke.

She shook her head. "Arrogant, until the very end." She crossed her arms and lifted her chin high. "That was a nice trick you pulled at the Temple, teleporting an entire group without being able to see them all, let alone be in physical contact with them." Joe sat motionless, offering nothing to her in response. She grew impatient and continued. "You are in much better shape than the last time we spoke. I still have no idea how you managed to get off the Square. I was sure I had that room sealed, but you always were a clever rat."

241

Joe moved his hands off his knees and folded them in his lap.

Erminia sniffed loudly. "Whatever passage you weaseled your way out of, I am clear it is just another one of the many secrets you kept from me. Was it the same one you used to spy on me before you slunk back to the Council?"

Erminia had begun to pace slowly. Joe followed her movement with his head, but did not respond.

"I heard your message, that you wanted to 'face me alone' and that I would know where to find you. It took me a while to realize you would be sentimental enough to come here. I searched for you in the Temple after I captured it but was surprised to find the place almost empty. You weren't there to see me tear the room where the Council sat in judgment of me apart, brick by brick. That was a small disappointment, but overall it was still very satisfying."

Joe nodded and dropped his eyes to the floor. "I have thought about that day more times than I can count."

Erminia stopped and spun on her heel to face him. "Really? Have you now?!" Her tiny body was rigid and her voice had raised almost to a scream. "I have also thought about that day! The day that the man I trusted more than anyone else betrayed me. The day you sat by and let them all judge me like a criminal!" She raised her arms and the delicate spiral staircase ripped out of the ground, taking the overhead catwalks with it, and launched skyward through the open roof of the round building. A muffled crash could be heard a few seconds later as it fell back to the ground somewhere outside.

Joe did not move or even blink. "Yes, Erminia. I have thought about it. I have had just as many years to consider my actions as you have. You are right to call me arrogant, and it is accurate to label me judgmental."

Erminia regained her composure and took in deep breaths. Joe unfolded his legs and slowly stood. She stepped back and clutched the master key that hung on the chain around her neck.

Joe shook his head gently. "I have already taken too much from you. I am tired of fighting. I am tired of everything. My heart breaks to see the anger in your eyes knowing that I was the one who put it there. I was so caught up in playing God that I abandoned the most important gift that had ever been given to me. I took your love for me for granted. For that, and so many other things, I am truly sorry."

The structure above them had been compromised with the central staircase and catwalks gone. Several heavy wooden beams broke loose and started to come down on top of them. He held up his hand and they froze in midair. His eyes held hers in an unblinking stare. With a flick of his wrist, he sent the beams crashing against the wall, destroying a delicate outdoor table in the process. "Erminia, I am so sorry. You were blamed for something that was not your fault. I do not deserve your forgiveness. When you took the key from me...well, at first I was furious. But then I found myself relieved. I knew you would come here seeking vengeance. I realized that I would rather suffer your wrath than spend another day carrying the guilt for what I had done to you."

He stood just an arm's length away from her. He reached out and took her wrists. She flinched slightly but then allowed him to touch her. "I took everything from you. Your whole world crumbled that day. Now I stand in the ruins of what was my dream. Destroy whatever you wish. Strike out in whatever way you need to, to heal the wound I caused in your heart. I would rather see everything crumble than spend another day knowing that you are in pain."

Her bottom lip began to tremble and she dropped her eyes to the ground. When she spoke, her voice was tiny and barely audible. "Why did you leave me alone?"

He took her hands and pressed her fingers to his lips. "Because I was young, stupid, and blind."

She kept her eyes on the floor. "I have wanted to hear you say those words for hundreds of years. I have dreamed over and over of how I would hurt you and the kind of destruction I would bring to this place. Now that I look at you..." She raised her eyes to meet his. She shook her head. "As much as I might want to, Joe, I don't know if I can ever forgive you. In fact, I know that I can't. You hurt me too deeply. I don't think there is any way to erase all that has happened."

Joe took in a deep breath and waited just a moment before he spoke. "Actually, there is one way."

She cocked her head and wrinkled her brow. "What are you talking about?"

"We could leave this place. We could go back to the world together."

Erminia pulled her hands away and stepped back to consider him. She shook her head as if to make sure her ears were working. "You said you would never enter a body again. Your dream was to be the Architect of the Ether until one day you could ascend the same way your teacher had. You said there were no more lessons for you to learn on Earth."

Joe scoffed with a tiny smile. "I think that statement proves my arrogance beyond any doubt. I miss the way you used to look at me. I miss the love and trust we used to have between us. You are right when you say you could not forgive me. The trust we had is forever broken. I am willing to wipe the slate clean." He stepped closer to her. "Look at Random! Talk about a soul who had a long line of dark memories. Yet look at him now! He has been reborn after his time on Earth."

She held her arms out. "And what about all of this? What will we come back to when our lives are spent?"

He walked to her and took her hands in his again. "Leave that to someone else. Isn't that what you always used to say to me?" He smiled at her lovingly. "As soon as I escaped and made my way back to the Conclave, I spoke to Cho about it. He found us two families. The fathers have been friends since boyhood. The two mothers are set to give birth at almost the same time. They are not the richest or the smartest, but the two families have adopted each other. They would love nothing more than to see their children fall in love. We could meet again as children. Imagine what we could accomplish together!"

She stared at him with her mouth open. "You are insane! Now you want me to go back to Earth with you? Now?! I am not just your doting lover anymore, Joe! I became the true leader of that city the moment I ripped it from the ground. I cannot just leave them all. The people on the Square trusted me and followed me to war. They are expecting me to show them the truth the Conclave has been hiding from them."

Joe walked past her to the gaping hole where the door used to be. "I understand. If you want to rule over this world, you are welcome to it. Tell them anything you want. Invent a God if you have to. But I cannot go on like this, Erminia. I will not fight you anymore. With or without you, I have decided to go back. Everything is ready; Cho is at Windmear's Portal right now. I will wait there for the next hour. I hope you will join me. If not..." He walked outside and then turned back. "If not, then this is goodbye. Goodbye, my love."

Joe's silhouette was swallowed by the bright light of the day. Erminia stood in the middle of the crumbling courtyard.

The sound of the tearing of the Ether let her know that he had left.

: : THE PORTAL : :

Cho stood in front of the simple adobe building that housed Windmear's Portal. It was on one of the highest and most remote terraces. The canopy of trees shielded it from the chaos that still tore through the Conclave, but the sound of teleportations echoed from the canyons and white discs zipped over the tops of the trees.

Joe appeared in the clearing. He stood for a long moment wringing his hands before dropping to his knees. Cho walked over to him. The monk reached under Joe's chin and lifted his face so he could see his eyes. Cho gave him a loving smile. "Will she be joining us?"

Joe looked over his shoulder to the clearing. "I am not sure…but I hope she will consider it. I have hurt her very deeply; I can see why she does not want to trust me. I told her I would wait for an hour. But either way, I have to go back; I cannot take the thought of her being in pain any longer." Joe composed himself and got to his feet. "Is everything ready?"

Cho nodded. "Yes. There's been a flood of souls returning to Earth, but I was able to shield the two we found. Come inside; we need to get you prepared."

The monk opened the door and led Joe in.

The clearing was silent. After a few minutes, Erminia stood up from where she had hidden herself. She had always been one of the very best when it came to teleporting. If she wanted to, she could plow through the Ether and come out with a sound no louder than the tearing of a sheet of paper. In

247

which to storm into the Conclave. She had always pushed aside the thought of what she would do with them afterwards.

The old woman became agitated again. "The window's closing! We must act soon or we will lose the opportunity!"

Joe sat on his knees stoically. His voice was almost mechanical. "I will not break another promise to her. I will wait for an hour. If the time comes and she has not arrived I will go back alone."

The old woman stammered. "You don't understand! They'll both be gone by then."

"If she does not come, it will not matter. I will take any body that chance would give me."

Erminia stood up quickly and made everyone in the room jump. "You would toss your soul to the wind? No! You stupid arse! I will not let you waste your gifts on a low birth to some gutter trash!" Erminia walked over to him and held out her hands. He took them and she brought him to his feet. "We are royalty, my sweet. We were made to rule others and be served by them. I will go back with you just to make sure you never forget that!"

The old woman went tense as she looked into the pool. "The time is now! You must go now!"

Erminia grabbed Joe and kissed him. He took her in his arms and they jumped feet first into the shimmering pool. When the key draped around Erminia's neck hit the liquid, a blinding white light filled the room. Slowly, the pool faded back to a warm, golden glow.

The old woman waved her hands over the liquid and stared hard into it for many minutes. She sat back and released a deep breath. "They have both made the transition."

From the darkness in the back of the room, a man in a thick robe emerged. "Well, of course they did. I don't see why you found it necessary to be so dramatic about it." The man pulled the hood of his robe back to reveal his shiny bald head.

The old woman chuckled at the wiry man. "It's been many a lifetime since I've seen you, Otto, but you're still a son-of-a-bitch."

Otto laughed a wheezing laugh. He dropped the robe off his shoulders as he turned back to the darkness from which he had emerged. "Well, I stand corrected. I never thought you'd be able to keep your promise to her. I'm impressed."

From the shadows Joe emerged. "The family that Tazir has just joined is a very high birth. If I did actually have any intention of returning to Earth, they would be a fine choice. Erminia has also found a place where she can be nurtured. The world has become a very different place in the last few thousand years. I have a feeling it will be to her liking."

Otto pulled his red bowler cap from the folds of the robe and dropped it on his head. "Yeah, as long as she doesn't become a dictator. What was all that 'we're royalty born to be served by others' crap?"

Joe walked to the edge of the pool and stared down into it. "She was royalty, Otto... Long ago. Her teacher was right; he told me a million times that she lacked humility and compassion. He often said that a lifetime as a common person would do her a world of good. Now we have the chance to test his theory."

Otto shrugged and moved to the curtain. "You mind if we continue this conversation outside? I'm never comfortable standing too close to one of these things."

Joe followed him outside and the floating monk followed them through the curtain. The old woman leaned against the wall and took a long white pipe from her robes. She packed the bowl and lit it, taking long puffs and blowing a perfect ring of smoke.

When the three men emerged into the clearing, they squinted as their eyes adjusted to the light. Otto looked into the bright sky and spoke. "So now what? I mean, don't get me wrong, that was one stone cold trick you pulled on the bitch queen, but this place is still crawling with thousands of her faithful servants who're going to rip it apart stone by stone looking for her-- that is, when they aren't searching for the God you supposedly have hidden somewhere."

"Otto, I would ask that you not speak that way of Erminia. She was a troubled soul, but one I happened to love very deeply. What I have given her is a second chance. I knew there was no other way for her to release the bitterness that has festered in her for so long. I was not pleased to have to deceive her, but I hope this will give her a chance to forget the pain and build something new. She believes that she re-entered the world with her true love by her side. That is not a bad way to start a new life."

Otto dropped his mocking tone and put his palms together in prayer position. "I'm sorry; I meant no disrespect." They shared a small silence together. "Please understand, I had no idea you two were ever anything but mortal enemies. I've also lived in her shadow on the Square for some time. She could be beyond merciless. Not many kind words are spoken of her by the merchants who have lived under her rule."

Joe nodded. "Thank you for honoring the memory of the woman I knew and loved. I do not take that lightly. I have heard of some of the atrocities she inflicted on those who live on the Square, but you saw them firsthand."

Cho spoke in a low rumble that made both their heads swivel to him. His eyes were closed and he was in deep meditation. "Mmmmm....I found him. He is safe, but he has much anger in his heart. Will is with him. They are near the Temple...the white-robes gather there in the thousands." Cho's eyes stayed closed as more words hummed from his mouth. "Alma is waiting for us near the shore. Harris..." The monk's eyes opened and his kind focus found Joe. "...Harris is no longer here with us."

Joe gave a sigh. "That is unfortunate. We will honor his birth another time." Joe turned back to Otto. "The questions you posed before are valid. The Truthers will never believe that she has abandoned them. They will also never stop looking for the god she convinced them was here. I have no intention of interfering with their search or trying to change their minds about anything."

Otto ran his fingers through the tiny tuft of white hair below his lip. "So what's the plan?"

A wicked grin seeped across Joe's normally placid face. "Am I correct in assuming that you still have the key Tazir gave you?"

Otto touched the small pocket of his vest defensively before he could catch himself. "The key was given to me in payment for a service."

Joe chuckled. "Do not worry, it is yours; I have no intention of taking it from you. I was simply hoping that I could use it. Under your personal supervision, of course."

"Use it? For what?"

Joe placed his hands on Otto's shoulders and looked him in the eyes. "You have already been of great service to me by helping Tazir escape and safely escorting her here. I am already in your debt. "Otto's left eyebrow jumped at the sound of his favorite words. "I need you to use your key to sneak the last of the Council on board the Square."

Otto's confusion deepened and was joined by disbelief. "You want to sneak the Council of the Conclave onto the Square? What the hell for?"

"Because I am going to steal it."

Otto broke immediately into laughter. "You want to steal Transit Square? I admire the audacity, but I ask again, what the hell for?"

Joe took his hands from Otto's shoulders and stood tall. "I have planned for this day for hundreds of years. As with most great schemes, not everything has panned out quite the way I thought it would, but this part is something I have thought about since the beginning. I have one more thing to set right with an old friend who is still on the Square. After that, we are abandoning the Conclave. The Truthers can have it."

Otto stood with a blank stare on his face.

Joe continued. "Look, much of what I said to Erminia was true. I do believe that I have been arrogant and stupid. We have sat in this cloistered little world too long. It is time for us to write a new chapter. Otto, we need to move quickly. Will you help us?"

Otto stroked his beard. "At the risk of sounding extremely self-serving, what's in it for me?"

Joe smiled broadly. "My friend, your payday will be one they tell stories about."

: : ASCENSION : :

The Temple was in ruins. The tower still stood, but great chunks had been torn out of the curving walls of the main structure. White discs carrying the disciples of the Truther rebellion surrounded it. Some of them waited on board the hovering discs while others milled around the perimeter of the building on foot.

Random and Will hid behind a broken wall fifty yards away. Will poked his head out to survey the situation, then ducked back behind the wall. "They aren't doing anything. I don't see their fearless leader anywhere; she must be inside."

Random sat still with his back against the wall that concealed them. He wasn't sure why he was here or what he intended to do, but he was filled with rage. He had escaped from the golem as the stone soldiers focused on ripping it to shreds. His giant may have been defeated, but he could still see the look on Saul's face in his mind. He was glad he had managed to find Will again in the confusion. "We need to stop Erminia. She's committed to nothing more than destruction and pain. We need to find Alma and the rest of the Council." He looked to the sheer mountains that surrounded them. "Do you think the students managed to evacuate everyone?"

Will peeked around the wall again and scanned the scene. "Looks like it. Nothing but zealots in white robes as far as I can see. On our way here I saw a few groups on foot headed in the direction of the pass." Will sat back down next to him. "But I have no idea how we're going to find anyone in this mess. Why don't we just join the others at the rendezvous? What are we doing here?"

Joe stepped out from behind a crumbling wall. "That is a very good question. What are you doing here, Random?"

Random's face was hard and his eyes blazed. "We can't just run away, Joe. I know she once meant something to you, but you have no idea what she's capable of. I saw it with my own eyes. We can't leave it all to her!"

Joe came over and sat beside him. "We are not leaving it to her. She is gone. I witnessed her exit this world with my own eyes. I am sorry Random. I could not tell you all the details of what I was up to. I can explain everything later. But we need to get out of here before her followers realize that she has left them."

"So we just slink off through the mountains with everyone else?"

"No, Random, it is too late for that now. You and Will need to come with me. We are leaving by a different path."

• • • • •

The rusted wheel in the center of the great iron door began to spin slowly in a chorus of groans and squeals. Water seeped from the riveted seams around the edges of the door as the wheel's spin increased in speed. When the wheel stopped, the door was pushed open from the other side and water spilled onto the steel floor. The flow became a trickle as the huge iron door swung inward.

The rusted hinges resisted Will as he pushed the door all the way open. Will stepped onto the metal floor and gestured to the others to follow. Alma stepped through first, followed by Random and Otto. The two men rushed to join Will, who was waiting for the signal to slam the door shut again. Alma had moved away from the entrance and was peeking her head around corners to make sure they had not been detected. Everyone was silent.

Joe stepped out backwards over the high threshold, maintaining focus as he moved and taking care not to slip on the wet floor. He looked back through the passage at Cho, who hovered in deep meditation in the middle of the transparent bubble from which they had all emerged. The deep green-blue water of the lake framed Cho. The fragile bubble was pushed hard against the hull of Transit Square, some fifty feet below the surface of the lake.

Joe spoke in a hushed tone. "Cho...we are ready."

The monk's face remained placid and his eyes remained closed as he hovered through the doorway. Joe walked backwards as the monk approached him. Then he took a deep breath and gave a nod.

Will and Random slammed the door quickly. Otto was on the wheel immediately, and spun it furiously to seal the door as fast as possible while Cho held back millions of gallons of water with nothing but the focus of his intention. Will joined Otto in tightening the wheel until it would no longer spin.

Otto stood up with a bemused smile. The key that had allowed them to open the door hung from a long chain around his neck. He gave a snicker and tucked it into the pocket on the front of the vest. "Well. That was interesting."

Alma came back from her scouting. "It looks pretty empty. Everyone is either topside or on shore." She gestured for them to follow her.

They walked the steel catwalks that wound through the pipes and valves of the engine room. Joe stopped abruptly when they came upon a large stone statue of Shiva, her many arms spread wide. Incense burned in a pot below the statue's feet. He turned to share a look with Cho, then they continued down a flight of stairs.

As they descended to the lowest platform, they could see the bare feet of a scrawny man sticking out from under a table piled with junk. He was on his hands and knees, rummaging around for something, causing items to fall off the tabletop and clatter across the metal deck. Joe led them onto the platform without alerting the man under the table.

Random and Will looked up in wonder at the giant man who sat with his legs crossed, towering above everything. The giant's eyes were closed. Flickering lights from all corners of the engine room danced over his huge form. Alma and Otto looked at the piles of junk strewn on tables around the perimeter of the platform. Joe stood firmly planted on his feet watching the man under the table as he tossed things out behind him and talked to himself.

"No, no... Wait! This is... No, that's not it at all... Everything's mixed up...stupid, stupid, stupid!" The scrawny man backed out from under the table and brushed dirt from himself as he stood up. He examined a brass bowl he had extracted and dumped ashes out of it with displeasure. He stopped moving as he realized he was no longer alone. His head swiveled slowly and

255

he found himself confronted by his guests. He froze in place like one of the many statues in the engine room. His eyes darted from one to the other in deep panic.

Alma approached the man with movements like billowing silk. "Don't be alarmed. I've brought you a gift." Her voice had a resonance that was intoxicating. She held up a dazzling crystal globe that emanated blue light. His eyes were locked on it and his body relaxed. She took his hand and placed the globe in his greasy palm. He looked greedily at the luminous object and seemed to forget the others. He dropped the brass bowl and cradled the globe with both hands.

Alma stepped back and held her palms out. With a shower of sparks and a violent ripping sound the light snuffed out. The crystal globe had been transported and the spindly man holding it had gone with it. Alma turned her eyes up toward the giant's head and called out. "Cho? How's he doing?"

The monk hovered five feet from the giant's face, examining him like a physician. "They have made him work very hard recently. I don't think we will be able to make a jump."

Alma tied the sash of her robe tighter and began to gather her hair in a ponytail. "Looks like we'll have to do it the old fashioned way and just fly the city over the mountains." Random watched the way she moved and the joy in her every action. Neither he or Will had told her about Saul's departure. Now was not the time.

Joe motioned Otto over to where Random and Will were standing. He gathered the three men in a small circle. "As soon as we move the city, whoever is left aboard who is loyal to Erminia will undoubtedly rush down here to try and stop us. Since there are only the three of us to assist our large friend here, it is going to take a huge amount of focus, so we must not be disturbed. I need the three of you to watch the stairs and stop anyone who tries to interfere."

Random looked at the four different sets of stairs that led down to the platform. It would be difficult to guard. He put his hands to his temples and focused. With a groan of metal, all four sets of stairs began to fold from the bottom up. The metal flooring of the catwalks rolled up like paper, leaving only the frames. Soon there was no way left for anyone above to walk down to the lower platform.

Joe put a hand on his shoulder. "I have missed you." He turned to Otto and Will. "It is still best to stay alert; they may be determined enough to find another way down."

Joe turned to the massive being towering above them all. With a small hop into the air, Joe rose up, levitating to meet Cho. Alma had finished gathering herself and ascended silently to meet the other two Council members. Joe hovered in the middle, Alma and Cho flanking him. They stared at the giant's face in silence and synced their breathing with the rise and fall of his massive chest.

The giant's glowing white eyes opened suddenly. His great head pivoted to assess the three beings who hovered in front of him. He spoke and the walls quivered with the rumble of his voice. "It has been a long time since I have seen these faces."

Joe answered him. "It has been lifetimes, my old friend. I beg your forgiveness. You kept your word to me all these years. You kept her safe and followed her orders. Now, Erminia has returned to Earth. We need to move this city one last time. When we arrive at our destination, I will free you from this room. You need not be confined here any longer."

The giant took a deep breath. He no longer seemed tired. "I am ready."

• • • • •

When Transit Square rose from the lake, all eyes turned to watch its ascent. The faithful gathered around the Temple pointed. Salvo came rushing out of a building to look into the sky. The city moved straight up, trailing long streams of water and gaining altitude rapidly. Some white discs attempted to catch it, but their effort was in vain. The city did not slow until it had reached nearly five thousand feet. Then it paused for just a moment before it headed due west at high speed, still climbing as it approached the sheer mountains.

Those on the ground watched as the massive city crested the highest peaks of the mountains, then disappeared over the horizon as it descended down the opposite slope.

: : LETTING GO : :

The open plain where the Square had landed was covered in high green reeds for miles in all directions. The city rested heavily on its immense landing gear. The lower superstructure had a ragged hole where the thick metal of the hull had been ripped open. The interior of the former engine room could be seen from the ground. It was now just a tangle of pipes with a large, empty platform at the lowest point.

They stood on the ground in the shadow of the city. Joe shook Otto's hand. "Thank you for your help."

Otto smiled. "A pleasure doing business with you. I always fancied myself the real ruler of Transit Square. Never thought one day the whole damn city would be given to me."

Joe gave him a look. "You might have to come up with a new name. Given the state of your engine room, I do not see the city traveling anywhere soon."

Joe turned away and joined Alma, Cho, Will and Random. Otto gave them a wave. Alma raised her arms gracefully, and the section of earth on which they stood tore itself from the ground. The hunk of grass-covered dirt carried them aloft and they soared away from the wiry man in the red bowler hat.

As they flew, Will stood proudly next to his teacher, chatting with her as she piloted them over the grasslands. Cho sat quietly on the ground, chanting softly. Random sat looking backwards, watching the alien shape of the Square grow smaller on the horizon as they moved farther and farther away from it.

Joe came and joined him. They sat in silence looking backward for a long time.

Random finally spoke. "You know, the moment I stepped on the soil of the Conclave, I felt at home. It was the first time since I returned here that things were familiar. Then I saw it all destroyed. The sight of the things I built helped remind me of my past." He turned to Joe. "There's still so much I don't remember about who I was before."

"What is important is who you are now."

Random set his jaw. "Because before I went insane?"

Joe did not blink. "Before you lost sight of who you were. You are a great creator, Random. You helped build some of the most lasting things in the Ether. You brought order to a world that was chaotic and frightening to those who had just lost their lives. But you struggled with the emptiness." Joe paused. "When you first started to breathe life into your creations, I hailed your achievement and encouraged you. You were always so scientific in your approach, recording every thought you had. I knew there was a risk. Creating beings that could think for themselves, no matter how crude, brought the danger that you might fall prey to the same fate as those trapped in Glory Bubbles or forever Hellocked."

"One day it stopped being a canvas that called you to dream and became a void that sent you tumbling into despair." Joe looked at him with eyes filled with regret. "I was too caught up in my own delusions of grandeur when you came to me for help. I told you it would pass. I often think about how different things would have been if I had put everything else aside and listened to my friend in his moment of darkness. For that, I am truly sorry."

Random sat up straight. A great wave of emotion rolled over him. Suddenly he was there in that long-ago moment, reaching out to Joe. He felt the despair. He felt the disappointment as Joe dismissed his fears. He remembered leaving the room where Joe and Erminia continued to laugh and pore over their notes, their plan for a better world.

"Your downfall was rooted in your obsession for ever more resilient materials to breathe life into. When you left the Conclave to continue your work in seclusion, I was worried. When I learned that your experiments had led you to viewing the very souls who walk the Ether as a material to be reshaped..." Random's eyes grew wide at the thought. "Well, that is when I knew I had lost you. I could not allow you to continue. I chose to put you to sleep."

Joe pointed at him. "Your ideas were always better than anything I came up with. They were better because they came from your heart. It is a good heart, filled with compassion for others. Just remember never to lose that compassion again. Who you become without it...is frightening."

Random let out a breath he hadn't realized he'd been holding. He chuckled as he looked at Joe. "Your ideas weren't so bad. Look at us now, off to build the whole thing all over again."

The smile left Joe's face. "No, Random, you need to build something new. All the students of the Conclave will help you. Alma will need something to distract her from her grief, and Cho will provide balance as always."

Random cocked his head at the obvious omission. "And what about you?"

"It is time for me to go. The last thing I needed to set right was the war with Erminia. I had to settle it in a way that could bring her peace, and break the chain of lies that we forged so many lifetimes ago."

Random was shaking his head in disbelief. "No... Why would you go back into a body now? I don't understand."

Joe gave a soft grin. "I am not going back Random, and I am not staying here. I have finally completed the last lesson my teacher assigned. I know how to let go."

A gentle wind blew over them as their little clump of grassy earth flew over a wide, twisting river that wove lazily through the grasslands. Random could see the peace on Joe's face. He was saying goodbye. "My time is done. I'm ready to move on. I have no idea what awaits me. No one who has ever ascended into the mystery has returned to tell us what lies beyond the wheel of birth and death. I'm ready to take the leap and find out for myself."

The winding river met the shore of a vast sea. They began to see the former students of what had been the Conclave gathered on the shore. Thousands dotted the coast. They had built a few simple structures. Peppered on the ground were shimmering pools of liquid, wild portals that dotted the landscape. Random looked again at the vast ocean and noticed the glow of the water. It matched the liquid in the many portals. What appeared as an ocean was the limitless stretch of unformed Ether. This was the very edge of their world, the place they had stopped creating.

Joe put his hand on Random's shoulder. "Do you remember that job I wanted to talk to you about? I hope you will accept it and take my place. Be more than just a Builder. Be an Architect of something great. I can think of no one better." Joe stood and Random did also. "Stop here, please."

The small hunk of ground slowed, then halted. Joe took Random's wrists and turned his palms up. Random kept his hands together and waited. Joe reached up to the back of his own neck and unclasped the necklace he wore. He withdrew the three keys that had been hanging from the simple cord, close to the center of his chest. He placed the three intricate shapes into Random's hands.

"I used to be a fan of locking things. The master key Tazir gave to Erminia was one-of-a-kind. These are not master keys. Each one is unique and designed for a specific set of locks, much like the one I gave to Otto. They took years to make and are so detailed that they are nearly impossible to reproduce. I hope the world you create will not be one of locked doors." Joe winked at him. "But you should keep these, just in case you run into something I locked." Random looked at the keys and raised his eyes in question. Joe held up his hand, signaling that he had no intention of answering. "You will know one of my locks if you find it. The most important door has been opened, and the Conclave is no more."

Random nodded and fastened the cord with the keys around his neck. Alma walked up to Joe and gave him a kiss followed by a long hug. "I'm not sure what kind of world you've left us. I'm still not sure if this plan was a good idea but, despite all your stubbornness, you will be missed." She paused. "I'll miss you, Joseph."

Cho stood and gave a deep bow with his hands in prayer position. Joe matched his act of reverence. "Keep an eye on this one for me." Joe thumbed towards Random. "Hopefully he will be quicker to listen to your counsel than I was."

"I doubt it." Cho smiled and chuckled softly.

Will was confused. "What's happening? Are you going somewhere?"

Joe took Random by the hands and then gave him a warm embrace. He kept his eyes on Random as he backed away. "Yes, Will. I am going home."

Nothing happened for a few minutes. The sound of the breeze was all they heard. Then Joe's form became translucent. The highlights on his face where the sun touched him began to glow. With a soft whisper of wind, all the particles that formed the man they knew as Joe blew apart like a dandelion. The traces of light dispersed widely and soon could not be seen at all.

Alma, Cho, Will and Random were left staring at each other through the blank space where Joe had stood. Cho broke the silence with a boyish giggle. He focused his eyes on Random. "And where are we going?"

Random looked to the shore of the sea and the multitude of people waiting there. "Alma, please take us the rest of the way to the shore. I'm sure there are many students who are worried about you two." He went to Will and put his hand on his friend's shoulder. "We're going home, too. I could use a good friend by my side to help me remember what's important. I have a lot of things I need to build."

: : ACKNOWLEDGMENTS : :

The process of writing leaves you with a lot of people to thank. Thanks go out to Bill Missett who was the first to encourage me when I came up with the idea for the story, even though the first draft he read was shite. Thanks for the advice to start in the middle, Bill.

Thanks also go out to Mitch Jacobson, who provided the first round of editing and story advice. She had an amazing way of telling me never to use the word 'amazing' again.

Thanks go out to all my test readers, who provided wonderful feedback and helped shape the finished story. Tess Borden, Eric Weiss, Chris Hennes, Jessica Yurasek, Bill Missett, Jackie Cruz, Donna Foster, Lauren Hellman, Susan Collins, Essly Yeo, Jennifer Powell, Doug Powell, and Otto Penzato. Special thanks to Otto for letting me use his persona as the king of the underworld. I could think of no better character than him, right down to his funny little red bowler.

Thanks to John Couch who used his Aikido ways to get me to slow down and do it right.

The amazing skills that Kinga Toth brought to the final copy-editing cannot be understated. She is the mistress of grammar and word-smithing. I didn't run this part by her so I may be using 'word-smithing' incorrectly.

Thanks to my mother, Shirley Hawk for raising me with the mantra "You can do anything you set your mind to." You were right mom. Also giant thanks to all four of my sisters. Judy, Kay, Nancy and Kathy. Thank you all for being in my corner, all these years.

My most sincere thanks go out to my dear Kelly Kreuzberger. She was the first one to ask me "How many words have you written?" and gave me the yardstick to measure my progress. She helped lay the groundwork for Transit Square and define the more subtle motivations of the female characters, especially Erminia. She listened to me read the entire story to her over the nine-month writing period.

Thank you Kelly, for all the love and support. I love you.

COBURN HAWK

: : ABOUT THE AUTHOR : :

Coburn Hawk loves to tell stories, so writing a novel was something that was bound to happen eventually. He is blessed to be surrounded with a community of high quality human beings that he is honored to call friends and is very proud of his son Spencer.

Despite his new found love of writing, Coburn continues to produce oil paintings, spin fire, and work as a Director of User Experience. He lives in Los Angeles and spends a lot of time coming up with ideas that can best be described as ill-advised.

Amazon.com/author/coburnhawk

www.coburnhawk.com | www.randombridges.com

@coburnhawk | @randombridges

The story continues
in Book 2:

The Three Keys

∞

○

•

the half second when she heard Joe begin to transport, she initiated her own and arrived only a fraction of an instant behind him, using the sound of his entry to mask hers.

She walked through the grass and approached the door cautiously. They had failed to latch it behind them. She slipped her tiny body past it and peeked into the room beyond. The small anteroom was empty and all the curtains were drawn, leaving it rather dark. Erminia crept up to the thick red curtain and managed to peek in without causing it to move enough to be detected.

There he was. Joe stood inside. He wore a simple green tunic with long sleeves. Cho was waving the smoke of incense over his body with a feather fan as he chanted. An old woman knelt in the dirt and waved her hands over the pool of shimmering liquid. There were no other initiates in the room.

Erminia managed to get her tiny frame between the curtain and the interior wall during a particularly loud moment in Cho's chanting. Not all of the torches had been lit and the room was very dark. Erminia stayed low to the floor, her body covered by the curtain and her head peeking out so she could watch them.

Cho finished his chanting and put away his feather fan. He rang a bell and then waved it over the shimmering liquid. Joe knelt just behind the old woman, who continued to wave her palms over the pool.

Cho hovered off the ground and assumed lotus position. "Now we will wait for your beloved."

Erminia took in a short breath.

The old woman waved her hands with more urgency. "There's so much chaos in the Ether! I don't know how much longer we can shield these two!"

Cho spoke with a deep authority. "We have waited hundreds of years to pay back a debt. We can wait a bit longer!"

Erminia sat in the darkness and thought about the last few hundred years. She had spent every waking moment plotting revenge. The bitterness had become part of who she was. She thought of the mess unfolding outside. The faithful would not be pleased if they couldn't find the mystery she had told them was hidden here. Would she have to invent a god for them to worship? The Truther movement had just been a sham to help build a loyal army with

Made in the USA
San Bernardino, CA
23 October 2015